JULES DIXON

EVERNIGHT PUBLISHING ®

www.evernightpublishing.com

Copyright© 2016

Jules Dixon

Editor: Lisa Petrocelli

Cover Artist: Jay Aheer

ISBN: 978-1-77339-029-1

JULES DIXON

DEDICATION

People who've struggled with weight issues and/or bullying hold a special place in my heart. I've been there, experienced that. My hope is that this novel gives some insight into the pain that comes with feeling like you're not enough, inspiration to those who still struggle to stand up to their bully, or you'll take away an "I've been there, too" connection. For those who still experiencing the heartache of reflecting too often about what you see as wrong with yourself, whether it be weight or something else, please know that there is so much right in you. You are not a sum of any wrongs. You are just a whole lot of right, pinky swear promise, and I dedicate this book to you.

With love, Jules

JULES DIXON

RUN TO LOVE

Triple R, 1

Jules Dixon

Copyright © 2016

Chapter One

Presley

Beep! Beep! Beep!

Four thirty a.m. Seriously, time to get up already? The ridiculous schedule had been my life five times a week for the last two years, which only indicated how insane but committed I was. Maybe I should be insanely committed?

I threw on workout clothes, swiped my gym bag off the floor, and a packed garment bag from behind my door. On the way down the hallway, the corner of my bag got stuck on a decorative metal stand—which held nothing, but according to my roommate, "Its spirit told her it was meant to be there." This spirit-feeling, sixth-sense sensing, people-loving roommate, better known as Willow Harper, would be up in less than an hour for her morning shift as assistant manager and sous chef at the local coffeehouse, but for now she slept peacefully. Avoiding the urge to un-Zen-ly fling the shelf out the window, I deposited the spirit-filled metal back to its original location and tiptoed away.

"Bye!" Willow yelled from the comfort of her bed. "Love you, you loud bitch!"

"Sorry," I half-lied. "Love you, too. Bye!"

The late April morning drive blurred by. I arrived at Run-Ride-Rock Gym well before my five a.m. training time. My stretching routine was completed in full-on zombie mode. By ten after the hour my personal trainer still hadn't strutted his way to the warm-up area, and that wasn't like him. I snagged my towel and water bottle from the floor and made my way to find out what was going on at the front desk. Even though I'd met her before at the gym and a couple of times at outside social functions, the young woman manning the front desk wasn't high on my list of favorite people. If anything, she sat at the top of my most loathed.

"Hi, I'm Presley Bradenhurst. I have a standing five a.m. appointment Mondays with Mitch. Is he sick today?"

The receptionist, a human yardstick with a giant blonde horsetail high on her bobble-head, turned, and her baby blue eyes glared her sentiments. "Oh, yeah, I forgot to stop you when you waddled in. Mitch was fired Friday. Someone probably left you a phone message not to bother to come in today." She scanned me up and down and sneered, "…or ever again."

What? He was fired? Why?

I cleared my throat. "I don't think I received a phone call. Since I've already paid for the 100 Session New Year's Special and I've only used about thirty, I'll need to interview for a new personal trainer. Can you set up an appointment for me to talk to Blake, please?"

"I'll see if I can work it into my schedule," the snarky blonde replied. "Sorry, I meant *his* schedule."

Typical.

"Hi, there." The deep and serene voice was friendly.

I spun with a smile on my face. "Hi..." I said, stretching the word for so long I was positive drool trickled from my cavernous mouth.

A cocky smirk tilted the attractive young man's lips ... his luscious and kissable lips.

Great.

A swipe of my hand to my mouth verified that I was in fact drooling. The response was typical for me and bound to happen again as my nervousness around the opposite sex kicked into overdrive.

"I heard your predicament. I'm a new personal trainer starting today. I'd be glad to give you an impromptu training session."

"That's really not necessary, Jude," the gritchy blonde inserted her opinion over my shoulder.

"I disagree. If she's made such an impressive 100-session commitment to the gym, she should get our undivided attention in return." He winked.

My skin tingled and goose bumps trailed my arms. "Thank you. Jude, right?" I asked, to confirm what my brain barely heard while it was stuck in mid-gape.

"Jude Saylor. Nice to meet you..." He stretched the words like he was looking for a name and extended his hand.

"Presley," I answered slowly.

Too slowly. Wake up!

"Presley, it's nice to meet you."

"Nice to meet you, too."

I noticed we hadn't stopped shaking, or at this point, holding hands. I jerked mine away but not before noticing how manly and large his hand was, while still soft.

"I appreciate you offering your time, Jude, but I'm sure you have better things to do than watch me work out." I offered the out but kept my gaze lowered to prevent more physical responses.

The blonde receptionist huffed and mumbled something I didn't quite catch. I gazed up through my lashes as Jude gave blondie a furrowed-brow glare. She spun in her chair like there was something more interesting on the other side of the desk.

This wasn't the first time Emerson Welch had said something less than pleasant to me, around me, or about me, and I was almost positive it wouldn't be the last. She radiated nasty from her ultra-sculpted eyebrows to her manicured white fingertips to her perfect size two ass. It was a package meant for intimidation and it worked. On me, at least.

"Nope, really can't think of anything I'd rather do. Did you stretch?"

I raised my gaze and gave a curt nod.

"Okay, let's go." He strolled toward the free weights, and with my mind on autopilot I followed.

The view is am-a-zing.

Jude's shoulder blade length brown hair pulled back into a low ponytail at the base of his neck just fit him, and his lightly tanned skin and a five o'clock shadow with long sideburns emphasized his oblong face. He was tall but not like NBA basketball-player tall, and he had an upper body full of muscles rippling with every masculine stride. He wasn't bodybuilder bulky. Firm. He was just … really … firm.

Drool check.

A sway of my eyes traveled down and across his toned back. I realized how thin his waist was—maybe smaller than mine, but I'd never been small by any stretch of the imagination. My eyes wandered lower and through his black knit shorts, his tight and energetic ass popped sinewy muscles every time he took a step.

Pop! Pop! Pop!

He spun around, and I brought my guilty gaze back up to his ... beautiful hazel orbs.

Of course he has awesome eyes. Geez.

I blushed at getting caught enjoying the view, but Jude continued like he hadn't noticed. "Let's start with a few free weights to warm up. Here." He passed me the barbells. "How about three sets of ten bicep curls?"

I started the movements without instruction. Staring into the mirror, I concentrated on my form. Elbows close to the body, knees slightly bent, I lifted slowly, feeling the muscles contract and release with each pump.

"Good. Okay, now three sets of ten front raises."

I completed the task as asked.

As much as I missed Mitch, I could tell Jude knew what he was doing when it came to personal training, and an at-ease feeling rode through me.

But it was short-lived.

"You have excellent form, Presley. Mitch must have been a great trainer." Jude stalked around me, taking in all angles. His predator-like movements returned my discomfort. I made a conscious effort to stop my breathing from altering even after feeling my heart rate increasing ... and not from exercise.

"He was. Do you know why he was fired?"

Jude adjusted my arm's ascent. He tipped the weight to give a different stress on the muscle, leaving radiating warmth from his touch on my wrist.

"I don't, sorry. Like I said, first day." He handed me something a little more substantial. "Now, let's try something different to work the smaller back muscles. Let's do a shoulder shrug with these weights."

Standing beside me, Jude demonstrated what he wanted me to do, and I copied his image.

"Only the shoulders, relax your biceps." He touched my bare arms, and I shivered. "Sorry, are my hands cold?"

"No. I'm fine."

Stop it, body!

I adjusted the raise of my shoulders.

"Perfect. This is great for these muscles back here."

He grazed his hand over my shirt, and I straightened to avoid the pressure. My best efforts to keep my body from reacting to his gentle contact only made any reaction seem worse, and I cursed myself internally.

"Okay, one more set."

Watching me in the mirror, he counted down from ten. I was thankful when he moved on, and I could take a deep breath.

He then directed me to do a variety of free weight-based exercises and so many crunches my stomach burned like it was filled with hot sauce. But the sensation was so good because the feeling meant something was happening to my stomach.

Something is definitely happening in my stomach.

"Great. Let's do some cardio." Jude pointed to the treadmills. "I haven't had a run today."

"I don't run, Jude. I jog … issues." I tried to give as little information as possible. Telling him I used to be significantly heavier sounded like just the torture I needed to shove me over the edge and into a complete anxiety attack.

"Then let's jog, Presley." He lifted his voice like the suggestion was the best idea in the world. No judgment. No questions.

We chose treadmill machines next to each other and began a decent walking pace. When Jude increased his speed, I did the same. Soon we were going at a good clip. Definitely a faster pace than I'd attempted in a long time, but I gave the intense exercise the old "if it doesn't kill me, I'll still hate it" try. We fast-jogged. *Who am kidding? This is an all-out run.* We continued for about fifteen minutes when I caught his puzzled look from the corner of my eye.

"So what do you do, Presley?"

"I'm a salesperson at Jessen Auto Mall. We sell both new and used." I stared ahead.

His tone changed when he asked, "Do you like what you do?"

"Most days, yes. Some days, no. It's decent money ... and I like my coworkers. My boss has never had a female salesperson who's able to hold her own with the guys on car knowledge." I inhaled a shallow breath as my chest tightened. "My uncle was a gearhead ... car buff ... grease monkey ... whatever you want to call him. He had the bug bad and passed it on to me. I knew how to replace a transmission ... in a car ... before I got my first period." I cringed and blushed.

Giant sinkhole gods, swallow me please!

Jude smirked. "And what do you like to do in your free time?"

I cleared my head of embarrassment and took another strained breath. "I volunteer ... at the Nebraska Humane Society ... cleaning dog and cat kennels ... on Sundays." I adjusted my stride but nothing was helping. I managed to finish on a squeaky exhale. "And I like to go biking around the area lakes."

"Good choices. I have a black cat, Ninja. He's sneaky and likes to jump from piece of furniture to piece of furniture. It's actually kind of impressive. I swear there are days he doesn't touch the ground at all."

"I ... like ... cats. He ... neutered?" My world started to spin in a counterclockwise fashion.

Jude jumped from his machine, reached over the side rail, and slammed the stop button on my machine. "When you start to breathe like that, you stop! Immediately, Presley!"

Mortified, I clutched the side rails as the machine ground to a halt. My legs wobbled like Jell-O.

"That's a sign you're overexerting yourself. No need to do that. Let's walk around the floor for a few minutes."

I scampered away from him, but he followed on my heels.

"Are you okay?" His hand skimmed my lower back and I slinked away.

While my breath came and went like a whistling duck call was stuck in my windpipe, I snuck out, "Yeah… just need … a minute."

At the water fountain I drank quick sips in between rasping breaths.

Damn asthma! This is a reminder of why I shouldn't run.

Jude motioned with his head. "Come on, let's do a stroll around the gym. I still don't know where everything is, so it'll do me good, too."

We walked together to the indoor track. Jude was an excellent conversationalist, moving from subject to subject with ease but never asking anything too personal. I kept my answers quick, without elaboration.

Walking beside him, I smelled his familiar soap scent, and it mingled in the air with his musky body spray. The mixing of soap and scents caused my childhood and high school days to flash both happy and not-so-happy memories in my brain. A little of his salty sweat socialized with the other scents and my body responded in two places—my nipples and my heartbeat.

I glanced in a mirror as we made a second trip around the track that wrapped around the outside of the gym floor. My sports bra was doing very little to hide my physical reaction. Jude smiled, catching my gaze in the mirror. His eyes dipped to my chest before he averted his gaze.

Agreed, not much to look at.

After we completed two trips round the gym floor, he stopped by the door to the female locker rooms. "Well, since I didn't have a plan set up today, I'd like to offer you a free session on Friday. If you're interested, Presley? Give me another chance to work you until you're dripping with sweat everywhere and your muscles are screaming for release?"

That didn't sound sexual at all ... holy shit!

I shifted in my tennis shoes. "Um ... okay, Jude. Same time, five a.m.?"

"Great!" He held out his hand for a shake but mine was all sweaty.

"I'm all sweaty," I said, rubbing my hands on my gym shorts and then waving them to dry.

He caught my hand on the way back down, forcing a shake anyway. A manly rumble released from his chest when he grasped my hand.

Probably just disgusted by the clamminess. I warned him.

"It was great to meet you, Presley." His eyes softened as his hand lingered over mine.

I stepped backward toward the locker room, and he released my hand. "Thanks, Jude, and good luck to Ninja at making his way around the house safely today."

"I'll let him know you send your best, and..." He stepped forward, closing the distance again. Lowering his voice, he leaned toward me and his hot breath filled my ear. "Although Ninja doesn't want the truth getting out to the slinky Siamese next door, I bet you won't blow his cover as a stud," he whispered. "He is neutered."

I giggled and blushed. "I promise I won't say a word. See you on Friday."

He backed away and raised his voice. "Yes, you will, Presley. Have a good week."

I turned and entered the locker room with a smile on my face.

Damn, he was too cute, and he likes animals. Like, my perfect guy ... if only I weren't the most imperfect girl. I bet he wants a perfect girl.

Wish I were a perfect girl.

Chapter Two

Jude

Well, that was an epic fail. First potential client and I almost blew it. And looked at her chest half the time.

"Jude, here's the form you need to fill out for Princess's session." Emerson waved the piece of paper petulantly. I wondered how Emerson could even stand herself. The minute I met her, her demeanor told me she was a miserable human being.

But hot ... miserably hot.

"It's Presley, not Princess, but I have a feeling you already knew that."

"Well, Presley definitely wasn't a princess when she started here." Emerson blew her cheeks out and puffed up her body, indicating that Presley put significant effort into getting healthy and fit.

"Then I think we should support her outstanding success. Good for her!" I walked to the other side of the large circular desk.

Emerson rolled her big blue eyes at me. "Whatever. You just want clients."

I shook my head while filling out the in-depth paperwork. "Okay, what do I do with the form once I've filled it out?"

"It goes in the inbox on Blake's desk. He likes to keep track of the progress of his best clients. Since Princess bought the 100-session package, she's considered a VIP."

Avoiding further conversation, I went to the office of Blake Carr, manager and owner of Run-Ride-Rock Gym, or Triple R, as the Omaha's workout scene nicknamed the popular and fully-loaded gym.

I knocked on his open door and raised the form. "Hey, Blake."

He pointed to the corner of the desk. "Welcome to the team, Jude. Glad you made it in early this morning, shows me how much you belong here. I saw you out there with Presley. Thanks for jumping in for Mitch." Blake's cell phone screen lit up and the metal buzzed across his desk. He glanced at it, a slight exasperation clouding his eyes.

"No problem. I set her up for a free follow-up session on Friday. I'll have an actual plan designed now that I know her needs better. She does a great job, excellent form and amazing effort."

"Mitch used to say the same. She's also an incredible car salesperson. Sold me on my Ford SVT Raptor before I even drove it."

"Interesting." Presley's innocence and nervousness would have screamed wallflower career choice, not outgoing salesperson.

Blake chuckled. "Yeah, she could rattle all the specs, packages, and engine info off the top of her head. It was quite impressive. I gave her a twenty-session trial as a thank-you and she's been a loyal member for almost two years. Lost some significant weight. Not that she wasn't attractive before, but now..." Blake tipped his head and raised an eyebrow.

I did the same in agreement. Presley made the word "beautiful" feel inadequate, with all that blushing and her fluttering eyes, and she was as sweet as Mom's homemade strawberry jam. "Well, if I need a vehicle, I'll be sure to visit this Jessen Auto Mall."

And Presley.

Blake's phone buzzed again. "Love my kids, but it's never a dull moment being a divorced dad with three pre-teens on spring break ... at home ... alone." I backed out of the room as he answered, "Hello, Jayson, what's Brighton done now?"

In the break room, I nabbed bottled water from the fridge, stopping to look over the local paper's sports section.

I only had one sibling to deal with—Zane. He'd gone to the University of Nebraska at Lincoln, UNL, for degrees in logistics management and business, then moved to Omaha for a job. After a weekend visit, I discovered the city was a good fit for what I wanted to do. I moved here to live with him on his offer. I didn't mind living with my twenty-four-year-old brother. He's entertaining, to say the least.

Zane worked for Union Pacific Railroad as a night train dispatcher, completing twelve-hour shifts for three nights in a row and then receiving five days off. The rotating schedule seemed to work, especially for the two young ladies who lived in the south side of the duplex he owned, whereas we lived in the north side. The beautiful tenants spent a lot of his off-time with him—both of them—in his bedroom. I didn't suppose they were having in-depth conversations about trains, but I didn't really care to know what they were doing either. I did know Mom wouldn't be too happy about the alternative arrangement. However, Dad would probably get a real kick out of it.

Chuckling to myself at my younger brother's open views on sexuality and relationships, I exited the break room and turned the corner back to the gym floor. I shuffled to stop as Presley glided toward me. In her skin-baring workout clothes she took my breath away, but now … now Presley stunned me to muteness with her beauty. She wore a skirt that showed off her mouthwateringly toned calves and a crisp white shirt unbuttoned at the neck that teased the curve of her round breast, plus the heels she wore made the sway of her hips all the more eye-catching. Each piece was simple. Simply sexy.

Presley's long, straight, and shiny-as-polished-onyx hair, combined with her polished-to-a-sparkle emerald eyes was a powerful fusion of sweet and sensual. Her dedication to exercise had created a tight and sculpted physique covered in a creamy layer of the palest skin I'd ever seen, almost translucent. She and Mitch had struck the perfect balance—tastefully toned with alluring curves. Personally, I would have worked a little more on her glutes to create a nice bubble butt, but I found most women preferred less over more in that department.

Taking in the whole picture, it was inevitable that my body would respond. And it did.

Control yourself.

As she approached, her eyes crashed to the floor. She shoved mirrored aviators onto her face, masking those striking green globes.

"Bye, Presley." My tongue felt like a foreign object in my dry mouth.

"See you Friday, Jude," she said, swaying out the front door into the morning sun.

Might need a cold shower.

I walked to the desk.

"Hey, Jude." Emerson rolled her eyes for no reason at all. She huffed. "We had a call-in for a personal trainer. I set the WOM up with you, ten a.m. today."

"What's a WOM?"

"West Omaha Mom. The women who come in to keep their bodies all tight and perky so their rich hubbies don't go looking elsewhere."

I doubted her assessment that the women from Omaha were that insecure. If they were like past clients, they wanted to stay healthy for themselves and their families.

"Oh, well, thanks, Emerson." Not wanting to make small talk with her, I turned to walk away.

"Hey, Jude, you want to get a drink this weekend?" she inquired all sweet and demure.

And there it was, the change of attitude.

I'd met Emerson the week before on a tour given by Blake, and she'd immediately struck me as someone who used her womanly charms to get what she wanted. After working at a bar, I could smell-out her saccharine type, and I was immune to her kind of flirting.

"I work a second job on the weekends, sorry."

"Really?" She stretched the word. "Where?"

Shit!

I'd backed myself into a corner. "Two Fine Irishmen," I mumbled.

"I love that bar! I live around the corner from there. I'll just stop by and you can buy me a drink. They have a band this weekend?"

"I think so." The more questions she asked, the less I wanted to say.

"You work Friday night?"

"Yeah."

"Sounds interesting." Emerson went back to work, adding, "It's a date, Jude," as I walked away.

"It's *not* a date, Emerson."

She giggled. "We'll see."

I would invite my new friend, Kanyon Hills— he'd told me his dad had a warped sense of humor when it came to giving him his name—along on Friday and ask or beg him to run interference with Emerson. I'd met Kanyon a few weeks earlier, and I wasn't quite sure what his kind of woman was. The two times we'd enjoyed beers and conversation, the females had flocked to him and a couple of males did, too, which made him squirm a little, but he'd handled the propositions with class.

Overall, his tastes seemed ... eclectic. The first girl he'd taken home was a redheaded bombshell 90 percent covered in tattoos. The second was a pearl and pink sweater-wearing sorority girl who couldn't stop giggling. He might be willing to do a little colleague-blocking for me on Saturday.

I texted Kanyon during lunch to see if he wanted to meet for a beer after work, and he suggested Crescent Moon. I hadn't been there. As a recent transplant from Iowa, I was still getting to know Omaha, so I agreed.

The rest of the day at Triple R went well. My ten o'clock signed up for the twenty-session package, twice a week for ten weeks, and Angie wasn't a "WOM" like Emerson said. Tired of personal trainers who didn't listen to what she wanted, Angie was just plain frustrated. I understood that attitude. She quickly bored by a typical routine, and she wanted something new every session. The challenge intrigued me.

Normally, new personal trainers stalked the gym floor like hyenas waiting for fresh meat to show up, but Blake insisted that Triple R would never be high pressure. After observing the workings of the gym, I believed him. The clients appreciated not being constantly accosted and in return they signed up for complimentary trials from the new trainers, willingly. I guided two free spontaneous half-hour sessions during the afternoon, and one signed up for additional sessions. Training without commitment didn't bother me. I'd rather be busy and helping someone to better themselves than sitting on my ass in the break room.

I headed out from Triple R after a twelve-hour workday, four thirty a.m. to four thirty p.m. Physically I was spent, but mentally I was pumped. Two clients were in the books, and two more appointments were booked for tomorrow, mostly thanks to Emerson. I had a bad feeling that having her as an ally might be a necessity considering she answered the gym phone for the mornings and afternoons when most people called in to set up visits and trainer interviews. Wonder how close I need to keep Emerson so she continues offering my services to call-ins.

At home, I showered and dressed in jeans, a long-sleeve t-shirt, leather jacket, leather boots, and my expensive but totally worth it Dennis Kirk Arai silver and red Defiant Character helmet. I rode my bike to the bar. It was a laid-back, don't-give-a-shit kind of hangout with a kickass beer list. I chose a draft of a local brewery's lager. It was okay. I had both enjoyed better and spit out way worse in the past.

While I waited, my phone buzzed with a text.

Kiera: **Hey! How's Omaha? Have you eaten your weight in beef yet?**

I chuckled.

Kiera Maxwell was my first long-term girlfriend. We'd met a month into our freshman year of our undergraduate degrees, and I'd enjoyed those four years of college by her side. I really thought she was the one—marriage, house, kids, the whole picture-perfect life. But we ended as quickly as we began. While I decided to stay at ISU for my master's degree, she moved to Chicago for her dream job. There was no way I was going to ask her to stay. The dream of moving from Iowa and finding the perfect job was bigger than her dream of us.

Saying good-bye was more of a physical separation than an emotional one. Over time my feelings had morphed into only friendship. We'd stayed in contact, texting or talking at least once a week, and I'd had seen her a few times. A little friends-with-benefits action ensued, but neither of us acted like starting something up again was of any interest.

Jude: **Hey? Hay is for cows. That's what the Nebraskans say. Don't think this Idiot Out Wandering Around will ever be a true Cornhusker but I like the scenery.**

That was what Nebraskans nicknamed Iowans. IOWA—Idiots Out Wandering Around. I never found it totally offensive. The designation spoke more to their lack of creativity and humor, but unfortunately and occasionally, I kind of fit the humorless description.

Kiera: **You never pay attention to the scenery! You are 100% directionally challenged. I sure remember that time you got us lost in Chicago. I've never been that scared in my life. Roll 'em up!**

Yep, that's me.

Jude: **Just showing you where NOT to go in Chicago. Glad I helped!**

Kiera: **Whatever! :-) I think I may be coming to Omaha for consulting soon. I'll keep you informed, maybe we can get together?**

Jude: **Sounds good. Later.**

Kiera: **Hugs <3**

Kanyon arrived about ten minutes into my first beer and promptly ordered a porter beer, dark as blacktop and almost as thick as asphalt. The cute waitress called Kanyon by his first name like he was a regular at the establishment. Delivering his drink, she threw him a flirty little smile.

Kanyon worked in sales at the Ducati store on Industrial Road. The week after moving here, I went to look at what I knew I could only afford if I sold both kidneys on the black market. We struck up a conversation about our bikes. His collection made me almost hate him. Six bikes, including a '48 Harley Davidson Panhead *and* an '08 Indian Chief Vintage, and of course a collection of three Ducatis. My collection was one … one bike—a

2005 Kawasaki Vulcan 1600 Mean Streak with Vance and Hines performance exhaust pipes. I bought the chrome and black bike after working my ass off for a home-builder my final summer of college. We met up later for a beer to finish our discussion. He was a cool guy and since my brother wasn't a motorcycle enthusiast, it was good to talk to someone who shared the same hobby.

But maybe someday I'll have a real collection of bikes.

"How was your first day?" Kanyon asked after a long swig from his fancy beer glass.

"Good. What are you doing Friday night?"

"Why?" he asked suspiciously, like I was already asking him for a favor and he wasn't sure he was that invested in our friendship yet.

"I'm not asking you out on a date, dude."

Kanyon chuckled at my retort, but crossed his arms.

I leaned forward. "There's this girl that works at Triple R—Emerson—beautiful but annoying as fuck. Emerson's the daytime front desk staff and I need her to be on my good side so she keeps sending me new clients. She asked me out this weekend, but I don't want to get that kind of chummy with her. She got it out of me that I bartend at Two Fine and she's going to show on Friday night. Wondering if you could make an appearance to be a buffer between us to keep the night professional?"

"She's beautiful, huh?" The wheels turned in his sandy-blond-hair-covered head, his green eyes narrowed in on me.

"Yeah, early twenties, five foot five, blonde hair, gigantic blue eyes, well-shaped body, decent rack, and a bountiful booty to match her bountiful bitchy attitude."

He smirked at my assessment.

"But the right guy could probably fuck the bitchiness out of her," I added to pique his uncommitted interest.

"Nice, bro." Kanyon shook his head.

I shrugged my shoulders in a non-apologetic way and drank a long swig of my beer.

He sighed. "All right, I'm in. Don't have any plans, and I like Two Fine Irishmen. Good food, decent beers, I'll show. Considering my current predicament with Moriah, I can't promise my bitch-exorcism skills are working. Don't expect miracles, fair?"

"Fair."

We ended up eating dinner and having a couple more beers before leaving. I left alone. Kanyon left with the cute girl-next-door waitress, which totally confirmed he had no set type of woman. Unless *willing* is a type.

I walked in the front door of the duplex and heard noises from Zane's room. Noises no brother should ever have to hear. A tiled bathroom insulated out the sound between our bedrooms, but the noise carried under his door and echoed into the living room. In the middle of his five days off, Zane and the girls next door had been "talking trains" the last two nights. I'd think he'd be exhausted. I would be. But he seemed to thrive on the ... personal attention.

In the kitchen, I filled a glass with water, and Ninja jumped off the top of the refrigerator onto the counter.

"Hey, Ninj, you're not supposed to be up here."

He did his best to purr an apology. Talking to the cat made me think of Presley. Maybe she'd like to meet Ninja sometime.

"Just don't let Zane see you, he'll yell ... at me. Did you go see Sheba next door today?" I trailed my hand down his rail-thin back and long tail. "Did she find out your secret?"

Ninja decided I asked too many personal questions. He tightroped the edge of the counter to the breakfast island, making use of one of the stools as a pouncing-off point to the chair in the living room.

"Hey, I'm going to bed and I'm closing my door so I don't have to hear that." I nodded over my shoulder at Zane's bedroom door. "You in or out? I'm not playing the 'let's see how many times I can make Jude get out of bed' game tonight."

Ninja curled up on the black leather chair's ottoman and sent me one last "bite me" glare. I chuckled at his apathetic attitude and hit the hay myself.

Ninja woke me up four times during the night to come in and then go out and then come back in and then go back out of my room.

Chapter Three

Presley

Monday at the dealership was uneventful, which was never a good thing. If management had their way, the sales staff would be working with multiple clients at the same time, performing like car-selling jugglers. But that didn't happen. We were dead. The Internet shopping sites I visited all day to save me from my boredom saw more sales action than I did. I was ready for Tuesday to be a good day. It couldn't be worse than Monday in the sales numbers.

"Good morning, Presley," our general manager, Charlie, greeted me as I scampered through the door ten minutes late.

"Sorry for the late show, Charlie."

"No problem, figure there's a traffic issue. Drexel and Sam aren't here yet either."

I cringed. Just hearing the name Drexel had my skin crawling. Drexel Mason was my biggest competition at the auto mall. Always first loser to his first-place finish every month, I knew this month was shaping up to land me right back in the same pitiful category.

In my office, after putting away my lunch, I turned my attention to the referral slips on my desk. One benefit of being the only female salesperson was the front desk staff tended to treat me right. It didn't get past me that they were all female and treated just as shitty as I was by the male-dominated sales staff. I'd become pretty close with a couple of the girls. Didn't hurt that I brought coffee and low-fat blueberry muffins once a week for the morning girls, and an arrangement of chocolate-dipped fruit as an afternoon snack for the afternoon/evening girls. I'd discovered how to grease a squeaky wheel … and it wasn't with WD-40. Soft fluffy morning pastries and dark chocolate-dipped fruits—that's what made the wheel squeak-free.

I lifted the stack and it felt heavy ... like really heavy. I counted the slips. Six? Six referrals? I almost felt guilty. This could put me over Dixless ... I mean Drexel. "Dixless" is what Willow named Drexel in an attempt to support me in my never-ending professional pain. Screw it! He was an ass to the staff, and by this amazing gift, I imagined yesterday evening he was a bigger asshole than normal.

I did my standard background work based on the information written on the cheery yellow slips and phoned each referral. Three out of the six set appointments to come in for test-drives that day. I put in orders for the desired cars to be washed and readied. With the other three interest slips, I left messages on the contact number, praying to get a return call. I e-mailed the contact info, too, just in case they didn't check their voice mail. By noon, everything was set for the test-drives, and my confidence was solid.

The first couple test-drove a used Camry during their lunch hour. Nice car, fully equipped, zippy ... yada, yada, yada. It was clear that the car would be the woman's so I played to her. Asking general life questions, I found out she was an artist. Ah-ha! Something we had in common. The revelation bonded us quite well, and they agreed if nothing else piqued their interest, they would be back tomorrow. A good feeling rolled through me.

The second referral to show mid-afternoon was a young, single guy. I listened to Garrett on the phone, and he said he wanted something brand spankin' new and sporty, although my gut told me he was a bells-and-whistles guy. Especially after he recited all of the upgrades in the Mustang Club of America Special Edition

Package faster than I ever could. However, the client was always right—to start with—in my book. There was no use arguing over the phone. My job was to get him here then work my magic.

I moved the requested Ford Mustang GT to the front. Garrett rounded the car with little enthusiasm. We settled in for the test-drive, and he tore off, sending rocks orbiting into the atmosphere. I laughed and joked about his lead foot, but I was guaranteed flak from Charlie about the excessive wear and tear and potential liability factors when we returned. After the immature stunt, Garrett still seemed unimpressed. I told him I had something that would be a better fit, if he'd just trust me. He hesitated but agreed.

I drove back to the dealership to save the sports car from further damage, and walked him to a slightly used but priced better-than-new, fully loaded to the hilt, BMW 335i. I rattled off the list of upgrades and special features the car possessed. It was amazing that the feat of auto engineering didn't time travel. I almost added that feature to see if Garrett was listening, but I didn't. I could tell he was enthralled by the way he rounded the bright red car and a smile illuminated his face.

The smile.

He drove. He bought. That car sped away. Zero to sixty in 4.6 seconds.

Later, I was waiting in my office for the third test-drive appointment to arrive, when Drexel rounded the doorway. If he weren't such a jerk, I'd think he was hot as hell. An all-American look with vibrant blue eyes, styled wavy blond hair, and perfect white teeth. A fine representation of what the Heartland had to offer in a long and lanky body.

"Hey, Miss Perfect," slid off his slimy tongue.

I rolled my eyes and pretended to gag.

He chuckled through his words. "I just wanted to let you know that while you were out with Beemer-boy, your college sweetie came in and I took care of her. Hope you don't mind. You don't, right?"

Every hair on my body stood. This wasn't the first time the still-a-frat-boy-at-heart had stolen a potential sale from me. Complaining about the steal would do me no good. Charlie would listen, but "The customer needs to be helped immediately" would be his mantra. And the sales manager, Trent, was in a bromance with Drexel, so he was less than useless.

Don't think this is over. And watch your back, I'm out for blood now.

I kept my reaction in check. "No problem. Did she end up with the economy car she needed?"

"No, I convinced her to get a full-sized. Didn't take much ... I just gave a wink and she was putty in my hands." His gaze made a trail to my chest and then back up to my eyes.

I ignored his obvious eye-mauling. "Drexel, she is just out of college. She needs a fuel-efficient car because she's going to be a traveling nurse."

"Sorry, sweetheart, just part of the business. Plus, I got an eight thousand dollar up sale."

"Drexel, you need to think more about our customers and what they want. And not about your wallet."

He flattened his hands on my desk and leaned forward. "Well, you know, it's not the size of the wallet, it's how a guy uses his line of credit." His eyebrows flashed at me.

This was a typical Drexel Mason encounter. For the past two years, he had acted like an ass around me ... and *to* me. Drexel was simply distasteful and completely boorish and totally immature.

He added, "I'd be glad to let you abuse my line of credit, Presley."

"Get out." I stood and pointed at my door.

"I was just kidding, geez, you can never take a joke, Miss Perfect." He raised his hands all fake-offended.

"Drexel, out of my office. Now!"

He finally stepped backward toward the door. Before he moved into the hallway, he lowered his voice and wore a lascivious grin. "I love it when you get all worked up, Presley. I can imagine that's how passionate you are in bed. Maybe someday—"

"Out!"

You're a giant swine boy!

After Dixless retreated, I cursed for a minute to remove his foulness out of my head, only to replace the memory of him with other foul thoughts. Damn!

The third referral ended up being his anyway. Recovery was still possible. He didn't know about the final three referrals. Diligence and extra attention would ensure those three referrals would pan out. I would work my magic.

And I know what I need.

I texted Willow.

Prez: **Bad/good day. Have sweet tart martini ready, please.**

Willow: **Will do. Anything else? Need some B Cooper or J Depp tonight?**

Prez: **Johnny please … I need to be Depp'd badly!**

Willow: **LOL. Me too, dear, but I'm afraid both of us will be Depping ourselves tonight :-(**

Prez: **Ewwww!**

Willow: **I know you do it. The walls are thin … very thin.**

Prez: **Ewwww again! I'll be home in an hour.**
Willow: **I'll have the S.T.M. ready to be
chugged and extra AAA batteries waiting.** <3 u
Prez: **LOL. You are a true friend.** <3 u 2
Willow was the closest thing I had to a sister, and
I considered her my closest family member who didn't
match any part of my DNA. She listened to all my
Dixless problems, and I think she plotted to poison him
by luring him with her female wiles to some fancy tainted
meal.

I called the three remaining referrals one more
time and rattled off another sincere personal message of
my interest in helping them to find the perfect vehicle.
There was a fine line between interest and badgering, but
thankfully, I'd never been accused of the latter. After
finishing up some paperwork and powering down the
computer, I headed out to face the last of rush-hour
traffic.

At home, Willow stood right inside the front door
with in one hand, my purple and green tartan plaid lounge
pants and a ratty I Love NY t-shirt and fuzzy green socks.
In the other hand, she held my bright-blue-colored
martini. I stripped at the door and crawled into the
comforting clothes. Willow and I were way past the
embarrassed-to-see-each-other-naked phase.

"So tell me about your day." She examined me
from head to toe like I should have visible bruises or
scars if my day was that bad.

The tangy and sweet martini danced on my palate.
I plopped on the couch with a thud to give her the
highlights. Willow snarled and appeared to be thinking
up ways to give Dixless a few bruises and scars in
addition to poisoning him. I calmed her down to just
under furious with a promise to talk to Charlie about his

behavior before we ate the quiche and salad Willow made, while I enjoyed a second sweet tart martini.

The next news might upset Willow, but she would want to know anyway.

I cleared my throat. "So I didn't get a chance yesterday to tell you, Mitch was fired from Triple R. And before you ask, no, I don't know why."

"What? He didn't call me." She tipped her head and her face tightened. "And I didn't sense anything was wrong, but that's not new ... whole love-block thing."

Mitch and Willow dated for about a year when we were seniors in high school. He was her first boyfriend, · love, and lover. They stayed in touch and sometimes they still touched each other. She assured me they were only compatible in the sack, but I wondered if she didn't still hold a little place in her heart—her eccentric and wildly unique heart—for him.

She lifted her phone from the sofa armrest and texted, I assumed, Mitch.

"So, did you workout on your own yesterday?" she asked.

"No, this new trainer rescued me from the front desk piece of work while I was trying to get an appointment to talk to Blake."

Willow groaned. "Emerson?"

I rolled my eyes. "Yeah, she made some, I think, rude comment that I didn't catch when I tried to give him a chance to back out of training me on the fly. He told her he couldn't think of anything he'd rather do than help me." I ingested a long drink of my martini. "It was kind of sweet," I added, holding the glass to my lips to hide my smile.

Willow opened her mouth wide. "Oh! My! God! Prez!" She accented each word with a pop of her eyes. "You like him!"

"I do not."

I kind of do.

"What's his name?"

"Nope. Not going to offer his name up so you can use him in one of your perverse sexual fantasies."

"Fine. I bet you twenty dollars that you'll be Depping yourself to his mental image and screaming his name tonight."

I smacked her arm lightly. "Ewwww! Unlike you, I have control of my sexual appetite."

Considering I didn't get that many opportunities to satisfy my appetite, I'd grown accustomed to savoring sex when the magic happened. Two boyfriends in the last nine years, each one lasting about the length of a calendar year before we fizzled. The first took my virginity, the second my Xbox 360. And that's not a euphemism.

The first boyfriend was nice. The second one was like Satan on cocaine. Even though it'd been over a year since a casual one-night stand that ended up only ho-hum, I didn't think I was ready to hum again with anyone … yet.

But Jude, with his long silky strands of sable-colored hair that I could slide my fingers through, his long, perfectly trimmed sideburns that I could imagine grazing against my nipples, his incredibly tanned, muscular body that could be written about in books, and his amazing hazel eyes that I could envision looking down on me while we made love … well, he made me question my need for a good hum. However, past experiences taught me that men could look one way and act another. It was a fact that had left a sour taste for getting to know the opposite sex. Maybe it's time to have a sample taste again? Not all men are alike, right?

"Earth to Presley … *Presley!*" Willow yelled loud enough to make my ears ring.

"What? What!" I snapped away the scandalous thoughts with a shake of my head.

"So next Monday's training won't come soon enough, will it?" She shoved my shoulder.

"Actually, he's giving me a second session on Friday. For free."

"No shit!"

"Yeah, you're not going to believe what he said." She leaned in closer. "What?"

"He asked me to give him another chance to work me until I'm dripping with sweat everywhere and my muscles are screaming for release."

She fanned herself. "I think I'm dripping ... down there."

I made a disgusted face at Willow's uncouth comment but followed my reaction up with a closed-mouth giggle. "I know he meant the comment to be strictly professional, but damn, I about melted into the commercially carpeted floor!" I acted like I fainted into the sofa, and Willow laughed.

After we watched a Johnny Depp double feature of *Chocolat* and *Benny and Joon*, it was right before midnight when we turned off the TV and cleaned up the living room and kitchen. I had a noon start tomorrow since it was my night to work until close at eight p.m. I usually slept in a little before I went to work out. I hit my cozy feather comforter-covered bed right at midnight, but I tossed and tossed and turned and turned. My body wouldn't unwind.

Staring up at the ceiling, I realized what needed to happen. Damn, I'll owe Willow twenty dollars.

I opened the drawer in my nightstand and took out my special pink vibrator, hoping Willow was already asleep after her three martinis.

I turned on the quietly humming soft plastic to the lowest buzz and imagined Jude's full lips started at my nipples as I grazed the toy over each raised peak, his wet lips encircling each of my quarter-sized light pink areola, pulling on my erect nipples. I moaned softly as the light vibrations sent an ache through my breasts. I glided the tip of the vibrator down my body, teasing my belly button, imagining Jude would do the same until I was writhing for more. Only when I couldn't take the heavenly torture, he would lower his tongue through my tastefully trimmed but not shaved mound. My vision morphed with him guiding himself down so he was face-to-face with the part of me that was blistering heat from the inside out. His hot breath scorched the delicate skin between my legs with want and need to please me.

I pictured him looking up at me from his prone position between my raised legs, licking his beautiful crimson-red lips and throwing me the twisted smirk he had on yesterday as I walked past him when I left the gym. I stopped for a moment to tease my clit with the bulbous tip of the vibrator, and my whole body responded with a shiver of pre-delight. Lowering my hand, I slid the soft plastic through my already dripping wetness, fantasizing that Jude's lips and teeth were skimming over the outer and inner folds of my body, teasing, pulling, and licking until I was ready to explode from his tender yet confident attention. I guided the toy into my wetness, where the bulb end hit my G-spot perfectly and the little butterfly vibrated right against my engorged button, sending zings of pleasure throughout my body.

I hit the second setting on the push-button control, imagining his tongue alternating between my wet core and flicking my clit, teasing as he held me on the edge, building my internal tension until he plunged deep into my core with his tongue. I imagined his large hands holding my thighs at his will.

I thrashed on the bed, my body readying for a release, my thighs tensed, as pants and moans of extreme enjoyment escaped my mouth one after another. I pressed the button for the highest vibration setting and exploded in a thrilling rush of heat that seared long and unforgivingly through every muscle of my body like lightning through a June Nebraska sky. I murmured his name in reverence as the waves of climax washed over me for so long that I lost my breath and all reality, fully immersed in the fantasy.

I removed the toy and dropped my orgasm-shattered and totally relaxed arms to the bed.

"Holy shit!" I mumbled.

"You can say that again!" Willow said dryly through the wall. "And you owe me twenty bucks!"

We both laughed so hard and for so long that it was well after midnight before I got to sleep.

One of the best nights of sleep I've had in a long time.

Chapter Four

Jude

    Wednesday was my day off from Triple R. After I completed a ten-mile run in the crisp April morning air, I showered and dressed in comfortable cargo shorts and a Foo Fighters concert t-shirt. I spent mid-morning doing some basic cleaning. Zane wasn't a slob and neither was I. Still, we were bachelors, so bedsheets got washed less often than they probably should be, a layer of dust coated everything, and the bathroom wasn't eat-off-the-floor clean like our mom's.

    I woke Zane to tell him I'd wash his sheets if he carried them to the washer. They were a human petri dish of fluids, and I wasn't about to touch them. He stood, and I gave him a few choice cuss words for the birthday suit view and left the room shaking my head. His fondness for walking around nude didn't bother me, but that didn't mean I enjoyed constantly seeing his multi-pierced junk. This being his place and me living here practically rent-free, I didn't complain. I heard him divesting his bed of the covers. He walked into the living room and before I could move, the disgusting bedsheets covered my body.

    "What the hell! Dude!" I scrambled from the sofa, to get out from under what I could only imagine was semen, lady-part juice, and K-Y Jelly-coated material. "Zane! Take your nasty sheets to the washing machine, you douche!"

    Zane laughed at my reaction, picked up the fabric, and headed off to the laundry room. In a minute, the washer whirred and when he returned he was wearing a pair of lounge pants from the dryer. *Thank God.*

    "Have today off, bro?" Zane planted his ass in the leather chair. He slid his feet onto the ottoman and nudged Ninja to move from his favorite place to curl up.

Zane's eyes narrowed in on the cat as he stretched and jumped onto the coffee table, also designated a "cat-free zone". I grabbed Ninja and moved him to the sofa before my brother threw a fit a two-year-old would be impressed with.

"Yeah, Wednesdays and Saturdays and most Sundays, it's rotating." I rifled through some magazines on the coffee table.

"Your boss agreed to that?"

"I explained to Blake that I already took a bartending job at Two Fine for the weekends and coming in three hours after closing would be rough. Still, I kind of thought I'd have to quit Two Fine. Glad I don't. I like it, fast-paced, good tips, and great staff."

Zane grabbed the TV remote from the table. "So how did your first two days go at Triple R?"

"Better than I expected. I already have four clients booked for weekly appointments, one for twice a week, and I'm thinking I'll get this girl, Presley, to commit to me tomorrow."

"You make it sound like she's going to marry you." He switched the TV channel.

"What did you say?" I suspended my searching of the magazines. My heart tripped in a weird and fast rhythm when I replayed his words in my mind.

He shook his head. "Fuck. I don't remember." His shoulders shrugged away his interest in the question. "Anyway, did you ever call Yori's sister?"

"Yes."

Zane's lips tipped into a creepy smile and raised his eyebrows. "So are you going to do it?"

"Yes." I attempted to read a magazine article on nutrition.

Zane knew better than to continue asking questions, especially when I only gave him one-word answers. Soon I would stop answering the questions, which were grating on my patience and none of his business, and ignore him.

"Wanna go to lunch?" He smartly changed the subject.

"Only if you're buying, little brother."

After he showered and put on more than lounge pants, we drove to Petrow's for delicious burgers with combo onion rings/fries and chocolate shakes. I didn't eat like this every day, but my brother did.

Zane inherited Mom's incredible metabolism. Plus, his all-night workouts with the wonder twins probably burned whatever extra calories he consumed during the day. He was an avid soccer player during the summer, and quickness was a benefit to staying trim. He accomplished whatever fitness goals he had in our home gym in the basement. I tried the machine. Didn't hate it. Just preferred the Triple R atmosphere.

I worked hard to maintain my chiseled body. Zane liked his leaner—a personal choice that I supported as long as he was healthy about it, but eating this greasy, albeit delicious, crap every day was a ticket to cardiac problems. That said, I was far from obsessive about my own body. I didn't ingest a protein/supplement shake for every meal, and I didn't cut and bulk like competitive bodybuilders. I stayed healthy with reasonable nutrition and smart training.

When we arrived back at the duplex, we spent time cleaning up the yard. It had been a long winter, and as far as I could tell, Zane hadn't made an effort on the yard the last two years he owned the place. My brother was less than thrilled with my suggestion to get the work done, but he didn't complain.

After we finished, we sat in the living room watching DVR-recorded comedy shows.

"A, a, a, a, a ... b, b, b, b ... c, c, c, c..." Zane imitated the gut-busting instructions to improve his oral skills in the bedroom.

"Shape up, Saylor! Vaginas deserve respect!" I added.

"That's 'cause penises is easy and vaginas is hard." We both cracked up.

We watched several more episodes to pass the time and entertain our inner immature teenage boys. Our dad had raised us right and the immaturity would cease quickly, but it was still entertaining to let go with Zane. I'd never tell the pain in my ass, but I'd missed him.

After making and sharing dinner, I packed a bag with a robe and flip-flops.

"Have fun, bro. Don't get too excited," Zane quipped as I left through the front door.

I flipped him the bird and slammed the door. Had to admit, I was a little nervous. Maybe that is a good thing in this case.

As I entered my black Ford F-150 XLT, the girls from next door, Yori and Britney, walked down their steps and across the driveway for their nightly Zane visit. Yori was an Asian-American woman in her early twenties, a petite beauty at 5'1", with perfectly shaped, classic red-rose lips and dark, shiny, chin-length hair. Britney had long, wavy chestnut-brown hair with big brown doe-eyes. She was at least 5'8", an All-American cowgirl in her mid-twenties. They made an interesting duo. As long as my brother was happy with the attractive grouping, I would stay out of whatever it was that was going on.

"Hey, Jude, have fun tonight," Yori yelled with a shit-eating grin when I rolled down my window. Her sister Simi probably had talked to her.

"Thanks, Yori. Don't have too much fun with my brother. He's starting to look like he's dehydrated from fluid loss."

She laughed. "I think it's only movie night, so the poor baby can recover."

"I never agreed to that," Britney said, stomping her boots across the concrete.

Yori sent her an annoyed headshake. Trouble in paradise?

"Good night, ladies." I didn't want to know anything more.

"Night," they both said as I leaned back into my truck and headed off to show what genetics and years of training had blessed me with.

****

Presley

My morning started with semi-disappointment. No Jude sighting at the gym. After last night's amazing semi-pornographic use of his image to get myself off, I could have used a little inspirational reminder of his handsome face. It was almost like I missed him.

You barely know him.

Emerson worked out before she started her queen-bitch shift at the front desk. In the locker room, I heard her talking to another gym member about her plans for the weekend. Because I had no life, I listened in on hers.

"You know the hot new trainer?" Her voice was what I imagined a Barbie doll's would sound like.

Please, don't let it be Jude.

"You mean Mr. Fuck-me-eyes?" The other blonde adjusted her boobs in the mirror.

Probably Jude.

"Yeah. Well, I'm meeting him for a drink on Friday, and before breakfast the next morning I'm going to find out what size man missile he's hiding under those gym shorts."

I rolled my eyes at her vulgar comment but quickly fantasized about what hidden treasure might await a lucky lady. I bet his manhood epitomized perfect. Long, but not excessive or porn length, and he'd know how to work what he had. Veiny like the rest of his body, and probably warm like his touch. I imagined the rim of the head bulged like a mushroom and was ready to rub on a G-spot to give the ultimate in pleasure. I am already hornier than last night ... lovely!

Compared to Emerson, there was no way Jude would ever see anything in me. She was beautiful, and I was ... just Presley. Always a crisis away from overeating or becoming a couch potato. If I settled for having Jude as my trainer and enjoyed mind-numbingly fantastic Jude-based fantasies until I came across the next guy who found me tolerable, it had to be enough. That had to be enough because believing I could be more to Jude was a different kind of fantasy. It was a delusion.

I stopped off to pick up an arrangement of fruit dipped in chocolate for the front desk staff at the auto mall. They giggled with happiness when I delivered the treat. From that point on, like a nitro-boosted car, the day ran super fast. I finally got ahold of two out of three other referrals from yesterday, and there was another slip on my desk when I returned from a late afternoon meal. That tasty fruit always did the job.

To my benefit, Drexel had done nothing to endear himself today. He called both of the phone receptionists by the wrong name in front of me. At the same time! It's Jillian, not Jill, and Avery, not Ava. You self-centered jerk! They rolled their eyes when he turned away and we giggled like schoolgirls. I made three test-drive appointments for the next day. An hour before closing, the Camry couple from the day before rolled back into the dealership and in a surprise move paid cash for the vehicle and the sale closed successfully.

GM Charlie met me on the showroom floor.

"Excellent month, Presley."

"Thanks, Charlie."

"You do know with only one day left in the month, you're only five closed sales from overtaking Drexel, right?"

I spun my head to face him. "What?"

"He's had a pretty good month, but you've been keeping him on his toes every day."

And two of those sales technically should have been mine, so I would be only three down.

"I'm doing my best."

"I know, and someday soon you'll be on top. I can just imagine it. You can do it, Presley."

Charlie always quietly cheered for me. I questioned what he thought about Drexel as a person, but since Drexel knew how to sell cars, Charlie put up with his childish behavior.

"Why don't you head out? Only ten minutes left for the day and I know you have your class to get to." He gave a head jerk toward the front door.

"Thanks, Charlie!" I was mentally ready to go so I physically moved away before he could take the offer back. Not that he ever would.

After changing my clothes into jeans and a baby blue screen-print t-shirt with sneakers, I made the short trip across town to the local West Omaha art studio, Graphite and Acrylic. I participated in a sketching class to keep up on my art skills. Hadn't looked at the online schedule for tonight, but I hoped for something other than a bowl of fruit. Nothing was more boring than sketching a bowl of fruit.

My love life is.

I arrived early and wasted no time setting up my easel with a large sketchpad, arranging my graphite sketching pencils by tip size in the container. Out of the corner of my eye I caught movement at the front of the class, but in my effort to look around the cumbersome easel, I clipped my pad with my elbow and the already precariously balanced spiral-bound paper started to tumble to the floor. I scrambled to keep everything from crashing to the ground and missed what our instructor, Simi, said.

After adjusting the paper back to its original place, I watched my friend Edwyn's eyes pop wide open, and he produced an audible soft gasp. I'd sold him and his partner a fuel-efficient used Prius last year.

"What?" I asked.

"Um ... yum." He extended the *m* on yum until I giggled, but he didn't take his eyes off the sketching subject matter.

"More fruit?" I chuckled as he shook his head slowly.

I glanced around my large sketchpad and after my brain registered what was at the front of the room, I let go of a sexually frustrated sound that should have embarrassed me, but at this point, who the hell cared!

I do.

Standing at the front of the class—nude, full-frontal, buck naked, butt naked, stark naked, in a birthday suit, unclothed, bare, in the buff, *au naturel*, in the raw, leafless, without a stitch of clothing—was Jude!

I moved back behind my sketchpad and blushed every pink and red color creatable on an artist's palette.

"What?" Edwyn started his sketch. His eyes darted between the subject and the white paper.

"I know him!" I replied in a frantic whisper.

"Awkward." He tipped his head at me. "I'm sure he's a professional. Now professional what, I'd be interested in knowing. I'd be up for a threesome with that tasty piece of man-candy. Even if I had to pay for it." His eyes bugged out of his head.

"Ed! He's not a gigolo! He's my personal trainer."

"Well, he can personally train me any day." His words dripped with sensuality. Edwyn was always so straightlaced, he never acted like this. Frankly, I liked it.

"Jeez, Ed!" I returned with fake disgust and a genuine smile.

We both giggled behind our sketching pads.

"Okay, I can do this." I psyched myself up. "If he can be a professional model, I can act like a professional artist." *Or at the very least I'll try.*

I leaned slightly to take in the amazing male at the front of the room, hoping my placement at the back hid me from his sightlines. I put lead to paper, and in moments, I was sketching like a crazy woman, the graphite pencils flying like they were possessed. The vision of Jude's sinewy and flawless body scorched into my brain. Any fantasy I could've concocted about his physique was woefully misguided. He was a hundred times better in real life. *One thousand times better.*

Every muscle deserved flawless representation on the paper, and his man parts—although not explicitly porn-sized—complemented him in proportion. They were a specimen of male I'd never seen before, not that I'd seen a wide variety. Three. That was the breadth of my knowledge. Jude was all man down there, trimmed man, covered in a fine mesh of curly, sable brown hair, and his testicles dropped like two weighted golf balls. His penis curved perfectly, the pink tissue caressing against his sack like it was in the most comfortable place ever.

Before the hour of class ended, I'd downed three bottles of water because the tense and anxiety-riddled situation had me sweating like a high school slut at confessional.

Edwyn leaned over. "You okay, gorgeous?"

"Just overwhelmed."

"I can relate." Edwyn examined my sketch. "Holy crap, Presley, that's amazing!"

I scrutinized the drawing and swallowed hard while a bead of sweat trickled down my temple. It was my best work. What I'd created was almost a line for line, shape for shape, curve for curve exact replica of the original human work of art.

"Thanks."

I flipped the sketchpad to cover my efforts and packed my supplies, hoping to hightail out of the room through the back door and straight to the bathroom and avoid talking to the man whose mental image I'd masturbated to last night. The thought mortified me to the molecular level. In my efforts to pack up, I became oblivious to everything else happening around me, until a deep voice weakened my knees.

"Hi, Presley."

Squatting at my art bag, I mumbled a choice curse word and stood. "Hello, Jude."

"Um, so you're an artist?" He adjusted his black robe and retied the long sash.

"Yeah, as a hobby. Nothing da Vinci or Matisse would be proud of, that's for sure." I cringed as my bladder spasmed.

His brow furrowed. "Well, just wanted to say hello. I'll see you on Friday at five a.m., bright and early."

"I'll be there. Have a good night, Jude."

"Thanks. Bye, Presley."

The last smile he flashed qualified as heavenly and a memory that would probably keep me up tonight. My legs failed to move past the doorway, so I waited for him to brush ahead of me before I turned to run to the women's bathroom.

****

Jude

After changing in the men's bathroom stall, which was only big enough for a leprechaun, I splashed cold water on my face. My first time posing as a nude model, and although my horizontally oriented and absolutely-lacking-any-body-consciousness younger brother would probably be a better choice, I assumed he suggested my name because of his rotating work schedule, but maybe one of the girls had nixed the idea, too. I didn't know if they had that kind of pull in his life or not.

I didn't mind the posing, but I didn't realize Presley would be in the class. Watching her penetrating green eyes flash from behind that white sketchpad, teasing me every time I glanced her way, was enough to get the heavy-hanging weight lifter to start pumping up from his inert position. By sheer will alone, I kept him lifeless. I brought every penis-deflating baseball-like meditation to the forefront of my thoughts, instead of the wicked dreams I'd had for the last two nights about both normal and depraved sexual positions I wanted to see Presley contorted in, watching her coming undone under me and with me. The visions are killing me … slowly.

I collected my bag and walked out of the bathroom, not remembering which way the front door was. Before I had time to react to the wrong choice of direction, my body slammed into someone. I recognized a female gasp and the clatter of a bag, purse, and paper hitting the tile floor of the hallway.

"Shit!" I grabbed for the person, hoping to at least save her from following her belongings to the floor.

As I regained composure, I realized I was body to body with the apparition of my dreams. One hand grasped Presley's toned upper arm and the other slid around her waist, keeping our bodies pressed firmly to one another. Her slightly upturned nose rested against the bare opening in my black V-neck t-shirt.

I swear she just drew in a long breath ... of me.

"Sorry." I glanced down to the top of her head. Moving my hand from her arm, I brushed a piece of hair that chaotically sprawled across her forehead. She shivered at my touch. I rested the hand behind her neck and moved the other hand up her toned back.

Presley's face came up. Our gazes met, and her green orbs softened as her mouth opened in a soft *O* shape. I held her snugly against me for a few more seconds until I grasped the disturbing fact that the weight lifter had started pumping iron. Dropping my hands, I stepped back to keep her from being accosted by the part of me that found an incredibly awkward time to exercise his repressed will through my shorts.

I cleared my throat. "Sorry, Presley."

I squatted to pick up the items that were scattered at our feet, stopping when I came to the flipped-open sketchpad. I couldn't help but stare at the drawing. It was a photograph-perfect illustration of me.

"This is incredible, Presley." Looking up from my crouching position, I added, "I'd love to have a copy."

She dropped down to my level with a soft cotton-candy pink blush tinting her cheeks. She closed the sketchpad. "Thanks, Jude. I'll ... I'll have to think about it. I normally don't share my artwork with anyone. Sorry."

I handed over her purse and our hands collided, her delicate fingers resting against my larger ones. Our eyes connected again, and I couldn't help myself. Balancing ape-like on the knuckles of one hand, I leaned forward to her. Presley's eyes widened as my lips set on a mission to be on hers. Her hot steamy breath intimately interlaced with mine. We were only a hair's distance from touching when she heaved her personal items to her body, stood, and dashed around me.

I stood and watched her scurry across the entry to the front doors. I walked toward her. She turned and used her cute ass to push the door open and backed out of the building. "Have a good night, Jude. See you Friday morning. Bye." Her eyes flashed from my eyes to my crotch and back again.

Our eyes united intimately one last time.

"Bye, Presley." I brushed past her. "Was really nice running into you."

Chapter Five

Presley

The fact that I got no sleep last night shouldn't surprise me. The fact that I didn't masturbate to relieve the tension and encourage relaxation should. Running into Jude, or colliding like a wrecking ball into his firm but incredibly warm body, kept my brain dashing a mile a minute, every moment replayed over and over. When we were picking up my dropped items, I'd swear he was leaning in to kiss me, until I'd looked in the mirror at home and saw graphite smudged all over my nose. He was probably going to wipe the smudges away in disgust.

It was the last day of the month at the auto mall. I was determined to get as close to Drexel's sold tally as I could. I wore my best pantsuit, straightened my already straight hair, applied a little makeup, and chose sensible heels, ones that would allow me to move swiftly to any walk-ins that entered the dealership. Onsite, I reviewed my calendar and rechecked that I had the three test-drive appointments set up and all possible car prep was finished. All three requested vehicles were waiting around the corner to be driven to a spot in front. Only varsity parking for my clients. I was pulling out all the stops today.

My first appointment arrived. After I introduced myself, the middle-aged man went into a partially sexist diatribe about how a female car salesperson was the most ridiculous thing he had ever heard of. Well, next to women in the military, of course.

Of course...

Considering we'd handled all of his information and appointment details by e-mail and my name was kind of gender neutral. Not really though. I almost didn't blame him for not knowing, but another part of me needed to prove to him that he was simply wrong.

On my worst day, I do this job better than any man.

I walked him back to my office, made small talk, and then focused on business, asking the right questions, keeping eye contact, following up quickly, offering suggestions. By the time we were both out of inquiry, I'd made a valid argument that I was the woman for the job.

The buzz-cut grey-haired man leaned back in his chair. "So are we gonna continue to shoot the shit like we're old Army pals, or are you going to let me drive that hunk of metal outside?"

I escorted him outside to the Ford F-150 he requested by e-mail. He rounded the vehicle, entered and drove at what could only be called a Sunday/Grandpa pace, but I enjoyed his safe and fuel-efficient approach to automobile ownership. By the end of the drive we'd talked about his six grandkids and their numerous activities, from soccer and baseball to dance and music. They were why he needed more room than his single-cab Ford Ranger offered. He helped his two daughters to transport the grandkids around. One of the girls' husbands passed away last year from cancer, and he helped out where he could. Tears filled my eyes and I gave him my condolences. He sighed, relaying how hard it was to see his beautiful girl's heart still broken in two. It was times like this that regardless of whether they bought or not, I had a part in something I could be proud of.

Upon returning to the dealership, he spotted Charlie and beelined to him.

And here it goes. Somehow I messed this one up. Great.

"Charlie Johnson, you SOB! Why didn't you tell me you had a secret weapon at the dealership? I would have prepared myself for her assault. It was on level with the captain's bitch and berate that time after we almost flipped the Humvee at A.T." They hugged as two old friends.

"Gus Sheffield! Jesus, it's been forever. Presley's on track to be our best salesperson."

"Well, I can see why. I'm gonna need to call my daughter. Her eighteen-year-old son, you remember Ryker, right?"

Charlie nodded.

Gus wrapped an arm around Charlie, and they both stared at me. "Well, he's been looking for a dependable car and I'm sure he'd love to take a test-drive with that sweetheart in the seat next to him."

"Now, Gus, don't be lettin' your grandson make any moves on my favorite salesperson."

And oh ... my ... God!

Best feeling ever. The two of them continued fussing it up Grandpa-style over me. Gus ended up buying the truck, and Charlie took care of the details so they could catch up.

One down, four to go to beat Drexel Mason. If, and that was a huge if, he hadn't sold any today. Thinking of Dixless ... where is he?

"Hey Jillian, where's Mason?"

"Called in sick. I guess he figured he had the month sewn up. Prez, you have to do this. Kick his ass, sister! We all need that asshole to be brought down a notch and seeing your picture on the 'Shrine to Dixless' would be so awesome."

"Jillian, keep it on the down-low with the nickname, please."

She cringed. "Sorry. I just got all excited. Plus, Presley, I guarantee not another woman here isn't thinking the same thing."

"Okay, here's what I need you to do. I have to stay hydrated, so keep bottled water on my desk, please. Let me know if Dixless shows up, and if for some reason he calls in to talk to Charlie or Trent, please take a message or stall him the best you can. I imagine he'll try to sabotage me somehow. Okay, my next test-drive should be coming in."

"Will do all. Good luck!" She raised jazz-hands. "We're rooting for you!"

Drexel is out sick? This is the best thing to happen. Well, not for him but for me. I'm down only four to surpass him. I can do this. I think.

The next client, Alice Evans, test-drove and I could tell she hated, and I mean absolutely *hated* to the point of tears, the bare-bones new car she picked out online. The wiry tall woman needed something to fit her leggy and thin frame, not an undersized car.

I guided her to my office and explained the benefits of having an SUV, especially a four-wheel drive SUV, in the winter. Alice lowered her voice to let me know that her ex-husband messed up her credit, and she would have to pay cash. I asked how much she had, and she whispered $10,000 like it was a small amount of money. I could totally work with that. We found her the perfect SUV in the used lot. She fell in love with the handling, the upgraded interior, the heated seats, and the remote start for chilly winters. Now I just had to get the dealership's sales manager, Trent, to come down from $12,500 to her $10,000 budget. A challenge but not impossible.

After getting Alice a cup of coffee, I headed to Trent's office.

"Hey, Trent, have a minute?"

"Yeah. Whatcha got?" He moved paperwork to the side.

"Have a client who wants to buy that silver Nissan Pathfinder that's been sitting on the lot for almost a year…"

"Yeah?" He leaned back in his chair.

"Willing to offer ten grand cash for it." I waited.

Sometimes it wasn't what you said but how you said it. And other times it was knowing when to stop saying anything at all.

He tipped his eyes up to the ceiling, bouncing in his seat, clucking his tongue on the roof of his mouth. When he returned to a speaking human and not a chicken, he threw up a general wave of his hand. "All right, it's end of the month and I was going to send it to auction next month anyway. We'd get half that much there. Make the deal."

I practically ran back to Alice, and together we jumped up and down at the news.

Slightly unprofessional? Sure. But she was so thrilled I couldn't help it. I handed her a box of tissues when the moment overtook her.

"I really needed this, Presley. I got a new job yesterday and I knew my old POS car wasn't going to make it much longer. You saved me."

"Crap! Hand me one of those tissues, Alice." I half laughed and half cried. "I'm so glad I could help you."

I escorted her to the business office to finish paperwork and take ownership of her new used vehicle. I made sure the detail center shined the interior and exterior to almost brand-new, taking an extra hour to complete the transformation. When Alice finished with the red tape, I walked her to the detailed vehicle with a box of tissues ready to go with her on the road. Through tears she told me she would be back later with her teenaged son to pick up what would be his POS car from now. He'd be thrilled, too.

My last scheduled appointment of the day arrived after lunch. I met him at the front desk and we walked outside to the Porsche 911 Carrera S that he requested. It was an absolutely amazing car. And absolutely expensive, too. He rounded the car. Once, twice, three times. Never opened a door, never stepped foot inside, never asked a single question. I prepared myself to start exalting its better features when he interrupted my internal salesperson.

"Okay, I'll take it. My boss will be happy to have what he wanted for the weekend. Where's the sales or business office? I'll take care of the paperwork myself."

"I'm glad you like the car, Mr. Sullivan. I'd be glad to present your offer to the sales manager, Mr. Woods."

"I'm sorry, Miss Bradenhurst, I should've been clear. My offer is the sticker price, and I want to be gone as soon possible. I have three other important errands to finish for Mr. Buffett before the shareholders' meeting."

Holy crap! I didn't know if he meant *the* Warren Buffett, but even if he didn't mean the Oracle of Omaha, it was probably some relative. And even if it wasn't … it was a sale! I decided to let Trent handle this one. Especially since Mr. Sullivan was offering sticker and probably cash on a $100,000+ vehicle, without driving it.

"No problem. Let me check that Mr. Woods is available."

I offered him a seat in the waiting area and a bottle of water and walked to Trent's office.

I stuck my head around the corner. "Trent?"

"No, Presley, we can't go lower on the Pathfinder for your new BFF." His gaze stayed down and concentrated on his pile of papers.

"No, Trent, there is a representative here for a Mr. Buffett who wants to buy the Porsche 911 Carrera S. His name is Skyler Sullivan. He'd like to get the paperwork done ASAP so he can finish his list of to-dos for Mr. Buffett."

Trent sat up straight. "You're kidding, right?"

"Nope, that's what he says. Are you ready to work with him? I did my job. He wants to buy it sticker price right now."

Trent took over, introduced himself, and made like a kiss-ass. Mr. Sullivan thanked me and we shook hands. I left the room for fear of being sucked into the giant vortex of swirling crap gushing from Trent's piehole.

Yes! That was three down.

While I had a minute, I walked to the copy room and made some copies. By three p.m., I'd called every possible lead I'd ever spoken with and there were no loose ends to speak of. They'd either bought elsewhere, put buying on hold, or basically told me to F-off. I watched the clock on my computer click down. Slowly. The digits hit four p.m., and when my phone rang I jumped like my grandma at a fireworks show.

"Good afternoon, Presley Bradenhurst."

"Prez, it's Jillian," she whispered. "You need to go outside now, there's a guy milling around the lot. I've never seen him before. He might be new. But he might not."

I didn't even say thank you or good-bye. I threw the phone down, grabbed my jacket, and ran for the door. Outside, I watched Sam rounding the corner of the building, eyeing up the visitor.

"Hello, again!" I yelled and waved at the guy looking in the SUV's driver's side window.

The thin man stepped back from the vehicle. "Presley?"

My heels ground to a halt on the concrete. *How does he know my name?*

I took the last twenty steps and … my prayers had been answered. Mr. Miller. The neighbor I grew up next to and my high school math teacher. He stood next to a new, gray SUV.

"Hello, Mr. Miller. It's so nice to see you!"

The man tugged me in for a hug. Sam backed away with a scowl, acquiescing to the fact that a personal relationship already existed.

I cut to the chase. "Mr. Miller, have you been in contact with any other salesperson here at Jessen?"

"No, just stopped by to check out the new Explorers. Beth has been on me to trade up for a year."

"Well, you've picked a winner right here."

Mr. Miller took a step back and glanced me up and down. "Presley Bradenhurst, now, it hasn't gotten past me that you look different. I hope you're feeling well."

"Yes, Mr. Miller, I've been exercising and eating right."

"Well, you were always adorable, but dear, you're a beautiful young woman now."

A warm gushy feeling rode through my body at his sincere words. "Thank you. Hope all is well with Mrs. Miller?"

"She's got her bowling and mahjong. As long as she makes it to see her friends, we're very good and I'm not in the doghouse."

I chuckled. "So are you interested in a test-drive?"

"No, no. I really just wanted to sticker surf while Beth gets her hair done. You know, see the mix of metal, leather, and plastic up close."

"Well, just to let you know, the incentives on these models are great, but ... they end today."

"Like how great?"

Hook, line, and sinker.

My fourth sale of the day. I ended up tied with Dixless for the month. That was a whole lot better than first loser, but not what I'd really fought for. I was exhausted by the time I grabbed my purse and proceeded to the front door after five o'clock.

"And just where do you think you're going, Miss Bradenhurst?" I heard behind me as I clicked my heels across the floor.

I spun. "Mr. Sheffield? Hello ... again. I hope that truck is working out for you."

"That truck is perfect. My wife's driving it right now. I foresee having to get her one soon."

"Good to hear. Mr. Sheffield, is there something else I can help you with?"

"Actually, there is. Ryker! Grandson, come here and meet your salesperson."

A young man strolled over to us, and we shook hands. Gus introduced us formally, but I asked them to call me by my first name.

"Presley, I want to buy my grandson his first car," Gus said with a smile.

My eyes started to cloud with tears.

I'm actually going to do it. I'm going to beat Drexel Mason.

I cleared my throat and collected my thoughts. "Okay, let me set these things down in my office and I'll be right back." By the time I made it to my office, the shock had worn off. I awkwardly high-fived myself and giggled my way back to the front.

It took two hours to find the right car, but we did, and Ryker couldn't have been more thrilled. A used late-model Mazda 3, silver, manual, and sporty. He looked like he was going to break out in some sort of teenage jig in celebration.

When the deal was done, Charlie met me on the showroom floor to say good-bye to them.

After they'd left, I turned to him. "Did you have something to do with that?"

His eyebrows furrowed. "No, Presley, that was all you. Gus was thoroughly impressed ... with you. To see Ryker all grown up was great. He's so proud of that young man and since he's now the male figure in Ryker's life, he takes that role seriously. Presley, you did it! I'm sure Drexel will have a shit-fit tomorrow, but you deserve it. Can't wait to put your smile up there on the Wall of Monthly Best."

I pursed my lips, then I told Charlie thank you, and that I needed to get to an appointment. I was completely overwhelmed by the events of the day and partially exhausted to the bone. I gave the evening phone staff high-fives before leaving, and Charlie chuckled.

I got to my car and took a deep breath before pulling out my phone.

Prez: **U up for Chinese?**

Willow: **Are you trying to get out of paying the twenty dollar-holy-shit-tariff by charming me with food?**

I laughed. Forgot about that.

Willow spent the night out with friends. She didn't come home until really, really late—or early, depending on one's view.

Prez: **No, I'll get you the $20, too. Kung Pao Chix and crab rangoon okay?**

Willow: **Perfect!**

After calling in the to-go order at Golden Dragon and picking it up, I drove into the garage of the townhouse while I blasted my favorite Foo Fighters CD.

Willow greeted me with a beer and 'I'm-absolutely-not-going-anywhere' clothes.

"Okay, you have a shit-eatin' grin on your face, Presley. What's up?" she asked, plopping onto the couch and opening the brown paper bag to remove its delicious contents.

I sat on the couch. "I did it. I finally beat Dixless. I will be the top salesperson this month."

"Congratulations, Prez! I knew you could do it." Willow tackled me into a big hug. "I'm so proud of you."

I sat back and reveled in the feeling. Success and happiness. There was only one thing missing, someone special—other than Willow—to share the moment with. Willow was great, and I appreciated her support, but I wanted someone to fill the other voids in my life. I shook my head. Didn't need to find that tonight. Tonight is about celebrating.

I drank a long swig of Willow's favorite lemon-infused craft beer and set the brown bottle on the coffee table to start eating what Willow had dished out onto a plate.

After devouring a crispy crab rangoon, Willow wiped her mouth. "Why don't we go out tomorrow night to celebrate? Bring Jace along?"

"I haven't seen her in forever." I downed the rest of my beer as the meal seared my palate with the spice of chilies. "Maybe do a little West O barhopping?"

"I love it!"

While Willow looked over my shoulder, I texted Jace.

Prez: **Hey Sexy! Girls' Night Out tomorrow with W? You in?**

Willow and I watched some *Friends* reruns until we were quoting lines along with the characters. We both decided an early night wouldn't be a bad thing for either of us. The current activity was pointless if we'd seen every episode to the point of memorization. Plus, we both admitted to being worn out, me from the day's events and Willow from getting no sleep the night before.

In bed, I grabbed the latest romance book I was reading from the nightstand. My phone buzzed.

Jace: **I am in! Broke up with Taylor on Monday. :-(Could use a Girls' Night Out with my BFFs and a random forget-about-my-troubles hookup. I'm off at 4 tomorrow, so I can Happy Hour if anyone else can**

Prez: **Sorry about Taylor. :-(You will find the right person, totally believe that ... pinkie swear. Glad you can join us!**

Jace: **Are we celebrating or just going out?**

Prez: **Celebrating! I'm going to be Salesperson of the Month! I'm off at 5, but I'll let Willow know you could meet her, she's off at 2 or 3, I think.**

Jace: **Congrats sweetie! You definitely deserve it. Dixless can suck donkey-dix! Luv u!**

Prez: **Love you too! <3 TTYL**

I met Jaclyn (Jace for short) Zelensky at the University of Nebraska here in Omaha. We were in several business classes together. She accepted a job as a project manager for Wattier & Buchman, an advertising, public relations, and marketing company. Jace loved her bosses. They were a couple that epitomized true love according to Jace. I think they kind of made her jealous. I didn't blame her. Listening to her talk about them, I was kind of jealous, too. She deserved someone special to spend her life with. Jace's last partner, Taylor, was nice, but didn't understand Jace's professional drive.

Sometimes I wondered if that would happen to me, too. I worked long hours and, like tonight, I sometimes stayed long after I should have left the dealership. Selling cars wasn't eight to five. Ever. I needed someone who understood the need to put forth that kind of effort at work.

My phone buzzed next to me on the bed. Jace probably forgot something.

Unknown number. I opened the text.

Unknown: **Hi, Jude here.**

I stopped reading right there. How? Why? What for? A million questions spun through my head and my blood rushed through my veins at NASCAR speed.

Finish reading the text and find out!

Unknown: **Hi, Jude here. Just wanted to remind you-5am tomorrow. I'll be there. Can't wait to make you sweat. J**

"Holy shit!"

"Now you owe me forty dollars!" Willow chuckled and the sound carried through the wall.

"No, I don't. That wasn't an orgasmic 'holy shit' that was an I-can't-believe-what-I-just-read 'holy shit'."

"What can't you believe?"

"My trainer just texted me a reminder and he says that he, and I quote, 'can't wait to make me sweat'!"

"You need to jump that stud. He's sending signals, Prez. Trainers don't remind people of appointments. They get paid if you show or don't."

I remained quiet and stilled for a long time. My brain and body weren't communicating. Terrified that making a move would set off a nuclear reaction of overwhelming emotion, I was stuck in a weird frozen state of being.

"Are you okay, Presley?" Willow had this weird intuition that used to bug me. She predicted when I was going to crash into myself, the ripples of my psyche cracking and crumbling, but instead of telling me what was going to happen, now she supported me and let me work out the emotional fallout on my own ... most of the time. My coping skills had come a long way, but there was always a possibility that a giant emotional tidal wave would pull me under.

Relationship stuff like this could do that to me. I could drown in all the thinking and overthinking the details I'd already thought I'd thought about, drowning until I was a pile of human goo on the sofa watching every sappy and heart-wrenching *Lifetime* movie out there for weekends on end. Years of therapy helped, but I was still a bipolar worrywart. The worry rode slowly over me in extremes. The middle homeostatic good-type-of-worry area grew over time, but at that moment, I was 100 percent freaked out.

I inhaled a deep breath to calm my frantically beating heart. "Yeah, I'm okay. No Ben and Jerry's meltdown. I'm going to text him back 'thanks' and move on. He's going out with Emerson tomorrow night anyway. If he's into her, he definitely doesn't want me! I mean ... she's gorgeous and I'm—"

I swore I heard Willow growl or grunt or gargle or something.

What the hell was that?

When her voice came back, it was probably heard in the next county. "Presley, you are beautiful! How many times do I have to tell you that!" She calmed, then added, "You were beautiful before you started working out and eating better, but now, my sister from another mother, you are … Drop. Dead. Gorgeous. I swear. I wouldn't lie to you. You know that."

"I know," I mumbled.

Willow wouldn't lie, but the word "beautiful" just never came to mind when I weighed—what I weighed. I hated to think in numbers and I wouldn't ever again. Healthy physically, emotionally, and mentally was all that mattered.

Prez: **Thanks for the reminder. I'll be there.**

I went back to my book. My phone buzzed.

Jude: **My pleasure. How was your day?**

Small talk? Really?

I could have ignored him. But I didn't.

Prez: **Good, actually, really good. I will be the top salesperson for the month.**

Jude: **Congratulations! Blake told me you are a great car salesperson.**

Blake said that? How sweet.

Prez: **Thanks.**

I stopped typing and contemplated if I wanted to take the text a little further. I bit my lip and continued typing.

Prez: **Thanks. How was your day?**

My heart paused when I tapped the send button. I stared at his name, still kind of in shock that he was now permanent in my phone. And in my life?

I received a return text almost immediately and my heart played a quick tempo of happiness.

Jude: **Three new clients today. Loving Triple R. Met some great people.**

Prez: **Congrats to you, too. Triple R is lucky to have you.**

There was a long wait for another text. Maybe we're done?

Jude: **Sorry for surprising you @ art class yesterday.**

Prez: **No need to apologize. It was nice to see you.**

I pressed send and then panicked.

I didn't just say that! *"Nice to see you"?* He was naked! That sounds totally creepy!

Jude: **The whole me or just parts of me? ;-)**

OMG! I think he's flirting by text!

I sat up in bed and stared blindly at my phone. My brain was stuck trying to determine if he was, in fact, actually, positively, irrefutably flirting. I was sure several minutes went by, even if the lapse felt like seconds.

The phone buzzed in my hand and I flinched like it was a striking snake.

Jude: **Presley, I am sorry. I may have offended you. If I did, I didn't mean to. Hope to see you in the AM. Good night.**

Contemplating my next move from every direction, I closed my eyes and tried to absorb the emotions coursing through me, something I rarely did because the sensations were often overwhelming. Jude was a nice guy, and I wanted to like him, but I didn't want to get hurt either. I'd been here before. Putting myself out there and being rejected had eaten away the ability to see when someone was actually interested.

I typed slowly.

Prez: **No offense. Liked bumping into you as much as seeing all of you.**

After a deep breath, I closed my eyes and hit send. In less than a minute, there was a return text. I opened the message and then opened my eyes.

Jude: **My family says I never have my eyes open to watch where I'm going, both in my personal life and when it comes to turning the right direction.**

Trying to change both. However, when it comes to you, Presley, I have my eyes wide open and I like what I see, too. Good night.

Holy shit!

Prez: **Good night, Jude.**

I slept peacefully.

Chapter Six

Jude

It was finally Friday. Out the door early and to the gym in fifteen minutes. Omaha was an easy city to get around in. Similar to Des Moines, but with better grid-patterned streets. I was really starting to like this town. As well as other things.

I was curious how things would be between Presley and me. Last night's light text-flirting, where I thought she admitted she liked my junk, and when our bodies touched at the art place was ... interesting, and I was interested in learning more about her. There was something strong about Presley Bradenhurst and something equally as vulnerable about her. She was a puzzle of sorts. I love puzzles.

Sitting at the desk filing paperwork, I sat up straight when Presley came rolling in. In flat shoes, her head fit right under my chin, as I'd found out on Wednesday night. Her long hair was pulled back in a ponytail, like a black whip down her back, swishing side to side when she walked.

I left my long hair down this morning to dry. I was thinking about it the other night. Why so long? Mainly because I got lazy in college and let it grow, then girls started telling me the Jarod Leto-style looked good. So I left it that way. I'd thought about cutting it off—it could be hot during the summer and a bitch to take care of some days—but I didn't.

Just admit it. You're too fucking lazy to change it.

"Hi, Jude," Presley greeted me as she walked by to the stretching area.

I walked toward her, admiring the view.

You need to remain professional.

"Good morning, Presley. How are you today?"

"I'm good, a little tired. Stayed up too late reading and chatting by text with someone." She smirked and plopped onto the blue mat to grab her ankle for a calf and thigh stretch.

"That's too bad. I have new isometrics and a routine change-up planned for today. Do I need to bring the intensity down a notch?"

"Nope. Bring it on." She glanced up through her lashes and added, "Plus, someone promised to make me sweat."

Damn, she's being kind of playful today.

"I'll do my best."

She stood and completed a ten-second stretch of her graceful neck. "I'm ready for this day to get started so tonight can get here."

"Big plans?"

Please don't say you have a date.

She stretched her arms. "Girls' night out."

I started stretching, too. Not sure why. I'd already stretched. But it seemed weird to just stand and watch her.

"What about you, Jude?"

I really didn't want to tell her about the Emerson thing. "I have a second job bartending. I work tonight and tomorrow night."

Presley's face contorted. "Is there another new trainer working here?"

"Not that I know of. Why? Am I not doing a good job and you're ready to move on already?"

Stretching out her back, Presley twisted at the waist. "No!" She cringed at how loud she had said the word, and lowered her voice. "No reason. Anyway, you mean you work a third job? I'm assuming you get paid for..."—she lowered her voice to a whisper—"modeling."

Couldn't help but smile. "It's actually a favor to my brother's—" I tried to come up with what Yori was to him. She might not be a girlfriend, but she was definitely more than a friend. "—my brother's tenant's sister."

That was jacked up!

"Your instructor, Simi," I added quickly.

Presley beamed. "I love Simi. She's so talented."

I nodded. I'd only seen a couple pieces of her art, and I wasn't an art aficionado by any means, but they looked good to me. Presley's sketch was awesome.

Wonder if she decided on a copy?

"Okay, all stretched?"

Presley leaned over to grab her water bottle and the view was … oh, thank God I used her mental image in the shower this morning.

"Ready." She smiled.

I started Presley on weight machines to warm up, then moved to isometric muscle training with a special emphasis on developing a slightly different body form, filling in muscle. We moved to a medicine ball and ended with cardio. Soaked in sweat was a good look for her. The heat of her body intensified the scents and the salt-heightened, deep floral aroma caused my mouth to water and my heart to pound.

Presley started on the treadmill. I stood off to the side by the machine's controls and adjusted the speed. She moved at less of a clip than on Monday, but it was more than a jog in my trainer's book. Ten minutes into the jog-run, she broke the silence.

"How long have you lived in Omaha … Jude?" She panted a little and shortened her stride.

"About a month and a half. I moved from Des Moines and live with my younger brother."

"What's … his name?"

"Zane. Why?"

"Well ... with an awesome name like Jude ... I figured his had to be something cool, too. Wasn't ... wrong."

I smiled at her reasoning. "So, you have other plans for the weekend?"

"Probably ... recovery ... from girls' night out."

Her breathing was starting to get a little choppy and her face paled slightly. I backed her speed down and substituted a small incline.

She continued, "Maybe a bike ride. Supposed to be nice this ... weekend. And then cats ... and dogs, like every ... Sunday." The last sentence was on a quick exhale and she didn't seem to be improving.

"Sounds like a good weekend. Do you ever work on the weekends?"

Her amazing chest was at eye-level, and I became engrossed in watching the rise and fall of her perfect globes.

Mesmerizing.

"Only ... once ... a ... mon..."

Her one-word-at-a-time response and inability to finish the last word returned my attention. The tempo had compromised her breathing and her lips tinged with blue.

"Shit! Presley!" I slammed my hand on the stop button and caught her as the machine halted and her knees buckled. Cradling her in my arms, I carried her to a padded bench to lay her down, then knelt beside her head. Her eyes remained closed as her breathing wheezed in and whistled out. I checked her heart rate. Her carotid artery pulsed like a rock anthem beneath my fingers.

"Presley? Hey. Come back to me," I whispered close to her ear and cupped the top of her head. My heart pounded a frantic rhythm as if it were tied to hers.

A shallow rasp of air exhaled from her mouth. "I'm still here, Jude."

I skimmed her forehead with my thumb, gently. "God, you scared me. Are you okay?"

"My head is spinning, but I'm okay." Her body flushed bright red from oxygen reentering her bloodstream. "I didn't faint, just lost my wind." She gulped in a breath. "Can you get my water bottle, please?"

Her breathing settled slowly, and she fought to regain her composure. I bent over her and cupped her jaw. My thumb skimmed over her fleshy, supple, baby-pink lips, and her eyes flashed opened. I held her gaze. "I'm not leaving you."

I stood while keeping an eye on Presley. "Emerson. Emerson!"

Emerson ambled at a turtle's pace over to the bench. "I've seen her do this before, Jude. It's nothing new. She'll be fine."

"Please get Miss Bradenhurst a bottle of water from the staff lounge."

"Get it yourself, Saylor." She flipped her hair before turning her back.

"Emerson, get the bottle of water." I gritted through my teeth. "Now!"

Emerson turned back around and her jaw tightened. "Fine!" She threw a final remark over her shoulder, "Miss Overdramatic needs to find some endurance."

Presley squirmed with discomfort, then shook her head, her eyes clamped shut.

I squatted back down to be eye-to-eye. "Don't give what Emerson says a second thought, she's nothing."

A line formed between Presley's eyes. "Right … nothing. That's why you're—"

"Incoming!" Emerson yelled from about fifteen feet away, throwing me a cold water bottle.

I caught the airborne plastic rocket and turned to help Presley sit up. "Here. How do you feel now?"

"I feel like an idiot." Presley took a long drink. "This happened with Mitch, too. I can't go faster than a ten-minute mile. Never have been able to." She dropped her head. "Sorry."

I sat next to her and rested my hand at the small of her back. "You're not an idiot, and don't be sorry. I was too interested in our conversation. I like talking to you and I let my attention ... well, I just should've been paying more attention."

Presley's head came back up, and I smiled lightly. She smiled back and our eyes connected. Even with her pupils still dilated from the distress of almost fainting, it was easy to see there was attraction and desire running like wild horses through those green beauties.

The moment seemed almost more important than anything I'd said before, to anyone. "Presley, I'd like to take you on a—"

"What the hell happened here?" Blake's harsh voice bit through the air.

Presley's eyes widened as she stared up at him.

Rising to my feet, I faced Blake. "I pushed her a little too hard. Guess I wanted to make a good impression, and I overdid it. Sorry, Presley, and sorry, Blake."

Blake stalked past me to Presley. "Why don't you come to my office and rest for a while? I don't think you should drive. I'll take you to work and have Jamal drive your car there later. Okay?"

"Blake, I'm fine." Presley began to stand from the bench but her legs crumbled. She clutched my arm for support.

"Nope, not fine." Blake pointed a finger at me. "Jude, get her to my office now."

I scooped Presley up and started walking. She laid her head against my shoulder, her nose nuzzled into the side of my neck. Anyone looking from the outside wouldn't have noticed the move, but I felt it. My head spun with the thought that this woman had almost been hurt by my distraction. My heart swelled knowing she wanted this as badly as I did. And my gut churned wondering if I'd screwed up my chance with her and at Triple R.

But this is real.

There was something here, and whatever it was, I wasn't the only one who felt it.

Chapter Seven

Presley

I'd never been so embarrassed. Except for the first time that'd happened. At least that time I'd made my way to the locker room before I'd became totally incoherent and vertically challenged. A couple of other gym patrons had stopped and asked me if I was okay, and I'd said I had cramps. It was a good cover. They'd nodded like they understood and moved on. I was sure that was where Emerson saw me.

As Jude scooped me up from the treadmill to carry me to the bench, I almost felt like I was being rescued. But from what? Myself? Everything? His warm body was comforting, and he smelled woodsy with a hint of cherry and sandalwood. My whole body tingled with want or maybe it was lack of oxygen. Whatever was happening, the reaction warmed me deep inside. Jude was beginning to ask me something that made his gold-glittered hazel eyes dart between mine. His Adam's apple rose and fell with a deep swallow, but then a very pissed-off Blake had interrupted us.

Now Jude carried me to Blake's office. His sultry scent inspired my body to respond and my nipples hardened through my workout bra and my pink cotton t-shirt, the tight peaks brushed against his shiny black performance shirt, causing zings of awareness to strike between my legs.

"I'll take it from here, Jude," Blake huffed, backing Jude out the door after he'd set me gently in a chair.

"I'd like to stay to make sure she's okay."

"You have another client in twenty minutes. She'll be fine with me. I'll talk to you later."

"Okay. Again, sorry, Presley." Jude's eyes displayed his apology.

"Not your fault, Jude, genetics and past health problems created this issue. Thanks for catching me before I crashed to the ground."

Jude's eyes brightened a little. "I hope I—"

Blake cleared his throat.

"Okay, I'll see you on Monday. Have a good weekend." He flashed one last strained but still heartwarming smile before turning back toward the gym floor.

"I'll be here!" I called out right before Blake shut the door.

Rounding his desk, Blake examined me from head to toe. "Are you absolutely sure you're okay?"

"Yes, Blake. I need to be clear with Jude what my physical limits are. I think maybe I was trying to show off for him, too. He's a great guy."

Blake scowled at my assessment.

"And personal trainer." I added, to cover whatever he didn't like in my initial statement.

Blake drew a piece of paper out of his desk. "I'm going to move you to Jamal for training."

"Why?" I asked with more than a touch of concern behind it.

Blake ignored me and tapped something into his computer.

"Blake! Why?"

"I have my reasons."

"Don't I have any say in this?"

"Not really. Jude is new, and if I don't like the dynamics of the relationship or his training methods, I have the right to remove clients from him." Blake brought his eyes up and forced a thin smile. "Especially my favorite clients."

My brows furrowed. "What's wrong with the dynamics of our relationship?" My heart skipped as I said "our relationship". They seemed to be two words that fit together but I couldn't wrap my head around why.

Blake leaned forward. "Presley, you almost fainted. I can't have him forcing you to exert yourself like that. It's dangerous."

"Blake, first, Jude didn't 'force' me to do anything. I'm an adult and by now I should know my limitations. Second, it was a one-time thing." I crossed my fingers at my sides hoping lightning didn't strike me for lying. "I promise I won't overdo it again. I'll train on a less intense level. Promise. Please." I leaned forward and rested my hands on his desk. "I like Jude's style of training and I was fine … until the cardio. Actually, I felt great."

Blake leaned back in his chair, rocking while holding my gaze. "You're positive you won't overdo it again?" His serious face spoke his concern more than the words.

"Cross my heart." I airbrushed an X on my chest.

"All right, one more week, and I'm adding back in ten sessions to your package just so you don't sue me."

"You don't have to do that. I would never sue you, Blake."

"Karma will bite me in the ass some way if I don't. Consider the next ten weeks on me. Really, I'd feel better if you changed to Jamal or Kai or Shannon."

"Let's give Jude a chance to redeem himself—not that any of this was his fault."

"Okay," Blake muttered reluctantly. "One more session. And I'm going to be watching him like a hawk."

"Fair enough. Now, can I go shower so I don't smell like a dead fish at work?"

Blake chuckled. "Sure, but if you're not out in an hour I'm sending the cavalry in to find you."

I nodded, then stood and made my way toward the door. "Please, just not Emerson."

"What?"

Had a feeling he heard what I said, but I didn't repeat it. "I'll be fine. Thanks, Blake."

As much as Emerson had never been my favorite person, I didn't need to be bad-mouthing another person. I'd had people say bad things about me. Even if they were true, they still hurt, and I wasn't that person.

Blake's eyes narrowed, and I turned to leave. "Have a good weekend, Presley."

"You, too."

I worked my way to the showers and was ready within the hour. Walking from the locker room, I watched Jude helping his next client across the gym. He gave a chin-jut my way, but I decided not to return his acknowledgment. I didn't want to get him in more trouble. Plus, my feelings tangled and twisted. He was my trainer. That was all. I doubted his interest went further than that relationship. Why would it? I was the anti-Emerson, and maybe she acted differently when she wasn't here in the gym. I bet she had a nice side, too. Maybe she had to be a bitch here to keep the trainers in line and the customers from running her over. Why did I even care? I was about to have a night out with the girls. I needed to care less about Jude and Emerson and more about … well, more about me.

I walked to the desk where Emerson was filing her claws. I mean nails. I cleared my throat but she acted like she didn't see me.

"Excuse me. Emerson, right?"

She scraped her eyes from her nails up to my face. I lifted a manila envelope from my bag and placed it on the counter.

"Hi. Can you please see that Jude gets this?"

She snatched the envelope off the counter. "I'll put it in his mailbox."

"Please," I said nicely, "don't fold it."

"Wouldn't dare think of it." She rolled her eyes while squeezing the rectangle into a tight tube.

"Have a good weekend, Emerson."

"Oh, I plan to. Jude's the thing that I'm going to do this weekend."

I inhaled a sharp breath. She smirked. Obviously, she enjoyed getting a reaction from me, and I gave her what she wanted. I walked away.

When I arrived at Jessen's to finish up my workweek, a "welcome" crew with congratulations posters, balloons, and a donut tower cake greeted me inside. The amount of cheering was embarrassing. The front desk girls chanted for a speech, and my skin blushed ten shades of red.

After the natives had calmed, I took a deep breath. "Wow. Thank you, everyone! I'm not going to lie, this is overwhelming, but honestly, it's awesome!" More cheering echoed through the dealership. "Each of you played a part in this. From the wonderful front desk girls who are the first representation of this amazing dealership, to the backroom operations who make sure we get our paychecks that keep us wanting to come back to work. I am glad to be a part of this family, and I hope to kick some you-know-what again next month."

"Miss Perfect's win wasn't much of a butt-kicking." Drexel didn't hide his dissatisfaction while talking to Sam behind me. "One lousy sale." They snickered like teenagers examining a porn magazine for the first time.

I ignored them and walked to the girls, Jillian and Avery, for a celebratory hug, donut, and orange juice.

"Thanks, you guys. You know this victory is also yours, right?"

"Then we can have some of that big fat bonus check you'll get?" Avery probed while nudging Jillian.

I smiled. "Maybe a lunch on me?"

"I'll take it. More than we've ever gotten as a thank you from Dixless."

Jillian agreed with Avery, and I hugged them both. Their support was one of the reasons I enjoyed what I did.

After getting my uncomfortable fill of office love, it was back to work. I set up a couple of appointments for Monday on two referrals the girls slipped me as I walked away. Sitting in my office, I enjoyed the morning with the balloons making me smile every time they waved from the breeze coming in the front door. I mostly worked on playing Internet games on my computer. Charlie rounded the corner, and I thumped the monitor power button off.

"I know you all play those damn games. When there are customers standing around waiting for a salesperson, I'll start screaming. Until then, no need to break your finger hitting the off button."

A guilt-riddled smile crossed my face.

Charlie continued, "Anyway, not sure you know it, but the top salesperson gets the afternoon off the next day they work, or at least that's how Drexel worked it, so I'm giving you the afternoon off."

"Really?"

"Yeah, go! Get gone. You deserve it. Remember, Monday you get your picture taken by Jillian's husband,

Mark, photographer to the Jessen stars. Oh, and Presley, there's a loaner car waiting for you outside. We can't have our best salesperson driving around in what you drive around in."

"You're kidding, right?" I tugged my purse and my jacket from the back of my chair.

"Nope, brand-new and all yours for the month. You like it and we'll make you a good deal on it."

"Okay. I'll be all dolled up on Monday, and thanks for the loaner, Charlie."

"My pleasure. Congratulations, Presley. Have a good weekend." He tossed me the jingling famous Jessen "J" key chain.

"Thanks!" I caught it in midair, then handed over the key to my well-cared-for car so it could be stored in one of the off-site lots. I practically danced out of my office.

I departed the dealership to the same cheers I'd heard on my way in, but this time I shook my head and grinned from ear to ear. Outside parked in the VIP spot was a brand-new white Ford Fusion Hybrid SE. I hit the unlock button on the key fob and smiled when the taillights flashed a wink at me. I took one last look at my red Chevy Cavalier and waved. It was well-loved and still in very good condition, but I'd admit, meeting the end of its long and winding road. This was totally a sucker move by Management to get another sale, but since I'd get the credit for the sale, I was almost okay with it. It was time to upgrade anyway. Not sure the car Charlie picked was exactly what I'd get, but it was a close fit.

The interior smelled like new-car heaven. Earthy leather and fresh plastic. They were my favorite scents in the whole world. Except for whatever Jude wore this morning.

Stop thinking about him.

At home, I texted Willow.

Prez: **Got afternoon off. Going to spend some girlie time and get a pedi/mani. Maybe get a new outfit, too. Will you style my hair tonight? What time you get off work?**

I passed by some local bars and contemplated adding them to the possibilities list I'd mentally started for barhopping. Maybe I'd check them out on my phone while getting girlied-up for tonight. The mani/pedi turned out to be a godsend of relaxation. I nodded off until my phone buzzed.

Willow: **Hey, get off at 3. I will be home right after. Of course I'll do your hair! After I do mine ;-)**

Prez: **Thanks! See you soon.**

After the almost catatonic state the mani/pedi placed me in, I carefully drove to the local outdoor mall, Village Point. A new celebration outfit seemed like a good idea—to me, probably not to my pocketbook. I chose a new pair of skinny jeans at my favorite boutique store, a size smaller than I'd been wearing for the last two months. Vanity sizing strikes again!

I picked out a gorgeous spring floral bustier top with a pink grosgrain ribbon around the waist that showed off some of what I'd been working so hard to accomplish this year. The salesperson created such a fuss about how great the top accentuated my figure. I was a total chump and spent a ridiculous amount of money to buy the scrap of fabric and added a lightweight pink sweater to wear over the revealing piece of clothing. After I'd consumed enough alcohol to lower my inhibitions, I'd ditch the cover-up. Two doors down, I discovered the perfect pair of pink wedges that helped me to be about four and a half inches taller. I would almost be eye to eye with Jude.

Seriously, stop thinking about him!

Back at the townhome, Willow arrived about twenty minutes later.

"Hey, roomie!" Her greeting resonated down the hall as I stepped out of the shower.

"I'm in the bathroom."

"What's up with the new car?"

"Oh, yeah, forgot to tell you. It's a loaner for a month as a top salesperson incentive to buy something with that bonus check I should get on the twentieth."

"I like it. How's the ride?"

"Like ridin' on a pillaaaah."

Willow chuckled as she stripped her clothes off to get in the shower. "I had coffee spilt on me by that new girl, Frazier. Three times. Look at this!" She pointed to where there was a three-inch long burn down her left arm.

"Oh, my God, Willow. You're gonna need to put something on that."

"Yeah, I stopped off and got some burn balm and wrap. So where are we going?"

"I was at Village Point and saw Kona Grill. If we get there before five p.m., we should be able to get seating on the patio for happy hour. That sound good for a starter?"

"Damn straight! Five-dollar cosmos all around!" Willow exclaimed from the shower. "I'll text Jace when I get out."

"I can do it." I snatched my phone from the counter.

Prez: **Thinking of starting at Kona Grill … good?**

In my bedroom, I dressed and stood in front of the full-length mirror on the back of my closet door to do a little modeling. Loved the jeans and the top was pretty but sexy, too. Maybe I'll break my losing streak and partake in a little horizontal fun tonight? Maybe.

I headed back into the bathroom and dried my hair as Willow exited the shower all pink-skinned from the hot water.

"Holy shit!" she bellowed.

"Now *you* owe me twenty dollars." I shouted over the hair dryer noise, catching her eye in the mirror.

"Ha-ha," she replied snottily. "You know what I was talking about. Looking to get some tonight?"

"Honestly, yes. I need to forget about my hot-as-blistering-coffee personal trainer. He's going out with Emerson tonight." My eyes rolled as my brain clouded with confusion over what he'd said about having to work. The slip was probably a cover.

Why would he feel the need to cover?

"I think." I turned the blow-dryer off. "Anyway, I need to keep our relationship professional. I almost got him in trouble today. I almost fainted."

Willow stopped moving to listen.

"It was nothing." I waved away her narrowed eyes, boring into my skin.

She tipped her head at me.

I leaned back against the cabinet. "The only reason I got all worked up and out of breath was because I could smell him next to me. He smells incredible, like cherry, sandalwood and salt. Apparently it's my Bermuda Triangle of man scents. Plus, his eyes are this amazing hazel – green and grey with gold speckles. They make me drool." Cringing, I added, "He was watching me run. I was worried I was jiggling everywhere and forgot to breathe. Damn asthma."

Willow ran a comb through her hair. "I think I'm repeating myself but maybe you should just find another trainer and go for it, Prez. Might be worth the effort, even if it ends up the guy isn't the one, fun for a while is better than no fun at all. Jamal's a great trainer. Mitch used to consult with him early on in his career. You deserve it to yourself to give whatever could be a chance. Even if it doesn't work out, you can't keep holding your gut in while you run ... not that you have a gut! What are those jeans? A size...?"

"Eight."

"Damn, Presley! That's amazing! They show off that booty well. Love the shirt, too." She softened her voice to a creepy southern belle imitation, "Very, you can look, but I'm a lady, so if you're gonna touch, you need to ask."

I frowned in the mirror. "Not sure the shirt speaks that much, but I liked it and thought it said, 'I wanna get laid.' So that was good enough for me."

Willow left the room to get dressed, shaking her head in honest amusement.

My phone buzzed on the counter next to my perfume, reminding me to spray down with my favorite scent. I read the flashing text.

Jace: **I'll be there early to make sure we get a seat. Hoping for some eye candy for you and for me**

Prez: **Getting all done up. Be there soon.**

Jace: **You are beautiful. Come as you are!**

Prez: **Some of us aren't instant beauties like you**

Jace: **Ah, flattery will only get you to second base, my dear ;-)**

Prez: **Wish I was your type, it would make dating a lot easier ... I think**

Jace: **We all have issues with striking out before we hit a home run and it's hard to navigate the bases without getting tagged out. Experiencing the** game makes us better at knowing what balls to hit and which ones to let sail by.

Prez: **Nice baseball metaphor! Can tell why you're in marketing. LOL. Tonight we both will find, not necessarily the right one, but one that will be a home run for tonight!**

Jace: **Wow, Prez! Way to say you want to get screwed on (or rather in) home plate! You go girl!**

Prez: **You can't pull off a "You go girl!" LOL**

Jace: **You're right :-). I take it back. C U soon**

I finished my makeup while Willow styled my black hair into soft spiral curls. After I was all made-up she completed her makeup and hair. She was like that, putting me first, even after she said she wouldn't. And maybe she shouldn't.

Willow was one of those beauties where her inside beauty radiated through her skin. Her hair had gone a gamut of colors over the last few years. Right now she sported a beautiful royal purple color with streaks of lavender. She and her sister, Sierra, had bold hair color in common—that, and eyes so dark blue they affected men and women alike making them speechless, awestruck by the shimmering sapphire orbs. Willow blow-dried her hair into a messy, beachy style and gathered one side up into a fancy pin with a watercolor-blue butterfly attached. She chose a sapphire blue short-sleeved cotton shirt that showed off her elegant tattoo sleeve of a Japanese geisha holding a beautiful fan over her face on her right arm. She finished her look with torn jeans, a fitted black leather jacket and black platform heels, which added four inches to her normal five feet four inch height. Sexy and unique-looking but still approachable, that was Willow.

Kona Grill was already hopping with twenty-somethings and early thirty-somethings when we rounded the corner onto the patio. Jace chose a table near open windows that let in the cool spring breeze. Her long, straight blonde hair slipped over her shoulder as she stood to greet us. I loved her sparkling iridescent cerulean-blue eyes, and her bright white smile made me wish I'd whitened my chompers this week.

"Oh! My! God! Presley! Look at you!" Jace released every word at a decibel that guaranteed everyone in the restaurant probably *was* looking at me. I cringed from the inside out. "And that table of guys over there sure is, honey." When she gave me a hug, her tiny body enveloped me like she was six-feet tall, when in reality even in her tall four inch heels she was probably only five feet six inches.

I noticed the table of hotties when we walked in, but none of them was even half as cute, sexy, or interesting as—

Stop it! It's not gonna happen with him, move on.

Jace had already ordered the first round. We enjoyed appetizers and another drink and a couple of hours of talking about my achievement and general life details.

Jace had just started to tell us what happened with Taylor when a very attractive silvery blue-eyed, dirty blond-haired young man crossed the room to our table, focusing on Jace. He cleared his throat and we all scanned up his body admiring his perfectly pressed chinos and blue-as-his-eyes button-down.

"I normally don't do this. Promise. But, I can't help but stare at all of you beautiful ladies." He turned to Jace. "Hi, I'm Logan Higgins. Would you mind telling me your name?"

Willow and I sent each other *the eye*. Logan was flirt-humping the wrong female, but Jace would let him know.

Jace stood, holding out her hand. "Hi, I'm Jace and these are my friends, Willow and Presley."

Or maybe not?

"Nice to meet you, ladies." He shook our hands. "Can I buy the next round in apology for the amount of staring I've been doing?"

"That would be nice. Cosmos," Jace replied. Her bright smile lit up his face in return. "Are you with the table of hotties over there?"

He chuckled. "They'd all be racing over here if they heard you say that, but yes. The eight of us are in town for a meeting."

"The Berkshire-Hathaway shareholders meeting?" Willow asked, and he nodded. "So, not from Omaha?"

"Only one of us, the rest are from all over the country—San Diego, Dallas, Kansas City, Phoenix, somewhere in Florida, and I'm from New York City. College frat buddies."

That piqued my interest. No commitment or chance of running into the guy again, that could work. But after experiencing Drexel's frat-boy ways, the frat comment was a huge turnoff.

"The Big Apple?" Jace asked. "Never been there."

"You should visit." Logan stepped closer to her. "Maybe someday."

"I have a very comfy sofa, be glad to offer it up for a visit, Jace." Even in the busy bar, his whisper in her ear wasn't quiet enough. Willow and I heard the comment and we both raised our eyebrows.

Way to skip the whole chase, Logan.

Jace's eyes twinkled up at him. "Sorry, Logan, you're super cute and have a real gift to charm, but I prefer a lot less penis on my lovers."

Logan dipped his head back down to her ear. "Any chance you'd be willing to change your mind for the night, Jace?"

"Nope."

"Well, can't blame me for trying." He straightened his posture, and they exchanged a small handshake.

"I don't, but I still expect that round of Cosmos and if any of your friends have been gawking, they can repent with a round, too." She winked at him to let him know she was kidding.

Logan chuckled. "God, don't think I've ever been this bummed about striking out. Smart, hot body, and a spunky attitude, that's a triple win. But really, it's my loss. I'll just have to settle for a good-bye hug?"

Jace nodded her acceptance. He reached around her, and she hugged his thin six foot frame like she was saying good-bye to someone she had known all her life.

"It was nice meeting you, Logan." She backed away.

"You too, Jace. Nice meeting you ladies. Have fun tonight."

Returning to his table, the other eye-catching guys dished Logan crap for not pulling digits. I assumed he informed them of Jace's sexual preferences but then again maybe he didn't. He seemed like a pretty upstanding kind of guy, plus, who knows what kind of crap those guys would pile on Logan if they found out he went for the lesbian at the table.

Three Cosmos were delivered, courtesy of Logan, and we finished the delicious concoctions faster than the first ones.

Jace stood. "You guys ready for the next bar?"

"What about sweet tart martinis at Upstream?" I suggested.

"Perfect!" Willow and Jace replied in unison.

We closed out our tab and stopped to extend a 'thank you and good night' to Logan and acknowledged the rest of the hottie table, but we didn't stick around to make conversation.

Upstream Brewing Company ended up being low-key and that wasn't what I was in the mood for. The drinks were excellent, the bartender was cute and working hard for a generous tip, but I craved excitement. Celebration.

Jace abstained from drinking. I suspected she would drive my car to wherever we ended up next, leaving her car here. Willow and I consumed a couple of martinis each. I was definitely enjoying the alcohol in my system. A bouncy buzz, not a drunken daze.

We spent a couple of hours pulling the breakup details out of Jace. A few tears trickled down her cheek and the sight broke my heart because hers was broken, too. Same story, different woman. Jace tried to pretend the breakup wasn't that big of a deal and she claimed it wasn't the forever kind of love, but I could tell she was more invested than she let on.

Restless to move bars, we paid our tab and stood outside in next-bar-limbo.

Jace suggested Twin Peaks next, a bar that was a cross between Coyote Ugly and Hooters.

"No!" Willow and I responded in unison.

The scenery wasn't our thing. We had twin peaks of our own. We could see them anytime we wanted.

Jace rolled her huge blue eyes. "Fine. Willow, you pick."

"Let me look up something." She started some sort of search on her phone. "Yes! There is an excellent band at Two Fine Irishmen tonight."

"I could go dancing." I performed an alcohol-induced jig.

Jace laughed. "Me, too. Let's go."

Like I suspected, Jace suggested she drive. She wasn't a real drinker and her slight body composition made her a lightweight. Plus, I suspected she planned to work tomorrow. That whole 'loves what she does' thing kept her busy even on the weekends.

Inside my car, oohs and ahs were showered liberally.

"It's a loaner," I repeated, over and over and over.

When I committed to a car—or a man—it would be for a lifetime or until significant and irreparable maintenance or damage to the car and/or the relationship before I made another change.

As I drove to the nail salon today, I'd thought about adding Two Fine as a possibility. Willow and I used to be regulars but hadn't been there in a while. Hopefully the crowd kept up the reputation of a twenty-something meat market and the cute West O guys came out to play.

I'm ready to play all night long.

Already after ten when we got inside the front door, the band rocked a popular song. We paraded to the dance floor and danced in a group. Jace noticed a high-top open up in the back by the bar, and she practically elbowed down two big guys to claim the seats first. Jace always won the table game, and when she didn't, she turned on the charm until she did. Willow and I finished out the song, and the band blabbered about needing a short break to fix equipment.

I plopped into the pleather-covered high-top chair, feeling the need for a glass of water as my mouth dried from the exertion of dancing.

"Did you order a round?" I asked Jace.

"Yeah, lemon-drop martinis for you two, and waters all around."

"Whoa!" Willow fanned herself. "Okay, now that's a breed of gorgeous you don't see every day."

Jace glanced behind me toward the bar. "Not gonna lie, that even gets my lady parts humming."

The waitress placed three waters on the table. "Be right back with your martinis, ladies." Her sage-green eyes glowed in the florescent neon bar signs.

I downed a long drink of the water while Willow and Jace continued their drooling and ogling over whomever or whatever was behind me at the bar.

"What?" I turned around to see for myself.

"He went behind the other side." Jace waved across the room at a table of girls she apparently knew.

The waitress returned with our martinis. "That's fourteen dollars, ladies."

I pulled out money and paid, waving off Willow's offer.

"Thanks," the sun-kissed, brunette waitress acknowledged my payment and tip with a friendly smile.

I sipped the martini. Perfect. Both tart and sweet and so so lemony. Delicious.

"Say, before you go…" Willow stopped the waitress as she turned to the bar. "The bartender," Willow pointed with her head. "What's Ponytail's name?"

The waitress laughed. "Why? You want his number?"

"Maybe, but for now just a name to go with the fantasy bang I'm already starting in my head."

The waitress rolled with laughter, appreciating the humor in Willow's drunken clarification. I took another look but still didn't see the guy Willow was blabbering about. I sipped my drink faster than I should've but it was so incredibly tasty, fresher and more balanced than the usual concoction served here.

The waitress regained her composure. "Ponytail goes by Jude."

My heart crashed to my stomach. I sucked in a breath and carried the drink into my lungs, experiencing the sting of the alcohol and the waitress's words all the way down.

The waitress offered a concerned look at my coughing, but continued, "Jude Saylor, but I'm sure he'd love to hear you call him Ponytail. Really nice guy and as far as I know he's available." She walked away shaking her head and mumbled on a giggle, "Ponytail."

I was still choking on my drink with my back to the bar. Now I really didn't want to turn around. There couldn't be two Jude Saylors in Omaha and someone probably didn't steal his identity to bartend, and the ponytail thing would be a huge coincidence.

Wasn't he supposed to be on a date with Emerson? But he also said he worked a second job, right?

"Prez, are you okay?"

I continued to sputter after clearing my throat for the tenth time.

"I need to go to the bathroom. Be right back." I scuttled around the corner away from the bar to clear my head and catch my breath.

And to panic.

Chapter Eight

Jude

"Hey, Jude. The girls at table twenty-six in the back have nicknamed you and are looking for a foursome," Sage said with a smartass smirk. "And one might need the Heimlich maneuver."

I shook my head while I filled her beer order. I didn't do random hookups and especially not at the bar where I worked. That was asking for trouble.

"The three of them are gorgeous," she teased. "You might want to rethink your not-from-the-bar stance." She walked away with two pints.

"I'm up for a twosome, Jude." Emerson slurred every word. After only two vodkas with lime, all 110 pounds of her was officially trashed.

Kanyon chuckled. "I think this one is up for some water."

I agreed with him without saying a word and poured a glass full of lemon-lime soda, throwing in a lime for good measure. I traded the glass with the actual alcoholic version while Emerson's head was turned. Her glazed-over eyes came back, and she smiled a drunken crooked smile.

She took a long sip through the tiny straw. "Mmmm, this is delicious."

"Glad you like it." I walked toward the back to see what Sage thought was so special that I had to see for myself.

I rounded the corner and stunning emerald eyes met mine. I smiled, but Presley didn't smile back. She diverted her eyes from mine. Her eyes stayed down and a tiny furrow of her eyebrows appeared as she made her way back to the high-top table. Okay, what was that?

I caught up with another bartender. "Rahl, I'm going to take my fifteen."

He acknowledged my declaration with a short-tempered grumble.

The band started back up.

I crossed to the other side of the room. "Good evening, ladies. The waitress tells me I've warranted a nickname but she won't tell me what it is."

I never took my eyes off of Presley—her eyes, her hair, the clothes. I was close to crawling across the high-top table and pulling her to my body and covering her with my scent caveman-style.

All three of the girls stopped talking, and everyone but Presley smiled pleasantly. She fidgeted with the cocktail napkin under her drink.

"Hi, Presley. Want to introduce me to your friends?"

The two girls glanced from me to Presley and back again. Presley's face paled and her chest rose and fell quickly. It was a beautiful sight. *She* was a beautiful sight.

I reached out my hand to a young woman with stunning dark blue eyes and funky purple hair. "Hi, I'm Jude Saylor, Presley's personal trainer at Triple R."

"Holy shit!" Her volume made me jump and then chuckle. She spun to Presley. "And I don't owe you twenty dollars! I guarantee you owe me forty dollars and I imagine you lied to me about that second Depping!" She turned back around, regained her composure, and reached out her hand. "Hi, I'm Willow Harper." Her eyes sparkled with some inside joke between her and Presley.

"Nice to meet you, Willow. And you are?" I offered my hand to the blonde with eyes a shade darker than baby blue. They held to mine. I smiled because even her eyes smiled at me.

"Hi, Jude, Jace Zelensky and you're Presley's trainer ... hmmm. Interesting. Very interesting."

"Nice to meet you, Jace." I rounded the table to Presley, leaning down to her so she could hear me. "How are you feeling?"

"I'm fine. How are you and how is Emerson?" Her eyes flashed to mine but found something else to stare at across the room.

Fucking great.

Presley hopped down from her chair as if she was going to make a break for somewhere that was nowhere near me.

Moving closer, I leaned in and asked a question in her ear. "Can I talk to you in the hallway, Presley?"

"I don't think..." She moved her upper body away from mine. "I just want to have a little fun with my friends tonight." Her normally delicate voice sounded tight and forced.

"I understand, but I think you have the wrong impression of what's happening with Emerson."

Her perfume saturated the air and a craving to touch her caused my biceps to jump.

Presley's eyes widened. "None of my business. I came here to dance so I'm going to go do that. Have a good night, Jude." She skirted around me and clutched Willow's arm, dragging her to the dance floor.

I stood stunned. I wouldn't follow her. I wasn't that guy. She had to know I was interested, but she skittered away like a mouse. The evasive moves didn't bother me. She didn't owe it to me to listen to my excuses. I didn't know Presley was going to end up here. It was a public bar and Emerson was here because of my inability to think before I spoke. That made the fallout my fault. Still, I wished I were the one on the dance floor with her.

"So, Ponytail, I've seen that look before. You're interested but in what?" Jace said with protective female undertones flowing through the question. Her eyes looked me up and down, as if she was measuring the size of my manhood. Not the manhood in my pants, but the one in my head and heart.

Talking to the girlfriend was a crapshoot. Either she found you completely objectionable or she would go to bat for you. Let's see which it is.

"Ponytail? Did Presley come up with that?" I watched her dance. Her curls bouncing up and down like a Slinky, and her hips swaying to the beat. Every gyration, bounce, and side-to-side shimmy had my crotch taking notice.

"No, Willow did, but I'd bet Prez was the first to think it. I know she'd kill me for telling you, but I don't want to see her get hurt again. She's been through hell when it comes to guys and people in general. She needs someone who can understand her and treat her right, almost better than she treats herself." Jace followed my gaze back to the dance floor. She shook her head and sighed. "Unfortunately, she's trying to find that connection by getting laid tonight."

"What?" My hands fisted at my sides, and my nostrils flared.

Jace brought her gaze back and viewed my reaction. "Obviously, you heard me. She's attempting what generally turns out to be a disastrous effort to forget what she really wants. Which, I'm imagining, is all you, Ponytail."

"But I ... I..."

I can't get away from work. I can't imagine she normally does that. I can imagine being the one with her. That's not going to happen. Shit!

My brain viciously mauled the fact that Presley wanted to have sex with anyone that wasn't me. What could I do to change her mind or did I even have a right to? I had a feeling anything I said to her tonight was going to be the wrong thing.

I stared at Presley. She laughed and enjoyed herself on the dance floor with Willow.

"Don't worry. I'll do everything I can to keep her from making the thinking-with-her-vag mistake. For her sake, not yours. But if you're into Emerson, who is a raging bitch and treats Presley and most people like crap, then leave Presley alone. She deserves better."

Emerson who?

I glanced to the bar.

Right, that Emerson.

"I have to keep Emerson on my side because of her position at the gym. That is the only reason she's here."

"Fucking bullshit." I heard the words but when I turned back Jace didn't look like she had said it. She stared across the room.

"Jace..." I touched her arm, and she brought her attention back. "I won't wait. I'm interested in Presley, and if she gives me a chance, I promise to treat her right."

"All right, I'll give you a chance to prove it. Let's hope she does, too."

I motioned to the bar. "I have a friend keeping Emerson company. If you're interested in meeting a nice guy I'm sure he'd enjoy a break from the monotonous crap spewing from Emerson's drunken mouth."

"I like the ladies, too," Jace said unapologetically.

"Figures, the beautiful and interesting ones do."

She tipped her head and smiled. "Save those silver-tongued lines for someone with emerald eyes and ebony hair."

"Will do." I couldn't help but like Jace. She didn't mess around when it came to her friends.

"Hey, Jude! Less sizzling hot girls and more help!" Rahl yelled over the bar and gave the wooden surface a loud slap.

Jace rolled her eyes at him. Rahl raised his eyebrows back at her, and Jace shook her head with a smile.

I chuckled at the bar's resident ogre. Rahl was always a little grumpy with me, but I couldn't say why. I hadn't gotten to know him well, but there was always a grey cloud hanging over him. He was the Eeyore of great bartending.

"Guess my break is over. Have fun tonight, Jace. Thanks for your help."

"You're welcome. Don't piss the info away, Jude."

I trekked back behind the bar and helped Rahl through the rush of orders, all the time keeping one eye on Presley on the dance floor.

Kanyon snapped in my face to get my attention. "Who's that?"

"The black-haired girl is Presley. She's one of my new clients. The other girl is her friend."

"She just a client?" he asked in a low tone.

"What are you two little girls whispering about?" Emerson snapped.

"Nothing," we both said.

"I don't think these," Emerson hiccupped, "shrinks are doing anything. I'ms outta here." She slithered from her stool and fell to the floor, laughing uncontrollably. "I fells ... down."

"Great." I gave Kanyon a dude-help-please stare.

After cussing me out under his breath, he stood and lifted her up, holding her at arm's length.

"I guess I get the privilege of driving No Tolerance Barbie home?"

"Please." I grabbed her purse, pulling out her driver's license and apartment key. "She lives around the corner on 180th and Harrison."

"Fine, but you owe me one, like introducing me to the gorgeous purple-haired girl when I get back."

"Willow."

"Willow's a bitch!" Emerson slurred while swaying on her legs. Kanyon's arm tightened around her waist.

I lowered my voice to Kanyon. "No, she's not." Even after a short meeting I could tell Emerson was way off on that one.

"Where are you taking me?" Emerson stared up at Kanyon.

"You're going home."

"Yous gonna stay with me?" Her glazed eyes rolled across Kanyon's chest as she pawed at his shirt.

"You have a roommate?"

"Yeah, but I don'ts do threesomes and she wouldn't wants your penis. She likes baginas." Emerson wrinkled her nose, then smiled crookedly. "But I might wants your…" She ran her hand down Kanyon's shirt, past his waistband to his crotch. He gripped her wrist before she assaulted him in public.

When drunk, most people went the opposite of what they were normally, but not Emerson. She continued to spew evil bile like a broken water pipe and someone direly needed to find her shutoff valve. Told me how miserable she actually was.

"Then I'll drop you off in her capable hands." Kanyon carried Emerson next to his hip, dwarfed by his six foot three inch frame. "Be right back."

"I'll buy your next round," I called out.

"Next *two* rounds," Kanyon clarified.

I nodded in agreement as he scooped Emerson up in his arms like he was carrying a sleeping child. She laid her head on his shoulder.

"Bye, Jude!" she yelled from across the room as Kanyon kicked the front door open, spinning to give me one last 'you fucking owe me big time' glance.

The band pulled in a full house, and the next forty minutes flew with no breaks. People needed potions to ease their pain or stimulate their happiness. I recognized both kinds of need in Presley, which had me wondering the real whys of her pain. What got to her? What hidden secrets would I find with time and effort?

I thought the risk was worth the effort so I tried a friendly gesture. I made another round for the girls and paid for the drinks myself, asking Sage to say, "Congratulations, Presley! Ponytail got this one."

Sage rolled her expressive eyes and delivered the pale yellow libations. Willow and Jace smiled and waved in polite appreciation, but Presley bit her lip, breathed deeply, and stared at the glass sitting in front of her. Her hand slowly inched to the stem, and she sipped. A smile crossed her face, and her eyes flashed to mine. It wasn't a clear expression of acknowledgement, but it would be enough for now.

"Hey, where's the barkeep who forces his so-called friend to drive a tiny beast from hell home?" Kanyon's voice boomed across the bar.

"Light or dark?"

"Dark. That girl is *definitely* from the dark side."

I chuckled at his play on words, filled a pint, and handed the beer off to him. "How bad was it?"

"She got really handsy in the truck, almost found an empty lot and took her up on her insistent and slurred offer, but I don't do a trashed girl, ever. Little tipsy and feeling no pain ... sure. Drunk ... never. Plus, I don't think anyone could fuck the nasty out of that woman. She's Satan's handiwork in the flesh." He acknowledged my agreeing glance with a shake of his head. "Emerson's roommate gave me shit that she doesn't take care of passed-out or puking blondes, because unfortunately, the roommate has to be up at four in the morning. I dropped Barbie off on the sofa and told the fuming brunette, 'sorry, but that's why I don't have a roommate.' I think Emerson slurred that her roommate's name is Kai? She works at Triple R?"

"That's her roommate?" I was highly skeptical of that information.

"Thin, short brown hair, and a high and tight ass, the likes I've never seen before?"

"That's Kai. She's way too nice to be living with that dump truck full of bitchy and crazy. Guarantee I'll get to hear all about it tomorrow morning at the trainer's meeting."

My phone vibrated in my jeans, and I assumed the text was from Kai telling me she would kick my ass in the morning.

You deserve whatever she sends your way.

I tugged my phone from my pocket.

Kai: **Just remember I have training in how to kill a man in one move!**

I cringed. She wasn't kidding, as ex-military she did have the skills. I might avoid Kai for a few days until she calmed down.

After filling drink orders, I returned to where Kanyon sat.

My motorcycle-loving friend took a long drink of his Guinness. "What are you gonna do about your *client*?" He scanned the dance floor. "Damn, that's a beautiful woman, Jude."

"I know." An intense spasm tightened my pants as I noticed her glancing my way. "Her friend Jace said Presley's looking to get laid tonight." My head clouded with thoughts of being the one to make that come true.

"By you? Does she have *any* standards?"

I shook my head at his dig. "Unfortunately, after seeing Emerson, I think Presley's looking for anyone *but* me. Honestly, I'm really hoping your ugly ass isn't in the running." Kanyon chuckled at my attempted return-dig. "There's some history between Emerson and Presley, I just don't know what. Jace certainly isn't impressed with Emerson."

"I'll second that impression."

"Jace says she's going to do what she can to prevent a random hookup from happening. I'm going to let Presley know I'm interested tonight."

"Good luck, bro. I'll root for you, but don't chase after what isn't interested."

Can't promise that won't happen.

The bar owner approached me and asked if I'd be interested in being first to clock out. There was still half an hour before closing, but mostly regulars occupied seats and the band was finishing the last set. I agreed, finished up with the glasses I was washing, and made my way through the small inebriated crowd to Willow and Presley on the dance floor.

"Can I have this dance?" I asked Presley from behind. My hands gripped her slender waist lightly.

Her head spun before her body turned and she lost her balance. I slid my arm around her waist and tugged her in close, chest to chest. The heat of her hands burned through my t-shirt and my pecs hardened in response.

Sucking in a deep breath, she stiffened in my arms but soon her actions betrayed her tense body language. Her slender hands skimmed my chest to my neck and her nails grazed my skin. An involuntary growl escaped from my throat as she relaxed fully and her eyes softened. She lowered her head to my shoulder and her toned body swayed in my arms, some from the alcohol, some to the music. I joined the movement when she swallowed deeply and raised her head.

"I'm not feeling very well. Sorry, Jude."

I could see it in her eyes, the scales had tipped. She was past tipsy. Way past.

"I'll go get Jace," Willow offered.

"No, no, I'll go get her." Presley pushed off of me and staggered toward the table.

I wanted to follow but I needed to perform a little payback. I turned to Willow. "My friend, Kanyon, would like to meet you. He's the tall blond at the bar." I pointed with my eyes, but she didn't hide her interested gaze. "Are you at all interested? Or should both of us cut our losses and head home?"

"I'd be glad to meet him, Jude."

Thought so.

We walked to the bar, and Kanyon climbed from his bar stool. As we stepped closer, he shifted his weight in his boots and his eyes held on the purple-haired girl next to me. And hers were never on anything but him.

"Willow Harper, this is my friend, Kanyon Hills. Kanyon, this is Willow. Now there's a green-eyed girl over there who needs a little of my attention. Excuse me."

As I left, I heard Willow ask Kanyon if he was related to some other Hills family she knew here in Omaha and him confirming they were cousins.

I stopped before rounding the corner to Presley. I inhaled a deep breath and checked any concerns.

Just tell her what you want to and let her get some rest.

The two steps around the large wooden pillar brought me face-to-face with something unexpected. Rahl was typing Presley's digits into his phone. They were laughing, and her fingers on his arm gave a flirty squeeze.

What the fuck!

Now I was pissed, mostly at myself, some at Rahl, and a lot less at Presley.

The band had finished and the overhead lights flooded the bar.

I approached the table, keeping my eyes on her. "Hey, Presley, did you have fun tonight?"

Her eyes were glassy, and she weaved on her long and shapely legs, her tall heels still accomplishing wonderful things for her ass.

Presley slid closer to Rahl and grabbed his arm. I started to tense, but after a moment I realized it was mostly for balance, not flirting.

"Yeah. But I think that last martini … woo." She flailed a hand through the air with her words. "And thanks, Jude. But it wasn't a good idea."

Jace touched my arm and I leaned toward her. "I'm going to get her home, Jude. She's too far gone to be of any use to any guy."

True.

"Are you okay to drive? Need help getting Presley to the car?"

"I'm fine. I didn't drink at all here. Presley chugged the extra lemon drop martini you made for me, after downing hers. Probably should have stopped her from doing that." Jace examined Presley's deteriorating state. "A little help would be appreciated, by me, not sure her."

"I should have noticed you weren't drinking and sent something nonalcoholic, sorry. I'd be glad to help with her."

Presley continued to talk with Rahl. She had issues with some pronunciation but after bartending for six years, I was seasoned in drunk-a-nese. Rahl contributed to the conversation and Presley seemed to be listening. Every once in a while, there was a glance from the corner of her eye. I didn't hide my observation. She wouldn't remember half of this in the morning anyway. Plus, I wanted to send clear signs to Rahl.

"Let me go talk to Willow and see what her plan is." Jace stepped from her stool.

"I'm gonna stay right here."

"Ponytail, let her have tonight. I think she's mostly upset by Emerson's presence, not at you. Patience."

"Not a virtue I am familiar with," I muttered under my breath as I took a seat.

Willow intercepted Jace before she got very far, and they chatted.

While leaning over the back of a chair, Rahl asked, "How was your first week at Triple R, Jude?"

"Good. Presley is one of my new clients." I said the words as casually as possible, but hopefully gave Rahl the "I saw her first" vibe.

The pitiful, juvenile and underused "I saw her first" vibe.

Presley hiccupped. "For now. Blakes isn't happy. He wants to moves me to Kai or Jamal. I asked him to gives you another chance."

"I appreciate that, Presley. I thought we had good chemistry going."

Presley's eyes met mine. "Me too, Jude."

The sudden lucidity of those three words was what I needed to hear. She would remember some things tomorrow.

Rahl broke our connection, squeezing her arm. "I'm gonna get going. Presley, I'll call you to get together." He turned to me. "Later, Jude."

"You work tomorrow night?" I asked, mostly so I could know if he might call Presley for a date. That way I knew how straightforward I needed to be with an inhibition-lowered woman.

"Yep. See you then."

"Later." I gave a final chin-jerk to send him on his way.

Presley and I sat staring at each other. The desire in her glossy eyes was still there, along with a significant martini haze.

"Did you get the envelope I left for you?" Her quiet voice broke the silence and her eyes dropped.

Envelope?

"I'm sorry, no, I didn't. What did it look like?"

"A large manila." She motioned the size with her shaking hands. "I gave it to…" Presley closed her eyes and shook her head. When she reopened them, those green orbs flooded with jealousy. "Emerson."

"Presley, there is nothing going on with Emerson." I lowered my voice. "I can't think about anyone but—"

"Ready to go, Prez?" Jace interrupted.

"Yes," Presley said firmly but stood on shaky legs. She rounded the table. I shifted in my spinning chair as she stopped in front of my spread legs. "It was a copy of the sketch of you." Her eyes dropped to my crotch and returned to meet mine. "Hope you find it. I wouldn't put it past Emerson to use the reality in some weird-ass fantasy she features you in."

I rounded her waist with my arm and gently dragged her closer to me. Pushing her hair over her shoulder, I whispered in her ear, "I don't care what fantasies Emerson Welch has. I only care if I appear in any of your fantasies, Presley." I watched goose bumps rise on her exposed upper chest as her breathing shallowed. My hand dropped to her lower back, tracing small circles over the thin fabric of her shirt. "So, do I?"

She turned her head and our lips were only an inch apart. Her lemony breaths made my head spin. I wanted to taste her equally tart and sweet tongue. Her green eyes widened and the already-dilated pupils expanded until the green was a tiny rim around the black.

Her words came out sluggishly as her breathing turned to panting. "Let's just say that I'm pretty sure I'll legitimately owes Willow forty dollars soon and my roommate's going to wish she hads earplugs. Goodnight, Jude."

Damn. Fucking hot!

Presley backed away from my arms and stumbled toward Jace, whose tiny frame struggled to keep her upright.

"Let me help you, please." With an arm around her waist, I guided her toward the door. She didn't argue.

"Thank you, Jude." She sighed with slits of eyes as I pulled out the seat belt, then leaned over to click her in safely.

"Anytime, Presley. I'll remind you of our appointment Sunday night by text."

"Okay." Her eyes flickered as she curled into the new leather seat.

I hovered over her for just a moment, taking in her soft floral scent one more time.

I dropped a peck of a kiss on her forehead and whispered, "Good night, Beautiful."

She was already passed out. I shut the door carefully.

"Is someone going to be home with her?" I asked Jace.

"I'll make sure she's okay before I leave."

"Thanks, Jace."

"No problem, Ponytail. You've got my vote, just don't campaign too hard, Presley's not used to…" She shook her head as she climbed in the car. "Never mind. Hope to see you around. Good night."

"Good night."

Kanyon met me near my truck with Willow at his side.

I chuckled at Willow's singsong voice of a famous Beatles song line. Wasn't the first time I'd heard my name announced that way, certainly wouldn't be the last.

"Hey, Willow. Kanyon."

"Jude, I overheard you talking to Jace. I live with Presley. I'll make sure she's okay tonight."

"You have a…" I was about to say "ride", but Kanyon's shit-eating grin was a clear sign, and I gave him one back.

Kanyon clapped his hand on my shoulder. "I'll call you this week, Saylor. Maybe go to Quaker Steak and Lube's gathering Thursday?"

"Sounds good. You two have fun."

They both snickered and walked to Kanyon's red Chevy Silverado.

Definitely no set type of girl for Hills.

I had to rise before the sun for an early meeting at Triple R, so I headed home and fed Ninja before hitting the hay. That night, my dreams of Presley woke me up several times with a hard-on that wouldn't go away without intervention. If Zane were home, he would've wished for earplugs, too.

Chapter Nine

Presley

I woke up. Alone. And pissed. At myself.

Just rolling over slowly, the pounding in my head indicated it had been a one-too-many kind of night. I glanced to the clock ... *4:44 a.m.?*

WTF! I was asleep for only two and a half hours! Seriously!

Wasn't like I had much to do today, but sleeping in was the one luxury I wanted to enjoy. Unless I woke up with someone in the bed with me, then I would have re-enjoyed that luxury. I guess getting up at four thirty was routine and my body clock had adjusted. Not one to waste a day, I tagged my phone from my nightstand and headed to the kitchen to make my hangover cure—fried egg on toasted white bread with a smear of tangy white sandwich spread, paired with a cup of delicious, steaming-hot coffee.

Willow's door was closed, and I could hear soft snores coming from her room. I didn't blame her for staying in bed, but I imagined she had to work sometime today.

No, wait. Jace dropped me off. Right? Maybe she stayed here?

I walked back down the hall and knocked lightly on Willow's bedroom door. No answer. I cracked the door and what met my eyes wasn't bad at all.

Awkward? Maybe. Unpleasant? Definitely not.

On top of her dark blue comforter was a rippling-with-muscle male lying stomach-down, his amazing ass shining to meet the morning sun. I gaped at the tattoo of a griffin winding its way across his back, its tail trailing his leg and between his thighs. Willow's soft hair draped over his neck as her head lay on his bicep. Her lithe body snuggled into him.

I stared for a few seconds. The fact that she allowed Bachelor Number One to sleep here was interesting. That rarely happened. Actually, that had never happened, not even with Mitch.

I backed out of the room and closed the door. A jealousy spasm clutched at my chest. To stop the intense feeling from engulfing my entire psyche, I repeated over and over to myself that there was someone out there for me.

I also reminded myself that guys were like spreads for toast. Not everyone likes grape jelly. Maybe they should taste orange marmalade. Don't like the bits of rind? Try strawberry jam. Can't stand the seeds? Give peach preserves a sample. Me? I wanted to try lots of flavors and have a taste of each.

Halting just inside the living room, I shook my head at the obscure thoughts. They sounded explicit and suggestive even in my brain. My point was that there is a flavor of guy for every girl's palate.

Still sounds sexual. Maybe I am just sexually frustrated and my fuzzy-lack-of-sleep-head is in the gutter.

I fried my egg and filled my coffee mug in an attempt to change my brain chemistry. I took a couple of pain relievers to end the pounding behind my eyes. Sitting at the kitchen table, I enjoyed my breakfast and perused a smut magazine.

Who cares what twenty-two-year-old JLo is screwing today? And no, I don't care who has the most cottage-cheese ass of all the female celebrities.

I didn't know why Willow bought this horrible, woman-bashing, celebrity-stabbing crap. Oooh, a crossword ... the only good thing in this colorful pressed dead tree.

It was well over an hour before Bachelor Number One made his way out to the living room, dressed.
Is it a walk of shame if it's a guy? I doubt it. Maybe a walk of "I got game?"

"Good morning," I offered as he neared the kitchen.

His body froze as he mumbled an expletive in surprise. He walked into the kitchen and snatched a coffee cup from the hooks under the cabinet and filled it with black sunshine. After taking a long sip, he finally returned my greeting. "Good morning."

Way to make yourself at home, Bachelor Number One. Maybe ask first before drinking my java?

He sat at the table across from me. "We didn't get a chance to meet last night. I'm Kanyon Hills."

"Presley Bradenhurst." I shook his offered hand.

"Nice to meet you, Presley. So Jude's your personal trainer at Triple R?"

"He was." I let the words slip before I thought about the finality of the statement. My chest constricted and I inhaled a tight breath.

Kanyon eyed me up. "I'm pretty sure he thinks he still is."

I looked away and sipped my coffee. "Probably, but I'm going to go with Blake's advice and change to Jamal or Kai."

"Not that it's any of my business, but is there a valid reason?"

Valid? Not sure you know me well enough to judge my reasons, Bachelor.

"You're right," I snapped. "It's not your business." I cringed at my bitchiness. I wasn't Emerson.

Kanyon sat back in his chair and crossed his arms.

"I'm sorry, Kanyon. It's the hangover talking. I promise, I'm not usually a bitch."

He beamed at my apology, and I melted into gushy protoplasm at a smile that was probably a dentist's wet dream.

"No apology necessary." Kanyon's attitude changed as he leaned forward. "Presley, Jude likes you and I can read women—it's something weird in my DNA. You are *really* into him. You two need to get on the same page before one of you does something to prove you don't like each other and what could be is over before it even begins."

Jude likes me? And that smile is deceptive.

I felt verbally assaulted, but Kanyon was right. His ability to read women was borderline eerie. I had issues with sabotaging myself.

Kanyon continued. "Yes, Jude is interested and probably disappointed with how last night went. Not that he wanted to get horizontal, but…" He raised his voice, "Hell! Who am I kidding? What man wouldn't? You're beautiful, Presley."

I blushed and stared into my coffee cup.

Kanyon continued. "But Jude's a gentleman. He'll wait and get to know you first before making his way to the bedroom with you. And there is nothing going on with Emerson. He has to be friends to encourage the obnoxious monster to send him business at Triple R. At least that's what he thinks. I suspect he's good at what he does and word would get around either way. He'll learn he doesn't have to rely on that bat-shit crazy woman for his meal ticket. I'm not sure he'll be excited to hear you aren't going to be his … *client*."

His emphasis of the last word sliced into me. "I haven't done anything yet."

Kanyon swallowed a mouthful of coffee. "Then give him a chance, both professionally and privately."

Willow rounded the corner. When she saw Kanyon sitting at the table, she floated across the room in her hot pink short nightgown, and her sapphire eyes softened. Happiness I'd never seen glowed across her face as she approached. He looked her up and down, and his smug face told me everything.

"Good morning." She grabbed a mug and filled it, adding her traditional two packets of the pink substitute and a splash of creamer.

"Good morning, Gorgeous," Kanyon returned like he'd said it every morning for years. He finished his coffee. "Willow, I have to get going. Have to be to work at eight. Would you like to get together for dinner after you get off work?"

God, I liked this guy, he was no-nonsense. Confident but not jerk arrogant. Something about him said, "You can fuck off if you don't like me!" He might be a perfect fit for similar Willow's attitude.

"Sure. I close at four p.m. I'll need to shower. Six?"

Standing from the table, Kanyon took what would be four steps for an average-height person in two long strides to the sink, then rinsed and placed the used mug in the dishwasher.

He cleans up after himself? That's refreshing.

He approached Willow, pinned her against the counter, and lifted her arm, placing a soft kiss where her bandage was. He whispered something in her ear that had her squirming against him.

"Six thirty. I'll pick you up. Dress warmly, it won't be my truck."

"You own a horse?" Willow asked on a laugh.

I chuckled to myself.

Kanyon wrapped his long arms around her, sliding a hand to the base of her neck. It was like I was watching a romantic movie right in front of me. But this was better. It was real life.

"Of sorts." His playful grin was cute, like take-him-back-to-bed cute. He laid a long kiss on Willow. Before it ended, I questioned if I should leave the room (or the house) so they could make use of the kitchen table or sofa or floor or counter. The kiss was blistering-coffee hot.

When he came up for air he kissed her nose and backed away. "Okay. Have a good day, ladies."

"Bye," Willow returned on a soft gasp.

"It was nice to meet you, Kanyon," I added.

He stepped backward to the front door. "You have Jude's number?"

"Yes."

"Use it." He opened the door and before I could tell him he sure was bossy, he was gone.

Willow took a seat at the table. "What was all that about?"

"What did you think of Jude?"

"It shouldn't matter what I think."

"Don't pull that bullshit, Willow."

The hangover was talking for me, but after eighteen years of friendship she should know better. I trusted her opinion, and more importantly, I valued it almost more than my own. Probably more than my own.

I leaned my face into my palm, waiting.

"Okay. Honestly, I really liked him and I thought you really, really like or liked him, too. Right?"

What I did or didn't think was melded into a pot of self-doubt, slight trepidation over my behavior—that I can't remember most of—last night, and my ever-present need for a friendly voice of reason. I'll go with a large helping of self-doubt first.

"I don't know." I shrugged. "Maybe it was just the endorphins from exercising causing a hormone overload that led to an attraction. People fall for their hot trainers all the time. Remember Vivian? Her and Ramsay? That was a huge mistake. It ended with Viv almost destroyed. I never felt anything with Mitch, but that's probably because I was so—"

"Don't say it!" Willow snapped. "You were not whatever self-critical and unbecoming word you were going to put after that 'so'. Just don't say it, Bradenhurst."

"Geez, what crawled up your ass?" My face contorted in disgust.

"You do this every time, Prez. A nice, good guy shows interest and you make an excuse why it couldn't possibly be that he actually likes you and wants to get to know you. It's that he wants the discount you can get on cars. It's that he's looking to slum it for a while. It's that he's falling on the grenade when we're together. Or it's that you have endorphin or hormone issues!" Willow stood and stomped from the room, throwing words over her shoulder. "You are not a discount, a slum, a grenade, or a slave to endorphins!"

I got up and tracked on her heels down the hall. "You don't know how it feels to have to wonder what ulterior motives someone has because that's all you've experienced in the past. You've always been beautiful!"

She turned in front of the bathroom. "And you've always been beautiful, too. Not everyone has bad intentions. Truthfully, I was embarrassed at how you treated Jude last night. Your bitchy attitude was just a step above that of Emerson's normal attitude, and if I were Jude, I'd consider it a sign of what your truer color is, even if it isn't the truth."

I reeled back from her and my butt hit the wall on the other side of the hallway. I collapsed against it. Being compared to Emerson was the slap I needed to take me out of my self-loathing and into the present. Tears filled my eyes.

"I didn't know what to do last night. He was trying to explain about Emerson and from what I can remember, I think he was trying to tell me he was interested. But before he could say anything I'd already decided I wasn't good enough for him." The tears started to fall, and my body crumbled forward.

Willow came closer and wrapped her arms around me. "Sweetie, there's a way to make it right. Two words, 'I'm' and 'sorry', and if he doesn't accept your apology or decides you're not worth the little bit of extra effort, then he's not worth *any* effort. Make the call. Don't text it. He's a guy, so hearing your voice will mean more."

"I don't know if I can. 'I'm sorry' seems like it isn't enough." I sobbed into her shoulder. "Willow, why can't I trust a guy or believe in myself?"

She leaned back, then slid my hair around my shoulders and down my back. "Presley, if I knew that I'd be your therapist and not your friend, you would owe me a lot more than forty dollars."

I half-heartedly chuckled. "I only owe you twenty dollars."

"Maybe it's time to stop running from your feelings. Time to listen to your gut and your heart? What are they telling you?"

"I'll try to figure it out." I hiccupped a sniffle. "I like him and I'm tired of being afraid to have something real with a guy. I'm going to go for a bike ride to clear my head."

"Okay, I have to get to work. I'll see you after I get off?"

"Yes, and Willow, Kanyon—that's a good-looking guy and he was pleasant to talk with this morning. Of course Kanyon didn't compare me to Emerson, which by the way was both the worst and best thing you've ever said to me, like being hit with icy water."

"I wasn't trying to be mean. I was being truthful. I like Kanyon, a lot. And damn, let's just say I don't think I've ever been Depp'd and multiple times, like he did." She smirked. "Kind of glad I knew you were passed out so you wouldn't hear us."

"Ewwww! All right, you should get to work before you have to fire yourself."

And you're making me jealous again.

By the time she'd finished her shower, I was dressed in my biking gear and headed out the door. I rode the trail around Zorinsky Lake slowly. Biking and a hangover didn't seem like the best combo after I was on the bike. My phone buzzed in my pocket, and I waited until there was a safe place to hop off and take a short break. I lay on the soft dewy grass. The blazing sun reminded me of my lingering headache. I shaded my face with my bike helmet.

Jace: **How are you this AM? I have your car, in one piece. I'll be over around 11, if that works.**

Prez: **I'm good. On bike ride, 11 is fine. I'll drive you back to Upstream to get your car.**

Jace: **I walked to Upstream and brought it home this morning. See you soon.**

Let's see what Jude is doing…

I shaded my eyes from the sun to pull up his number. My pulse quickened, and I closed my eyes to make a concentrated effort to keep from hyperventilating.

The line clicked over to voice mail, Jude's calming deep voice greeting my ears. I cleared my throat while his sexy voice kept rattling around in my head.

"Um ... yeah, hi, Jude. This is Presley, but you probably already knew that from Caller ID. I want to apologize for how I acted last night. I'm sorry. I was short with you and I regret a lot of my behavior, probably some that I can't even remember. Anyway, have a good weekend. I'll see you on Monday. Bye."

That wasn't horrible. Not sure it was enough, but I'd wait to find out.

My phone rang in my hand. Rahl? Who is...?

Reality slapped me. What a total freaking bitch I was last night! Jude had watched me flirt shamelessly with another guy. How immature! Rahl was nice—and nice to look at—but there were no warm fuzzies—*or scorching heat*—like with Jude.

Why is being an adult so complicated?

It was better to get the conversation over with, so I answered. "Hello, Rahl."

"Good morning, Presley. Didn't know if you'd be among the living today."

I groaned. "Yeah, I was feeling pretty good last night. My hangover cure did its job and I'm out for a bike ride, just taking a break to enjoy the beautiful morning."

"McDonald's?" he asked, trying to learn my hangover cure, which was sweet but kind of creepy, too.

Is he sweet or is he creepy?

"Homemade fried egg sandwich and java."

"That probably did the trick. Glad you're feeling okay. Say, I'd like to take you out this week. You interested?"

Definitely sweet.

Now, this was my dilemma ... Rahl was a nice guy and definitely not bad to look at—dishwater blond hair, muscular build, soft brown eyes. And he came right out and told me he was interested in me. Not that I remembered exactly what he said due to my inebriated state, but I vaguely recalled something about watching me dance and liking my moves. He was sweet in a pound-his-chest-and-grunt, "me-man, you-woman," kind of way.

Jude was a nice guy and awesome to look at everywhere. I'd learned he was interested, although it was still hard to believe he could actually be interested in me. *If* Jude asked me out, I could possibly have two dates. That was so not like me.

I pounded my head with my helmet as if that would help make my decision easier. It only brought back my hangover headache.

I sat up straight and released the words in a flurry. "Okay. I'll meet you for drinks. After work on Tuesday, say, six p.m.?"

Even if Rahl wasn't the one who would curl my toes, I wanted to make friends and it was good for me to get outside of my comfort zone when it came to men. Just talking with one was a stretch. Agreeing to meet for a drink was like a hop, skip, and gallop all in one.

"Sounds good. Brix?"

"Great." I smiled and fell back to the grass.

"Have a good rest of your weekend. See you then, Presley."

"You, too. See you later, Rahl."

After disconnecting the call, something that wasn't quite regret but felt adjacent to regret hit me. My heartbeat revved like someone had stepped on my accelerator while my clutch was depressed. My blood roared like oil through my veins, and my stomach clenched like an engine sputtering to respond while reality spun out through my brain.

I didn't know if Jude and Rahl were friends, but they worked together. Would they talk? Do guys do that? Do they care who goes out with who and when?

In actuality, I hoped that Jude did care.

When I returned from the bike ride, I found a little morning energy, and after showering and making myself relatively presentable, I tackled my normal weekend routine. Willow was an incredible classically trained chef. But I was better at cleaning, and she hated domestic warrior duties. So we made a pact. She cooked something delicious, but relatively healthy, at least twice a week, and I cleaned once a week. Not sure what we'd do if either of us moved out. I imagined I might die from boxed-meal nutritional deficiency, and she'd be a six-inch-path-to-the-bathroom hoarding slob.

My phone buzzed on the kitchen counter.

Jude: **In a long meeting at Triple R. Will talk to you later. Sorry.**

I decided to read until Jace arrived. Lying on the couch, I fell asleep quickly from the lack of truly refreshing sleep last night. The doorbell rang, and I jolted upright. Yawning like I hadn't slept in days, I reached the door and checked the peephole. Jace smiled on the other side.

I opened. "Hello." My gravelly voice chafed my ears. I cleared my throat.

"Hi. How are you doing, Miss Bradenhurst?"

"I'm tired."

"Well, I'd imagine. You were pretending to be a *Dancing with the Stars* contestant last night." She took a seat in the chair at the end of the sofa.

"Was I? I can't remember all of it."

"What do you remember?"

"I remember being weird around Jude."

Jace threw her head back laughing. "Well, you remember one of the more interesting parts of the night. Presley, I could tell you're interested in him and that boy is into you, too. Why the attitude?"

"'Cause in the locker room I overheard Emerson saying she had a date with him. She was there. Mostly, I can't believe a guy that hot could actually be interested in—"

"You?" Jace scowled at me. "I know Willow tries to cram down your throat how incredible you are, thinking she can convince you to think it yourself, but I'm not going to do that because obviously that method doesn't work."

My eyebrows furrowed at her semi-mean but not-entirely-untrue words.

She continued with a small smirk. "Do you have faults? Sure! Prez, we all do. I'm a workaholic, my boobs are two different cup sizes, and I'm a freak when it comes to having clean everything—ears, car, workspace, and home. It's a certifiable and untreated disease."

"You are not diseased."

Jace huffed. "You know what I mean. Presley, we try to minimize the negative things, not faking anything but emphasizing our better side. Our strengths, otherwise known as 'our best side', are what attract someone. We do a damn good job of pushing people away by acknowledging the weaknesses that speak so little about us instead of accentuating our strengths that speak volumes."

"Strengths?" I searched my mind for mine and the fact that I couldn't come up with one was depressing. Surely I had at least one.

"Yes. So what are you good at, Prez?"

"I don't know. Art?"

"And?"

Her insistence made my breathing irregular. I didn't like to discuss me.

"I sell cars better than most of the staff."

"I'd say you sell them better than *all* of the staff, considering you're the top salesperson for April. And you love your friends like family. And you take care of animals with such heart."

"Okay." I held up a hand. "So I have some strengths. The bigger problem is I have a lot of baggage for someone to contend with, too."

"Whatever you think that baggage is, honey, it won't matter to the right person. He or she will understand and accept everything about you. Maybe you don't know everything about Jude, but if you see the strengths in him to make you want to know more, then I say you should go for it. If all you can see is weaknesses then you should let him go. The right girl will see his best side."

"How do I stop seeing *my* weaknesses?"

"You won't. Ever. Just be confident in yourself. If he's the right one, he won't care about your weaknesses. He'll love your strengths."

"I think Willow was saying something similar earlier."

"Good. Since we're on the same page and you've heard this lecture once before, please take me home." A yawn the size of Nebraska escaped Jace's mouth. "I need more sleep, too."

I drove Jace home. The fact that Jude hadn't called me back had me concerned. It was after noon and I'd called him at nine this morning. I doubted Triple R had a three-hour meeting. How much personal trainer training is there to do?

I pulled into our drive and a motorcycle was parked on our side. I parked behind the hot black bike. Maybe Kanyon's horse?

As I exited my car, I heard a greeting.

"Hi, Presley."

My body responded with a tiny shiver.

I walked around the car. "Hi, Jude." I stopped when I was facing him at the bottom of the stairs.

His body was covered in form-accentuating denim down low, and smooth leather up top. All I could think was how I'd love to shove my face into his jacket and take a big long whiff.

"Would you like to come in?" My legs finally found a will to move toward where he sat.

"No, thanks. I have to get ready for work at Two Fine. I'm sorry to show up unannounced and I hope you don't find it too stalker-like that I looked up your address in the Triple R system. I didn't know if you'd tell me where you lived after last night."

I tipped my head in consideration. There was a real possibility I wouldn't have.

"No problem. Jude, I'm very sorry for getting out of control last night."

He stood from the front stoop and took the two steps down to the driveway. "I understand why you were acting like you were."

My speech froze in my throat, and my body was trapped in place as we stared at each other. His hypnotizing hazel eyes caught the high afternoon sun's rays and the gold flecks sparkled.

He continued, dropping his gaze, "And thank you for the apology. The fact is, I am your personal trainer. Not concentrating on my job almost injured you and almost derailed my career at the gym. I don't want either of those things to happen. *Especially* the first. I think it's smart for both of us if we maintain a professional relationship as trainer and client."

I swallowed. Jumbled thoughts of how I didn't want him to be only my personal trainer sprinted through my brain. I wanted to tell him that I wanted him. That I wanted him to want me. That I wanted things to be different.

But I just nodded in agreement and stepped around him.

I steadied my voice but kept my back to him. "Okay, I understand. Have a good weekend, Jude. I'll see you Monday morning. No need to text a reminder. Promise, I'll be there."

I opened the front door and sank to the floor while his bike roared away.

It wasn't the first time a guy presented information that confirmed I wasn't good enough, pretty enough, thin enough, smart enough ... or just enough. Unlike before, this time the hurt was crushing me somewhere deep inside, instead of crushing me from the outside in.

Hours later, when she arrived home from work, that was where Willow found me. She helped me to my bedroom. Without asking me any details, she rubbed my back until I fell asleep. I slept all night and well into the next morning.

Around noon, I dragged myself to the shower and prepared myself with minimal effort to head to the humane society for my volunteer hours. Getting unconditional love from the animals seemed to relieve whatever ailed me, but today the funk was too great. Even the animals sensed the cloud of gloom I brought with me.

Except one. She had her own cloud of gloom.

There was this little white dog that had been in the shelter for weeks. I'd watched plenty of families, couples, and singles stop to take a look at her but they'd shake their heads when she would cower in the back of the kennel. They'd ask the standard questions to the adoption counselor: *What's wrong with her? Why doesn't she act like a normal dog? We're nice people, what happened to her that she can't trust us?* As a stray the animal control officer picked up, these were unanswerable questions. Sometimes there wasn't a reason. That was just how the animal was born. Sometimes there was an answer but knowing didn't always help either.

I waited until adoption hours were over to clean her enclosure. Even on her best day it took several minutes to coax her from her cage, and she would tremble like Jell-O being shaken on a plate by a two-year-old while I completed the task. I didn't want any distractions or loud noises to spook her.

"Hey, sweetie, time for cleaning." The white fluff tried to burrow into the cinder block wall. "It'll be okay. I promise."

I heard one of the adoption counselors behind me. "She's a nice dog, just has so many issues. Her behavior and her weight problems are too much for many good homes to deal with. I think she'd be a good dog, eventually. We're thinking if she doesn't get adopted in the next ten days…" She sighed. "Well, you know. Have a good week, Presley."

After that news … really?

I swallowed hard. Just being written-off as problematic or unfixable or unlovable wasn't fair. Being given ten days to transform your head and your body was a death sentence in itself.

With patience, the little lady finally crept her way toward me, two steps forward, one step back. I let her sniff the back of my hand as she passed by, and she did a butterfly kiss nuzzle before scuttling away. She sat next to the kennel door. Her eyes never met mine and her head hung low. Sadly, we had the same physical posture and wondered if someone in her past had walked over her heart, too. Someone in motorcycle boots and a leather jacket.

Before I let her back into the kennel, I sat against the chain-link door, and she sat next to me. Not close. The only people in the building were the office staff and me. They would finish in about an hour and it would be time to leave. In minutes her body moved to lie against mine. In a couple more minutes her head rested against my leg. In another couple she was on my lap. I still hadn't tried to pet her. It would scare her to be touched.

When I heard the office being locked up, I kept my voice low. "I'm sorry, sweetie, but they're going to turn off the lights soon and I have to leave."

She raised her head and for the first time I got to see her eyes. Grey globes of sadness surrounded by white hope stared up at me. I calmly raised my hand and ran it down her back. She shuddered at the touch the first time but I did it again slower and she relaxed a smidge. I grazed down her back a couple more times. As if she was saying, "I've had enough," she scooted off my lap, gave a small shake, which was great dog body language for "I'm feeling better," and walked into her kennel. She didn't look back. She went to her place on her pillow in the corner and curled into a ball.

I wanted to do the same, so I did. I went home and crawled back into my bed. Ignoring my phone when it buzzed with a text, then another, and later another, I kept my eyes closed and turned the grating-on-my-last-nerve metal off and sobbed into my pillow.

There was a knock on my bedroom door. Without invitation the six-panel wood door opened and light flooded into the room.

I pretended to be asleep, but Willow probed for information. "Presley, did you eat today?"

I ignored her.

"I'm not leaving until you answer me, and I might go get someone to start an IV line for liquid nourishment if you haven't and choose not to eat something."

"No, I didn't eat, but if I do, I guarantee every bite will come back up. You and I both know what that might set off. I understand your concern, but it's best I don't start that chain reaction, Willow."

I had an eating disorder for most of my teenage years, binging and purging meals until my body was crumbling from the inside out. I caused irreparable damage to my esophagus and the regurgitation had the not-so-lovely effect of triggering asthma. Thankfully, blessed with some hereditary graces, my teeth and heart stayed in good condition. There was always an undercurrent of potential relapse, especially if I attached an emotional issue to reversing a meal. The average stomach flu wouldn't do it, but binging and purging emotions in association with food was likely to send me into a downward spiral that Willow, or even a medical professional, wouldn't be able to fix.

"Honey, I understand. You know I do. Maybe we can talk about it and find a way to understand what happened together?"

I released a sob that had Willow moving toward the bed. "Thanks, Willow, but I want to sleep." I tried to calm myself, but it was a complete freefall of emotion. "I'll go to my training session in the morning and move on. I have a date with Rahl, the blond bartender from Two Fine, on Tuesday night at Brix. Maybe that will be something." An involuntary wail of sadness that it wasn't Jude hit the air.

Standing over me, Willow sighed. "Okay, Prez, but if you don't eat something tomorrow, I'm instituting a friendship food intervention at DEFCON 1."

"Understood, and I appreciate your concern. Good night, Willow."

"Good night, Presley. Love you."

"Love you, too."

She shut the door and I bawled myself to sleep.

Chapter Ten

Jude

Telling Presley that a professional relationship was the way to go was about the hardest thing I'd had to do in the last four years. After that morning's three-hour seminar at Triple R on sexual harassment of and by coworkers, bosses, and clients in the workplace, I protected my career.

While I was telling Presley the whys of being only her trainer, I caught a glimpse of those easy-to-read emerald green eyes and almost said to hell with my career, but she took the news relatively well, which led me to believe maybe she wasn't that interested anyway. I stuck with my reasoning but I couldn't stop thinking about her for the rest of the day. I *was* that interested. Being just her trainer was going to be a struggle.

You're being smart. Doing the right thing.

I barely made it through my shift at the bar Saturday night. Rahl told me he'd asked Presley out for drinks at Brix on Tuesday and asked what I knew about her. I gave a one-word response and acted too busy to elaborate. The Ogre—the waitresses had nicknamed Rahl the fitting moniker—commented about what he perceived as an attitude problem on my part. I responded that he would know. After all, he was the king of attitude. He huffed a chain of creative and noteworthy expletives under his breath. Jabbing the Ogre was never a great idea. I got the hell out of there as soon as possible, driving the backstreets a little too fast on my motorcycle to match the thoughts racing through my mind.

Sunday, I made a trip to the gym early in crazy hopes that maybe Presley would be there, and I could see how she was doing, but she wasn't. On my way out, I remembered her saying she volunteered. Legitimately and logically, I kept telling myself that remaining professional was a good decision, but when it came to attraction and lingering feelings there was a lot to be said for acting irrationally.

Zane left for work and the house was too quiet. Lying in bed, I texted Presley. I considered that she said I didn't have to but every cell of my body wanted and needed to know she was okay.

Jude: **I know you said I didn't have to but— 5am. See you then.**

A half hour went by. I didn't like what I was feeling when there wasn't a return text.

Jude: **Are you okay?**

Ten more minutes went by. I wondered if something was really wrong.

Jude: **Presley, can you let me know if you're okay? Please.**

Five minutes later, I couldn't stand it anymore. I called Kanyon.

"Hey, Ponytail."

I chuckled.

Seems the nickname is going to stick.

I started with a soft opener. "Hey, Kanyon. So how is Willow, stud?"

"That's a loaded question, dude."

"Why?"

"Are you really asking about Willow or are you actually asking about Presley?"

My chest constricted, pulling at something that was fresh and raw on the inside. I did a sit-up in my bed. "What happened?"

"I think I should be asking you that question."

"Kanyon, what's wrong? Is it Presley? Is she okay?"

Kanyon sighed. "Not that I should be divulging what Willow told me, but I think you need to hear it. Willow came home yesterday after work and found Presley all kinds of messed up, crying, mumbling incoherently, and lying on the floor in the living room in a daze."

I held my breath while he continued his relay of information.

"Willow cancelled our date for Saturday night to take care of Presley. I convinced her to let me come over to keep her company and we listened to Presley cry in her sleep all night long through the paper-thin walls, which was a *real* mood killer. I'm pretty sure Willow wants to cut off the man part of your body. Jude, what the hell did you do?"

I sucked in a breath. "What I had to do. We had this excruciatingly long but eye-opening training about sexual harassment at Triple R yesterday morning. I realized I'd blurred the lines of trainer and client. Not only could I be fired, but because of my actions, I might have made Presley feel uncomfortable."

"Okay, didn't she get a hold of you to talk in the morning?"

"I was in that meeting. She left me a voice mail saying she was sorry for Friday night and regretted her behavior. I didn't understand why she had regrets but it made me feel like I had to be the responsible one to get us out of something that might be causing her distress. I went to her house and told her I thought it was smart to stay in a professional relationship, but also I endangered her life on Friday by not concentrating on my responsibilities as her personal trainer and I didn't want that to happen again."

The silence that filled a minute or longer made me uneasy. I checked my phone. The signal was still there.

"Kanyon?"

"You're a fucking idiot!"

"What?" The question shot out of my mouth.

"Fucking idiot! She can find another trainer. When she does, where does that leave you? You told her you know what's best for her. You didn't *ask* her what she wanted to happen. When I left Willow and Presley's place on Saturday morning, Presley was all set to call you and make an effort to get to know more than the pretty picture on the exterior of your idiot body. Didn't she do that?"

"Like I said, she left me a voice message while I was in a meeting at Triple R. I don't remember all of it but I do know she didn't sound happy. I showed up at her home and told her what I needed to. She didn't really react anyway, so maybe she wasn't that interested."

I was trying to give legitimate reasons but everything I said came out with an uncomfortable edge.

"Again, you're a fucking idiot!"

"Stop saying that!" I grunted.

"No, I won't. Presley will probably call me an asshole for suggesting that you two could have something real together, something more than a trainer/trainee relationship. You turned around and told her everything I was spouting was crap. She probably didn't sound happy 'cause she had one hell of a hangover. You need to get your shit straight, Jude. I like Willow. I'm going to make sure she stays happy cause when Willow's not happy it makes me unhappy. Have you ever seen me unhappy?"

I went to answer "no" but he cut me off.

"It's not pretty, Jude. You cause that unhappy feeling again and I'll make your pretty face not pretty, too."

"Are you threatening me?" My jaw tightened and my legs rolled to the edge of the bed.

"No, I'm trying to get your head out of your ass! You had a beautiful girl right at your fingertips, a beautiful girl wanting you, ready to be with you, trying to trust you. Screw personal training. You can find another client, but you'll never find another Presley."

He's right about that. Fuck!

I swallowed the lump in my throat. "Is she okay today?"

"No. I just talked to Willow and Presley hasn't eaten since yesterday morning. Apparently this concerns Willow a lot. She wouldn't tell me why."

I lay back in my bed. "I tried to text her a reminder for our session, but I haven't heard anything back."

"And you won't. She's asleep, again. You and I both know that if Presley hasn't eaten tomorrow, she shouldn't be working out. Jude, I know we've only known each other for a month and you have no real reason to listen to me, but bro, you screwed up. Make it right. These are two gorgeous girls who deserve good guys, if we're lucky enough to be those two guys—"

"I hear you, Kanyon. Shit!" I sat back up and ran my hand through my hair. "Presley has a date with the moody bartender from Two Fine on Tuesday."

"So? Get her before he does. When she shows tomorrow, be the biggest pussy on Earth and get that woman to feel something for you again. Make it clear she shouldn't go on that date with that guy. I know you've got moves." Kanyon chuckled. "So use them."

"Okay, I hear you. Just don't call me a fucking idiot again. I really hate that and it makes me want to hate you."

He chuckled again. "I'll stop calling you one when you stop being one."

I released a small, uncomfortable laugh. "Different subject. Quaker Steak and Lube, Thursday night?"

"Sure. Meet at your house. Maybe with Willow and Presley?"

"Maybe. And hopefully."

"Good luck, Jude."

"Thanks."

And then it was 4:55 a.m. Monday morning at Triple R, and there was no sign of Presley. I turned to Emerson.

"Hey, Presley said she gave you an envelope on Friday. Where is it?" I leaned over the desk waving in her face to get her attention when she pretended not to hear me.

"I don't remember that happening. If Princess did, it would be in your mailbox."

Emerson shot her response back calmly, but I could tell she was lying. One, Presley wouldn't lie. She had no reason to. Two, Emerson would. She had every messed-up reason to.

"Don't lie to me, Emerson."

"Don't call me a liar, Jude, and don't have someone I barely know take me home. How did you know he wasn't going to rape me?"

I grumbled under my breath, rifling through my mailbox at the back of the front desk. "Sounds like it was the other way around to me."

There was no envelope.

"What did you say?" she spat.

"Nothing. I'm going to use the restroom. If Presley gets here, tell her I'll be right back. And be nice for once!"

"Aye-aye, captain." Emerson saluted me with her middle finger.

I headed into the locker room and pulled my phone out of my locker.

There was a text at 4:33 a.m.

Presley: **Not feeling well. Sorry for late notice. Won't be in today. Goodbye**

Jude: **:-(**

I was the biggest pussy in history for sending a sad face, but I held out hope that maybe the move would at least inspire a return text and then hopefully an invitation to a conversation and then...

I returned to the gym floor.

Emerson flipped her hair over her shoulder and said, "Princess is stretching and waiting for you, your highness."

But I thought?

I walked around the desk to the stretching area and sure enough, Presley sat on the mat, her back to me. Her eyes held to mine in the mirror as a forced smile trailed through her sad face.

How do I play this? The real me ... that's how.

I squatted next to her.

"Presley..."

She turned her head to me, and I searched her face for some emotion I could hold onto, to build us back to being solid.

"I'm really sorry."

But there was nothing.

"I'm here. Let's get this over with so I can go home to get ready for work. I didn't bring my usual wardrobe change with me." Her words were straightforward and detached from any sentiment other than distance. Her hurt dug into my gut as she cringed away from me. She stood and grabbed her water bottle. "Okay, I'm ready."

It was going to take some work to mend this. I'd done hard labor before, building houses. I'd buckle down and put in the time to fix the mess I'd created.

No, this was a colossal-sized fuck-up.

Since she may not have eaten, and I didn't want to betray Willow's trust in Kanyon, I kept the workout light.

"Let's start with a little cardio warm-up."

I had her walk at a slow pace and even that seemed to fatigue her. After she stepped off the treadmill, I walked her around the gym for a cooldown.

"How was volunteering yesterday?"

She took a little while and everything in me wanted to ask again, but I held my tongue.

"It was okay. There's this little dog that I can't get out of my mind. If she doesn't get adopted this week, she's going to be..." She rubbed her temples. The move told me the words she couldn't say. "She needs a family that will understand her. She's got a little extra weight around the middle and doesn't warm up to people immediately. I can see a great dog in her. I hope someone else can too, before it's too late."

"Why not adopt her yourself?"

Presley's eyes, which had been dropped to the floor, met mine as we approached the mirror. It was obviously something she'd considered. She refocused ahead of us as we walked and stayed quiet.

"Ninja is a stray I found at a construction job site. Either he'd crawled into the dumpster and couldn't get out, or someone had put him there. I don't know which is worse to think happened. As soon as I heard him I knew he was mine. He helped me through a pretty rough stretch after a long-term relationship ended. Maybe this little dog was brought into your life to be there for you like you could be there for her."

"I just don't know if I'm ready," she said while she finished her last steps around the track and followed me to the warm-up area.

"Did you get my texts last night?" I asked.

"Not until this morning. I went to bed early."

"Your text this morning said you're not feeling well. How are you feeling now?"

"Honestly, like crap and a little hungry."

"Maybe we should call it a day so you can go eat and rest?"

"No. I need to keep up my workouts. It's the one thing that keeps me sane and in tune with my body."

After making our way back to the stretching area, I grabbed an elastic band and instructed her on exercises that wouldn't overexert her already fatigued body. Yet, she would definitely feel the effects tomorrow. I stood behind her and gave her encouraging words softly and gently in her ear. I made sure to watch her breathing and for any signs that she was pushing herself too far. This workout was more mental than physical, getting her to a place where she was feeling something other than upset—a change of focus.

I asked her when she had to be at work today, thinking that maybe I could take her to breakfast after this to talk privately. She said she had to be in early for a meeting and she wasn't looking forward to seeing some Drexel guy.

"Why not?"

Presley did some woodchopper core exercises with the band. Her intense focus in the midst of her depressed mood amazed me.

She sighed. "Cause he's an ass to every woman in the place. He makes the crudest remarks. Mostly innuendos and juvenile jokes, but since he's usually the top salesperson, I don't think the management will ever do anything about it."

"Sorry to hear that. Guys can be jerks."

"You can say that again," she mumbled and her eyes darted to mine.

"Guys can be jerks," I said again, firmly.

She let out a muffled chuckle but quickly her mood deteriorated right back to where she was previously.

"Are you going to be okay, Presley?" I stood in front of her and adjusted the directional pull of the band.

Like many questions today, she chose not to answer. Instead, she asked me what I knew about Rahl.

I shared the truth. "Don't know him that well. I've only worked at Two Fine for about a month. Why?"

"We have a date tomorrow night at Brix. Was just wondering." She pulled the band taut. Her shoulders rolled forward, indicating she wasn't totally comfortable with the conversation she'd started. I placed a hand on her back, and she straightened her posture. I moved my hand to her shoulder. She recoiled from the touch like my hand was burning her.

"I hope you get some rest and feel better before then." The words were sincere. I was worried about her, more worried than I had been about any other person for a long while. I gave a supportive squeeze of her shoulder and stepped back.

On her last set of a chest-toning exercise, I stepped in front of her. My hands on hers, I helped the last movements be the best of the ten count. Her body responded very little and internally that lack of response tore a hole in my chest.

"Like that, Presley. Three … two … one. Good job." She dropped the band to the floor, and I tagged her water bottle from a bench, handing it over. "How do you feel?"

She drained the bottle. A little life came back into her cheeks. "Actually, better. Mitch never did anything with the bands. I really liked that workout. I can tell I'm going to be very sore tomorrow. I had a buildup of tension everywhere and every move helped release some of that." She met my gaze and her sad green beauties cut me with the raggedness of unpolished emeralds. "Thanks for a great workout, Pony—" Her eyes widened. "Jude."

I grinned at her almost slip-up. "You're welcome, Presley."

The small smile on her face was so much better than the frown she had been wearing for the last hour.

"Did you ever find that envelope I mentioned Friday? At least I think I did, right?" She walked to her bag.

"Yeah, you did. But no, I didn't."

"Here." Presley tugged a rolled and rubber-banded paper from her bag before returning to where I stood. "It's the original sketch." Her eyes flashed between mine. She sighed. "I should have known this was never meant to be mine anyway."

The light paper felt like a brick in my hand.

Presley threw her bag over her shoulder and walked out the door.

I hated the emptiness I'd brought on myself. I did what I thought was morally and ethically right, but every part of my body was screaming that nothing was right, and I got in return what I fucking deserved.

I moved to the desk to fill out the VIP info form.

Blake's voice rumbled behind me. "I'll take that when you're done."

"Good morning, Blake. Here you go." I handed him the form and waited to find out my fate as Presley's trainer while he perused the paper.

"I think you redeemed yourself today, Jude. I watched carefully and as soon as I saw Presley I could tell she wasn't feeling well. I think you realized that, too. It's good to have that intuitive side as a trainer."

I decided not to tell him it was more insider information than intuition.

He nodded over his shoulder. "Walk with me." We headed toward his office. "I liked what you did with her and I'm sure she's going to be feeling the effects tomorrow. Good job. I'm glad Presley convinced me to let you have another chance." Blake eyed me up. "She's quite the young woman. Can't imagine why someone hasn't snatched her up yet. Hopefully the guy who is lucky enough to earn her heart realizes what a treasure he has and doesn't piss it away. Good luck, Jude." He walked into his office.

I collapsed against the wall in the hallway. I'd never been punched in the gut with words, but Blake succeeded. Maybe he saw our interaction last week and witnessed the attraction we had, or maybe it was her pleas to let me continue as her trainer. Whatever it was, his speech was like his blessing to pursue her.

Maybe he thinks of her as a sister?

My brain ran through how to proceed. First, I couldn't be her trainer if I wanted to be something else to her. Maybe I could talk to Kai about what I thought would be the right training for Presley, and she could consult me before making any changes? Then I could ask Presley out, but one big problem stood in the way. The Ogre.

Rahl won't let you join them at their table if you're alone.

I needed a date for tomorrow night, and I didn't really have an alternative.

"Emerson?"

She raised her head. "What, Jude?"

"You want to go get a drink tomorrow after work about seven at Brix, just as coworkers?"

Emerson eyed me up with a scowl. "You're not going to dump me off on someone else, right?"

"No, this time, I promise, I'll take you there and get you home."

"All right. I'll go." She spun her chair to file something in a mailbox. "At least I've seen what goods I might get to enjoy if I play the night right."

It didn't surprise me that she'd lied about the drawing. I decided not to make her question my motives by dismissing her assumption of what might happen at the conclusion of our evening. She and I were coworkers and only coworkers.

I just needed a chance to tell Presley I'd made a big mistake.

I won't mess up this chance.

Chapter Eleven

Presley

Lounging on the sofa, I choked down a cup of minestrone soup. If I wasn't in such a piss-poor mood, the cup of shell noodles, beans, and veggies in a tomato broth would've been delicious, but my attitude even spoiled my taste buds. Willow made the thoughtful concoction before she left for work, promising intervention if at least two cups weren't gone from the container in the refrigerator by the time she returned. Now I could pour the food down the sink disposal, but I forced myself to make an adult choice to avoid the wrath of purple hair. I ingested the two cups, one at a time.

I called into work and claimed I probably had whatever Drexel had last week, even though whatever he had on Thursday was either brown-bottle flu or an overconfident attitude—or more likely, both. The first ailment he would've brought on himself thinking he could celebrate another successful month, and the second disorder was a character flaw he'd probably never get rid of. Whatever the reason, I wasn't in the mood to deal with the deluge of crap comments and wisecracks from his giant asshole of a mouth today.

My behavior wasn't productive, and I made a much bigger deal than I should out of something I never had. It was the thought that I could've had something special that kept me ruminating in a circle of unanswerable questions.

After I sent the text that I wasn't going to be at training, a tidal wave of guilt had rushed over me. More like culpability for continuing my training, with or without him. I'd worked too damn hard to let any man mess with my head in a way that would mess with my body. So I dragged myself from bed and made my way to my training session. I either proved I was a glutton for punishment or proved to Jude I was okay after his declaration on Saturday. Pretty sure I accomplished some of both.

Jude surprised me with a change in workout. I think I surprised him by handing over my drawing as if I didn't want to have the personal reminder of him anywhere near me. Whatever hadn't happened between us was never meant to be, and I needed to accept it. Believing I was at a point where I could be only his trainee was probably delusional but I pulled the illusion off that one time. The significant feat felt like I'd stood up for myself. Although, repeating the performance on a weekly basis seemed like a monumental act that I might not be able to accomplish.

Monday came and went quickly without much transformation in my attitude. When the sun came up on Tuesday, I rolled over to have the alarm clock glare that it was after seven a.m. I considered making my illness a multi-day event, but I didn't. I rolled out of bed and was at the dealership before my starting time of eight a.m., putting minimal effort into my appearance. I chose simple dark brown slacks, a creamy-white silk shirt, and a camel-colored sweater with kicky cheetah-print heels on my feet in an attempt to put a little boldness in my step.

I was sitting at my desk when my phone buzzed.

Rahl: **You still in for tonight at Brix?**

I took a deep breath. I could say I wasn't feeling well, and even if he asked Jude about my condition, it would have been a passable truth, but I needed to move on.

Prez: **I'll be there. See you right after 6pm.**

Rahl: **Looking forward to it.**

I'd use the date as a reason to keep the day going and not head straight to bed after getting home.

I forgot I was supposed to get my picture taken yesterday, so when Jillian's hubby, Mark, rounded the corner into my office, I made an annoyed sound that was probably very rude. Although, I'm not sure anyone loved to have his or her picture taken, except maybe models. Photographs were like going to the dentist. I did what I needed to do to get the unpleasantness over with, not because I enjoyed the attention.

He leaned against the doorway, arms crossed. "I guess you're looking forward to this."

Mark was a great guy, and we instantly hit it off when Jillian invited me over to their house. I taught him how to change the oil in his own car to save a little money. The dealership's service department probably wouldn't appreciate that. But as an artist, I knew saving a little here and there could make a big difference.

"I just haven't been feeling well and didn't put much effort into my appearance today."

"Presley..."

I plastered on a smile. I motioned to my face. "Just give me a couple of minutes in the bathroom to reapply, and we'll get it done."

His eyebrows furrowed. "Okay, I'll wait here for you."

In the bathroom, I applied a little powder to cover up the semi-oily parts of my face, added a little more eyeliner and mascara than usual, and a soft rose-colored lip gloss. I pulled my hair out of the low bun I had it in to dry and arranged the tousled waves around my shoulders.

It'll have to do.

Mark was standing outside my office when I returned.

"I want to do something a little more unconventional with your shots, Presley. Let's head outside."

After what felt like 5,000 photos, he extended his congratulations for beating the Great Dixless and indicated he would have the photo up on the wall in the morning. I told him there was no hurry. I wasn't a fan of myself in pictures even though I was sure he would do his best.

Mark sighed loudly. "Presley." His voice was so direct that I couldn't help but be rapt in attention. "Beauty may be in the eye of the beholder, but any man would love to be holding your beauty in his arms. It will be no challenge to make your photo beautiful because you already are."

My eyebrows were in my hairline when he was done speaking. If it were anyone other than Mark, I might think they were trying to get something from or maybe hitting on me. But he was so genuine that I inhaled a deep breath and swallowed to clear the lump in my throat.

Maybe he's right? Come on! You know he's right.

"Thanks, Mark. I can't wait to see it."

"Good. Have a nice day, Presley."

"You, too."

Pulling into the Brix parking lot after six, I sat in my car for a few minutes. Anticipation had my stomach doing impressive gymnastics moves, mostly because I ate more than yesterday and my stomach threw a little tantrum at the introduction of more than a cup of food at a time. If I was going to be enjoying a glass of wine, I needed sustenance to keep me from becoming a bawling idiot.

I texted Willow.

Prez: **Going into Brix for my date. Wish me luck.**

On the way to the door, I got a return text.

Willow: **Good luck. I'm out with Kanyon. Probs won't be home tonight.**

Prez: **You go girl!**

Willow: **LOL ... thanks. <3**

Inside, I located Rahl in a booth along the front wall.

He stood and kissed my cheek. "Hi, Presley, thanks for meeting me."

"Hi, Rahl. Sorry I'm a little late, traffic."

"No problem. What would you like, red or white?" He picked up a wineglass from the table.

"White, pinot grigio or sauvignon blanc, please."

"I'll be right back."

Rahl crossed the room to the white wine self-service dispenser. Solid from the tip of his nose to the tip of his toes, he wore jeans that skimmed his legs and emphasized that he wasn't a small guy. With the jeans he sported a button-down hunter-green shirt that brought out just the touch of green I hadn't noticed before in his soft brown eyes. Casual brown leather shoes shrouded his feet comfortably. His hair was styled differently today than on Friday at the bar. The short, thick, dishwater-blond strands were standing straight up in front and he was clean-shaven, unlike on Friday when multi-day dark-blond stubble sullied his young-looking face. I would say he was mid-twenties but he had a maturity about him that made me think he might be older. The whole package was quite handsome, but there was little real physical attraction to him.

"Here you go." He handed me a glass of wine. "Sauvignon blanc from New Zealand. My friend, Joe, suggested it. He's at the bar waiting for his wife." Rahl pointed to a muscular man with kind eyes who gave a wave when our eyes met. I waved back to him.

"Is he your date safety net if our time doesn't go well?" I joked.

Rahl's deep chuckle got a return of the same from me. "No, just coincidence. How was your day?"

"Decent. I dragged a little this morning, but doing better this evening. How about you, and what do you do?" I cringed. The conversation sounded too familiar.

"I guess you don't remember some things from Friday?" he teased.

"Honestly, not everything." I sipped a drink of the delicious wine, and grapefruit and kiwi flavors skimmed my palate.

A waitress stopped by our table. "Would you like an appetizer tonight? Cheese plate, margherita flatbread, or Brie with bread?"

Rahl didn't hesitate and didn't ask me if I was hungry, but I suspected as a big guy he was probably hungry all the time. "The Brie, hummus platter, and the steak frites, please."

She nodded. "I'll get it ordered right away."

Rahl turned to me. "If you're hungry after that, I'd be glad to buy you dinner, too."

He sipped his red wine. The sight was quite the contrast—this brawny, testosterone-dripping male with a delicate wineglass balanced in his large hand. A manly beer might be more apropos but somehow he made it work.

Still don't feel a thing for him.

My lack of interest made me wonder if there was something wrong with me.

Rahl cleared his throat. "To answer your question, I had a good day. I own a private security firm. Think mall cops with more than mace as a weapon."

"Ever have to use more than mace?"

"You really want to know?" His grip on his glass firmed.

"I think you just told me without telling me." I scrunched up my nose. "Sorry."

"I was in the Army, Afghanistan, four and a half years. So, yeah, more than just mace, unfortunately." A moment of sadness and maybe distress passed through his eyes. The emotion flickered in and out, but it was there.

"I think you told me that on Friday night, right?"

"Yeah, but I wouldn't expect you to remember. Was there a reason for the pitcher-sized consumption of lemon-drop martinis, or was it just an unwinding gone horribly wrong?"

In other words, was I an alcoholic or just temporarily messed up?

Our appetizers arrived and we dug in. My appetite seemed to be returning.

"I'm not an alcoholic, Rahl."

He chuckled heartily, dimples indenting his cheeks. "I wasn't thinking that, promise."

I took a sip from my glass after swallowing a smear of Brie on a piece of bread and contemplated how much to say.

"Honestly, I was supposed to be celebrating that I was the dealership's top salesperson for the month of April but unforeseen circumstances caused me to get a little out of control. I'm not proud of it. Just happened."

"Congrats on the success. Everyone has those nights where things get out of hand, Presley. I promise I wasn't trying to pry or judge your behavior."

"I know you weren't."

It wasn't so bad to be a friend with a guy.

I sipped the wine. "So what do you like to do in your free time? Not that you have any, working two jobs."

"I'm working the second job to add to the down payment on a home I'm having built, so Two Fine will be temporary. But in my spare time I like to shoot skeet competitively, and I brew my own beer at home."

"I thought you looked more like a beer guy than a wine enthusiast."

"Wine is okay, but, yeah, I'll probably move to a beer after this."

Our conversation was light and easy, nothing too-too personal—family, work, and hobby-related. He was a native of Omaha, like me, but he grew up in a different part of the city. He was older than me. His twenty-six years to my twenty-four. He shared that he's the oldest child of his family with two sisters and divorced parents. I relayed I was an only child, divorced parents. I could tell he was trying hard to make a connection. But it wasn't there.

Rahl's eyes pinched slightly and his jaw tensed into a line.

"Something wrong?" I watched his face soften again.

"Not really." The tight quality of his voice spoke the opposite. I sensed a presence approaching the table. "Hey, Jude, what's up?" He raised his voice with an unfriendly edge.

Jude? Really?

"Not much. Just out for a drink with a coworker from the gym. Hi, Presley, how are you feeling today?"

My eyes met his. "Hi, Jude. Sore, but overall, better. Thanks."

"Glad to hear that. We didn't make an appointment, but would you like another session on Friday?"

"Not this week. Appreciate the offer."

Jude nodded and smiled his crooked grin. My body responded, sending tingles all through my chest. I took a deep breath, which did nothing to calm anything; in fact, the surge of oxygen ignited the tingles to follow a path farther south. I cursed silently and kept my eyes on Rahl across the table. He was safe and didn't cause a single tingle.

"Jude, let's go to Kona Grill, there's no place to sit." Emerson's whiny voice had my eyes rolling involuntarily. Rahl grinned and elevated his eyebrows quickly at my reaction. I shook my head to indicate it wasn't a big deal.

Of course he's here with Emerson ... his line of "there's nothing happening" was only a cover-up.

Jude searched the busy room and turned back to us. "I'm sure something will open up soon."

Rahl and I met eyes and an unspoken question flowed between us. *Should we invite them to sit with us?* I nodded in acquiescence.

"Would you like to sit with us *until* something opens up?" Rahl offered reluctantly.

"That okay with you, Presley?" Jude stepped closer.

"Of course."

Not sure.

I slid out and back in next to Rahl, his bulky size made the booth a cozy place to be. Emerson huffed at me before she slipped onto the bench seat. Jude sat across from me. His eyes bore into me but I avoided his penetrating gaze.

The waitress returned to the table. Emerson ordered a chocolate martini and Jude a beer. Rahl added a beer for himself. I decided to stop drinking and asked for a glass of water. I didn't want to get out of control again, and considering my heart had already started to pound after catching Jude's brain-scrambling cologne scent, I needed to do everything I could to eliminate the potential for lessening my discomfort with alcohol.

During our conversations, several tables opened up. Emerson nudged Jude but he ignored her. Every time she touched him, the urge to rip her hair out strand by strand tensed my hands. I tried to remain calm and unaffected by my still-raw feelings.

Success was a grey scale at this point.

"You work this weekend, Rahl?" Jude inquired.

"No, I have this one off, you?"

"Yeah. I'm up this one and off the next."

"I saw your bike outside of the bar. What is that? An '05 or '06?"

"It's a 2005."

"Nice. I have a 2008 Harley Road King Classic. Haven't had it out this year. The weather's been too unpredictable."

"Impressive bike. I'd enjoy seeing it some time. I took a chance and it worked out Saturday night. Don't really love driving that late at night with drunk drivers out, but I took backstreets to get home. Also keeps me from drinking while working."

"Hear that." Rahl lifted his beer for a drink. "Speaking of drinking while working, did you notice Sage on Saturday night?"

"Yeah, what was up with her?"

"Not sure, but that was a whole lot of vodka she drank. I thought Sam was going to can her ass. I drove her home and she rambled on and on. Mostly incoherent things, like something about ogres finding happiness and eyesight issues with cats and dogs."

"Huh. That's weird?"

Rahl seemed genuinely concerned. "She's never seemed like the kind to drown her troubles. She did a fine job that night. I checked in on Sunday by text and she said she was moving slowly."

"Maybe it was a fluke." Jude drank his beer. "Sometimes people need a temporary outlet to express their real feelings."

"I think Presley's outlet used to be mass quantities of food. Right, Presley?" Emerson offered with a cunning smirk and a sip of her martini.

Jude and Rahl both frowned at Emerson. My face heated with embarrassment. I dropped my eyes to my water, drawing abstract figures in the condensation on the outside of the glass.

Everything was silent until Emerson exclaimed, "God, you were huge! I bet—"

"Stop!" Jude roared, and Rahl swore under his breath at Emerson.

I flinched at Jude's loud voice. My eyes watered, and my breath spasmed in my chest.

Emerson had killer instincts of what buttons to push. She'd perfected her intimidation skills, and with razor sharp accuracy, her words could cut a person open from the inside out.

"Not another word to Presley, Emerson," Jude growled.

"Whatever, grumpy butt. I need to use the restroom." She waved for Jude to move.

After she left, I could feel his eyes examining me, but mine remained safely on my water glass. I was afraid if he showed any regret or concern I might lose hold of my emotions.

Rahl's friend approached the table. "Sorry to interrupt. Presley, right? I'm Joe Weston. Nice to meet you."

I shook his hand.

Joe glanced beside me. "Hey, Rahl, I have a flat tire. And I just bent my jack. Could I borrow yours?"

Rahl said nothing. Then I realized he didn't want to leave me alone with Emerson and Jude. He glared across the table.

I leaned to him. "Rahl, I'll be fine. Please, help your friend."

Rahl's hand fluttered lightly on my back and he lowered his mouth to my ear. "Are you sure?"

"I'm sure." I slid out.

Rahl strolled out of the building with his friend, but glanced back.

I cleared my throat of the lump of emotion that had gathered as I returned to the booth, moving more into the middle. Jude followed my move so he was face-to-face with me.

A rush of air escaped his mouth. "Presley, I'm really sorry."

I closed my eyes. "For what, Jude?"

"Emerson. How she treats you. Lots of things."

"Are you sorry for me or embarrassed by Emerson?" I tamped my emotions and attempted to grow a backbone. Scary as hell but when I looked him in the eye it was as if he shared his strength and hope with me.

"I'm sorry for being an idiot and mortified at Emerson's behavior."

I shook my head. Didn't change anything.

He sighed. "Presley, if I told you I went the wrong direction, what would you say?"

"I'd ask what you're talking about. What wrong direction?"

"Presley, I find you fascinating. Strong, and yet so vulnerable. Open, and yet so guarded. Innocent, and yet so damn sexy. I made a mistake. A big one. I'd like to get to know you better, outside of training. Please."

"But I ... I thought..." My shoulders began to creep forward. I sat up straight to stop the physical response.

"I was wrong and rash for what I said. Presley, I can't stop thinking about you, day and night."

My hand dropped from my water glass to the table. He reached across the table and covered my chilled hand with his warm one. His long thumb stroked slowly along mine, dipping into the curve before my thumb. My body shook with a small tremor of suggestive thoughts.

He lowered his voice. "Please, Presley, can you forgive me? Will you give me a chance to make it up to you?"

I yanked my hand back to my lap and glanced out the picture window to where Rahl was helping his friend. "I don't know. I'm so confused. What about your date?"

"I know you're confused and I'm to blame for that, but I'm not confused. Emerson is nothing to me. You are what I want, not her."

Legitimately I wanted to just say "thank God" and give in to him, but I needed to know he was authentic and he hadn't shown me anything near that kind of commitment.

My eyebrows rose and I sat back. "Does Emerson know that? Who invited who tonight, Jude?"

He straightened. "I asked her to come here with me."

"So how am I supposed to believe you would like to be a part of my life when you invited a person who can tear me apart in two sentences or less?"

"Again, I'm sorry. Fuck!" He rubbed his face with his palms as if to erase some feeling. That move never worked. I'd tried it before. "Presley, when it comes to you, it's like I can't think straight. I go left when I should go right. If you want to know my real reasoning then here is the lame excuse. I'm sorry for asking Emerson, but I thought if I showed up alone I wouldn't have had a chance of sitting at the same table as you and she's the only female I knew who would say yes, and legitimately part of me was jealous that it wasn't me sitting at this table with you instead of Rahl."

"You're right. That's the lamest reasoning in the world." I scowled at the bouncing blonde making her way back to us. Our eyes met.

She narrowed hers. "What's your problem, Princess? You really look like you need to eat. I think there's an all-you-can-eat buffet open at the casino."

"Emerson, stop it." Jude stood and faced her. "Now."

"Why should I, Jude? She's nothing."

Jude stared down at Emerson. "That's where you are fucking wrong. Presley's more than you'll ever hope to be, Emerson. You are the nothing to me."

Emerson's head spun like something from *The Exorcist*, her eyes glared, and her jaw hardened. She rotated back to Jude. "Her? You're fucking interested in *her*? You have to be kidding! You want a fatty slab of porterhouse when you can have a fine filet mignon every night?"

My eyes popped open. I'd heard enough. Being compared to a cut of beef was beyond what I ever imagined could come out of Emerson's hateful mouth.

Rahl walked in the front door and waved his oil-covered hands. "I'm gonna go wash up."

I smiled lightly and nodded. He cocked his head at me in question of what was happening but after I waved him on he walked down the hallway to the restrooms. I didn't want to get him involved in what I needed to handle myself.

I stood and grabbed my purse. "Emerson Welch, grow up and get over yourself! Your opinion of me means less than you seem to think. Actually, I think you're all talk." I stepped closer and she backed up a step. "That's what I thought." I turned to Jude. "I'm not feeling well. Please give Rahl my apologies." I threw my bag over my shoulder and hightailed my way out the door.

"Presley, wait!"

I kept walking. Jude caught up to me as I got to my car.

"Presley, just one more minute of your time. Please."

I backed against my car door. "What, Jude? I'm tired of listening to your excuses and reasons. So make it quick." My purse fell off my shoulder as if it were just as frustrated as I was.

"I was a fucking idiot! There, I said it and I mean it. When it comes to last Saturday and telling you I should only be your personal trainer, I thought I was wrong in pursuing you because of a three-hour sexual harassment seminar at Triple R. I was totally off base because I knew there was something between us from that very first day." His posture was straight but his shoulders slumped. He rubbed the back of his neck.

He continued, "For some reason, I'm failing miserably at doing and saying the right thing, but I want to keep going because I know you're worth it. Normally relationship stuff comes easy to me. But nothing about this is easy. It feels kick-me-in-the-nuts and heart-twisting and I actually think that's a good thing. It means something when it feels this way. Presley, I didn't mean to hurt you. I promise you that." His eyes lifted. "Just one more chance, please."

"You *are* a fucking idiot," I mumbled quietly back.

I'd never said that to anyone and part of me didn't like calling him that. He wasn't an idiot. He was … Jude. Handsome. Honest. And he wanted me. I just said it so he knew I'd been listening.

Jude chuckled. "Right."

I sighed. "I'll think about giving you a chance, tomorrow." I gazed into his eyes and they seemed to relay the right words. "All right last chance. Good night, Ponytail."

His lips broadened into a big smile. "Okay, I'll see you after drawing class tomorrow. Good night, Presley." He opened my car door and I got in.

Tomorrow… I will see him … all of him … again. Crap.

Chapter Twelve

Jude

Emerson met me in the vestibule between the wine store and the restaurant.

"At least you stayed where I told you to."

"I can't believe you're interested in her, Jude! Don't you know what she used to look like?"

"Stop! Presley was right. You seriously need to grow up. I'm done with you and I don't give a flying fuck if you ever give me another referral. I can find another gym to work at, and no, I'm not giving you a ride home. Figure it out yourself."

She huffed and stomped her feet as I walked away.

"Rahl?" I walked to the booth and pulled out my wallet to lay money on the table. "Presley wasn't feeling well. She went home. She asked me to apologize on her behalf."

"I thought she was in the bathroom," he said. "I'm sorry to hear that."

His eyes told me he didn't believe for one second that was why she left. I'd have to come clean with him soon if Presley and I worked things out, but for now I'd just leave it. No need to give him more ammunition to be an ogre to me. Plus, tonight I'd seen another side of him and maybe there was a chance he and I could be friends. Maybe.

I finished my beer. "I'm going to head out, too. My coworker is staying. In case you're interested, I'm going to let you know that she's a complete monster and any guy who thinks the outside of that package is representative of anything on the inside is in for a rude awakening. She is possibly the most disrespectful and miserable person I've ever met."

"I'm surprised you didn't get that Friday. I could smell her foul stench a mile away. She ever talks about Presley or anyone else like that in front of me again, and—"

"Agreed." I held up a hand to stop him from finishing his threat. Or his promise. I assumed he was the second type of guy. "I'll bring a shovel and you can carry the body, Rahl."

He stood and clapped my shoulder. "Deal."

He really isn't an ogre. Huh, wonder if Sage meant him?

"Good night, Rahl. Have a good weekend off."

"If you need someone to fill in for you, call me, please. I could use the extra money."

"Will do." We shook hands.

"Later, Jude."

Outside, Emerson leaned against the passenger door of my truck.

"Just a ride home. I won't ever ask you for anything else." She flipped her blonde hair over her shoulder.

Since I wasn't an asshole, I'd do it. I told her I would get her here and home and I kept my promises.

"Fine, but not a word on the way there."

She pretended to zip her mouth shut. If only that could happen for real.

I drove her to her apartment in silence. She slammed the truck door. I accidentally honked the horn when she was right in front of the truck. Letting out a small shriek, she glared at me while I backed out of the parking spot.

I'm a nice guy, Emerson, not a pussy.

****

The next morning, my day off, I made it to the gym. I was halfway through my routine when I caught

Emerson talking to Blake, and she was flailing a fake fingernail in my direction. She brought a manila envelope from behind her back, pulling out the piece of paper, and Blake's eyes met mine in the mirror. I dropped the weights onto the rack and made my way to where they were standing.

Blake watched me do a set. "Jude, can I talk to you in my office, please?"

"Yes." I followed him, ignoring Emerson's childish glare while passing by.

Closing the door behind us, Blake rounded his desk and threw the manila envelope onto it.

Presley's drawing.

"Want to explain that to me?" He pointed with his eyes.

I wiped my face with a towel. "What did Emerson tell you?"

"She thinks Presley is sexually harassing you." His voice lifted like it was a ridiculous thing to say.

I laughed at the absurdity of that statement, then collected myself. "You want to know the truth or am I going to be fired no matter what I say?"

"I want to know the truth."

It wasn't lost on me that he didn't confirm I wouldn't be fired, but I didn't give a shit anymore. I could find another job. I was the best at what I did and by now Blake knew that. Presley was what mattered.

"I agreed to be a nude model for a friend's *private* art class." I stood my ground as Blake crossed his arms. "By fluke, Presley is a student in the class. I saw her drawing, really liked it, and told her I'd love to have a copy. She dropped the envelope off at the desk on Friday after her session. Emerson kept the envelope and is using the drawing as blackmail against me because I won't have a relationship with her."

Blake's eyes narrowed at me while we stood in a male showdown. "I need you to be honest with me, Jude, and I think I already know the answer to this question, so no bullshit. Do you want to have a personal relationship with Presley outside of training?"

"Yes." I met his eyes and said the word with no room for question of my intent.

Blake sat and rocked back in his chair. "Please, have a seat." He turned his attention to his computer and worked the screen silently for several minutes.

"Have you engaged in any sexual contact with Presley?" he asked.

"No."

He raised an eyebrow and typed something into the computer.

I have dreamed and fantasized about doing anything and everything with and to her, but no ... not yet.

"Have you engaged in any sexual behavior with Emerson?"

"Fuck no!"

Blake laughed at my response and typed additional information into the computer. He straightened in his chair and leaned forward. "Okay, now that we're both on the same page. Jude Saylor, are you ready to be the man that Presley Bradenhurst deserves?"

My heart beat faster. "Absolutely."

The word didn't even come close to the honest truth. For a woman I only met ten days ago, she'd made her way into my head and heart, and if I couldn't help her to see I was the right guy for her to take a chance on, I would compare every woman to her from here on out. None would compare.

Blake leaned back in his chair, his jaw tightened. "Here's the deal. I was ready to fire Emerson before this happened. She claimed Mitch sexually harassed her. I knew she was lying but she kept screaming 'lawsuit' and I let him go instead of her. That explains the excruciatingly long and boring seminar on Saturday."

"The seminar that had me nervous to pursue Presley?"

He shook his head. "That was unfortunate timing. Sorry. Anyway, I'd like Mitch and the clients he took with him back and to mend fences with him and those gym members. He's a great trainer." Blake leaned forward. "Maybe as good as you."

"Thanks."

"At this point I don't give a fuck about Emerson. She's toxic. It's a lesson in hiring family that I won't forget. She's my sister's daughter. I thought maybe she would mellow out over time but she hasn't. Should've known, my sister is a nutcase, too. Emie will be gone before the top of the next hour."

He went back to typing into his computer. In a few minutes, he raised his head again. "I'm moving Presley to Kai. Do you know what that means?"

"I'm hoping I'm not going to be gone with Emerson."

Blake's demeanor relaxed. "No, Jude, *you* are staying. Presley's moving trainers because you can't date someone you're training. It's unethical and you're not that guy. And I fully expect to hear that Presley and you are going on a date by the end of the week. Do I make myself clear?"

I nodded, smiling. "Yes, sir. Can I tell Presley about the changes tonight at drawing class?"

"Yes, but make sure she knows she did nothing wrong when it comes to Emerson being let go or to her being moved to Kai for training."

"I guarantee I'll be crystal clear with the information. You want to keep the drawing or can I take it?"

"By all means. Presley is quite talented." He smirked. "That's all for now. Good luck, Jude."

"Thanks, Blake." I stood, grabbed the envelope, and opened the door.

"And Jude?"

I turned to face Blake.

"Hurt her and I reserve the right to act as her big brother, kick your ass, and fire you on the spot."

"Understood, sir. I'll do everything I can to keep any of that from happening."

I left the gym without saying another word to anyone. I didn't want Emerson asking me any questions or pissing me off more than she already had. I spent the rest of the day hanging with Zane and explaining the Presley situation.

"Wow, brother, you are an idiot," Zane repeated the sentiment I was starting to accept.

"Will people stop saying that?" I mumbled semi-bitterly as Ninja jumped on the couch to see me. He'd been floor-friendly after he did an impressive gymnastics move off the top of my dresser last weekend.

Zane contorted his lips into a kind of smirk-scowl. "Yeah, when you stop being one."

"I've heard that, too."

He grinned. "Are you ready for tonight?"

"I'm packed. I'm hoping to talk to Presley before class starts."

"Um, bro … maybe it's not a good…" Zane made a weird face, then waved off whatever he was thinking. "Never mind. Good luck. I hope you get the girl. Now, can I talk to you about something else?"

"Sure."

While his leg bounced with nervous energy, Zane told me that he was going to enter into a committed polyamorous relationship with both Yori and Britney. He was in love with both of them, they wanted him to move in, and he wanted that, too. This meant I would be living alone. Zane encouraged me to get a roommate but I told him I was too old to put up with another guy's shit. I could barely stand his. Plus, he would need some place to crash when he was exhausted from all the polyamoring he was going to do.

He laughed but became serious. "Really, Jude, thanks for being cool with this. I'm shit-scared to tell Mom and Dad, but I was nervous to tell you. I value your opinion. You've never judged me in the past. I figured you wouldn't start now, but still, it's not exactly conventional."

"I think it's kind of cool." I stared at my baby brother and wondered how he'd grown up so fast. "It's hard enough to love one woman and let her love you in return. That you have enough love to share with two women and keep them both happy, you're probably more of a man than anyone I know. I guess my biggest question is—are you happy, Zane?" I watched for any signs that his answer might not be the case.

"Happier than the last eight years of mind-numbing dating. Now I have two wonderful and gorgeous women, and I couldn't imagine life without both of them."

"Then why would you care what anyone thinks? I like Yori, I like Britney, they seem to really like you, too, or at least what I hear through the walls indicates they do. On that subject, I definitely won't miss hearing their exaltations of your abilities. At all." I deadpanned the comment.

Zane laughed. "I bet. I'm going to start the move tomorrow."

"Sorry I can't help. I have to work. Maybe Saturday, but I bartend this weekend at four p.m., which sucks. Hoping to get a date in with Presley, if she'll forgive me."

"She will. Plus, as Mom always says, 'The best things in life are worth a wait.' No problem on the move. I asked a couple of friends from work to help and I think Britney can carry more than most women. She's very … solid."

It was my turn to chuckle. "And hey, don't worry about Mom and Dad. They'll come around. Dad will probably buy you a cigar for your impressive catch … *es*. And Mom, well, she'll probably come around to seeing Yori and Britney as the daughters she never had, and that, my brother, might be *far* worse than her disliking them."

Zane and I laughed at that truth.

I stood. "All right, it's go time."

"Good luck and go get 'er, pumpkin!" With the creepy pep talk, Zane followed me out to go to the girls' side.

"Fuck off!" I blew out a huge breath of nerves as I walked to my truck. "But thanks."

And said a small prayer to the relationship gods.

Chapter Thirteen

Presley

My day was about as bad as it gets. My brain was stuck on Jude and it caused me to forget about other things. *Important things.*

I closed a sale in the morning, but forgot to put the "In Transit" stickers in the windows and the wife got pulled over on her way back to work. They returned to the dealership in the late afternoon all kinds of pissed off. I had to fight hard to keep my career unsullied with the huge mistake. After apologizing over and over and offering the previously lovely couple, now my worst nightmare couple, complimentary factory all-season floor mats and a six-visit detail package, they had a reasonable, forgiven-not-forgotten attitude.

When I finished with my begging session, I was walking down the hall, and Dixless came up behind me.

"You have a beautiful body, Presley. Like a work of art that I could gaze at for hours, if you'd let me."

I turned to ask, "What the hell?" and, like the jerk he is, he ducked into the men's restroom. What shocked me most about the interaction was that normally I would've just walked away, or more likely run away. Not this time. I followed him into the bathroom, but had to pretend I walked in the wrong door when I absolutely walked in on Charlie using a urinal. I apologized profusely while exiting, all the time hearing Dixless laugh in the bathroom stall.

Later, I remembered tonight was my drawing class. I had no clothes to change into, and all my supplies were in my old car, which was stored in the used car lot. Three miles away. Thus, I had to retrieve my supplies at lunch instead of closing myself in my office like I needed and wanted and desired so badly. Once I was outside, I savored getting out in the spring air. On the way back, I caught my face in the rearview mirror, and I wore a huge smile.

When it was finally time to leave, I wondered if going to class would even be worth it. Since sleep was relatively nonexistent last night, as I couldn't stop thinking about what Jude would have to say, I dragged today. At Brix he was blunt with his feelings, but still, my trust in him wasn't high. I'd been burnt before, and I wasn't sure I was ready to expose the new skin to possible heat again.

And although I'd stood up to her and was slightly mortified at my behavior, the whole Emerson thing was in the back of my mind, rolling around and feeding my insecurities. I needed to know he was really done with her, and I didn't know how I'd get that closure. Without it I just didn't think there was going to be trust. And without the trust, there was nothing.

I drove on autopilot to Graphite and Acrylic Art Studio. My mind wandered to the fact that Jude would be modeling again tonight.

Ugghh.

Didn't know if I could handle seeing him and seeing all of him.

Edwyn met me on the way up the long walkway to the freestanding building. "So, Prez, think the beefcake will be our model again?"

"Probably, and nobody says 'beefcake' anymore, Ed." My shoulders vibrated with a reserved giggle.

He chuckled. "Kind of got the feeling he was happy to see you last week. Something going on there?"

"Not really. Just a little drama that no one wants to hear about."

Edwyn's soft hand on my arm stopped me and his eyes softened with compassion. "Oh, honey, my Philippe says that drama is my middle name. You ever want to share yours, you let me know. It's not misery that loves company, gorgeous. It's real life that loves company."

Jude stood outside of the classroom in his robe and looking absolutely edible, his hair all pulled back into a low ponytail and his muscular legs showing. Edwyn whistled under his breath until I gave him a shove toward the art room.

"Hey." Edwyn performed a blatant inspection while passing Jude.

"Hey." Jude adjusted his robe, trying to cover more skin but failing miserably.

Jude's discomfort was noticeable and amusing, but totally unreasonable. Ed was in love with Philippe, like forever-love. He rolled his eyes and fanned himself behind Jude's back. After a quick giggle at his antics, I brought my attention to Jude.

"Hi, Presley." Jude glanced over his shoulder, and Ed hightailed himself into the classroom.

"Hi, Jude."

"Ready for class?"

"I think so. Had a pretty long day, but class always seems to change my mood, so we'll see."

Jude stepped close. Only a sliver of light flowed between us, the knot in his robe belt grazed against my blouse, and a wave of butterflies rode through my stomach.

"Can you stick around for a few minutes after class so we can talk?" His eyes searched mine for an answer.

"All right."

"Thanks."

I stepped around him, getting the scent of his body stuck in my nose. I swore silently as goose bumps rose on my skin. He still affected me so easily. The reaction screamed otherworldly, maybe a curse of Aphrodite and Pothos.

Or is it a blessing?

Inside the room, Edwyn prepped his area and patted the stool next to his. He sent a fellow student off to another easel with a bitchy/friendly glare. The line between the two emotions painted elegantly on his face.

Simi relayed general directions for the focus of the session. The new pose would be challenging and our model would be holding for forty-five minutes followed by a fifteen-minute break and an additional thirty minutes after.

Getting my supplies organized, the same gasp exited Edwyn, and I rolled my eyes. Before glancing around the easel, my heart pounded in my chest, readying my weak mind for the image. And I was still not ready. Jude was still gorgeous, not that I expected anything to change in one week. The definition of his muscles sent a wildfire running through every vein in my body, ravaging me with a blast of heat. It took all my will not to combust into a pile of ash.

"I knew it!" Ed whispered.

"What?"

"You are into him, in a big way."

"It's just a crush."

"Prez, it's never *just* a crush." He returned to his sketch.

I took my time with the drawing, starting at his face. Jude braced on a stool facing my direction. Simi had arranged his legs so one was propped on the lowest rung of the stool. The other leg was straight and his upper body was turned toward us, showing off the muscles in his obliques and his toned arm and shoulder. The pose was innocent, but nothing about Jude was innocent. He radiated passionate human and skillful lover from every pore on his godlike body and face.

Our eyes met occasionally. Over the thirty minutes of sketching, I noticed his face gradually tensed. He shifted uncomfortably, until he called Simi over and her eyes widened when she got close. They discussed something, and she handed him his robe. He slid it on and left the room.

Ed lifted his eyebrows. "That was interesting."

"And weird. Hope he's feeling okay."

"I'd say he's feeling something ... *big*."

"Okay, enough with the juvenile innuendos."

"Presley, he popped a boner," Ed said matter-of-factly.

"What?" I exclaimed loudly. "Sorry," I offered to the room and blushed until the heat of my cheeks spread to my ears.

"Yes, probably from looking at you like you're naked, too. You really need to get it over with and ride the pink pony."

"Ed!" I slapped him lightly, and he laughed it off.

Interesting that he said pony ...

I was so focused on sketching what was above the waist that I didn't even look at what was happening down below.

Damn, bet it was a beautiful sight.

I continued to sketch and attempted to concentrate on anything but Jude's big issue.

Jude

Simi arranged my limbs in a pose she found aesthetically pleasing. She instructed the students on some principles of drawing, then left them to their creativity.

The way I pointed on the stool gave me a full view of Presley. She'd obviously come directly from work. In grey slacks with a grey and white striped shirt, the arms rolled up and open at the neck showing off her white skin and delicate collarbone, my thoughts wandered through what kissing that delicate neck might do to her.

Halfway through the forty-five minutes, Presley stepped out of her black heels and her hot-pink painted toenails were all I could look at, like I told her—innocent but damn sexy. The graceful tap of her foot while she worked was adorable and the scrunch of her long toes when in deep focus fascinated. Our eyes connected briefly a couple of times but the last time, she held the gaze, as if she was studying my eyes for an answer to one of life's great mysteries.

When she dropped her gaze lower on my body, I became very aware of my sans clothing situation. Before this moment, being a model was only doing Simi a favor, but now I shared a part of myself that should only be for Presley.

And then my biggest fear became a reality. My lifeless weightlifter decided to show off, in a big way. I did my best to change the progressing physical reaction with deep breathing, repulsive mental imagery, and silently cursing the weightlifter's existence, but it was no use. The front row of five twenty-five to thirty-year-old artists began to snicker, and a one of them seemed genuinely offended.

"Um ... Simi?" I called, covering my lap with my hands the best I could.

Her eyes opened wide as she walked closer. The tiny woman giggled. "Having an ... issue?"

"Yes, sorry. Can I take a break, please?"

"Yeah, here." She handed me my robe, then turned to the students. "Class, we'll be taking our fifteen minutes a little early."

After I slipped into the black robe as discreetly as I could, I walked awkwardly and directly to the bathroom. Pacing along the front of the stalls, I came up with two possible actions and only one of them was probably an intelligent choice. First, I could leave. Grab my bag, extend my apologies to Simi, and text Presley that I'd talk to her tomorrow. Or second, I could man up, jerk off, and go back in with a flaccid member to finish the job I started.

I'm wrong. They're both horrible choices.

I rubbed my face, hoping to erase the memory of my penis faux-pas. I chose the second ridiculous option, because even though I was mortified, my erection was still as hard as stone. Plus, every lucid thought trailed back to the green-eyed, black-haired siren in the art room ten feet away and how badly I wished she were in this men's room with me to help me with my raging problem.

I chose the bigger of the two stalls and locked the door. Standing over the toilet, I wrapped my hand around my cock and started long, slow strokes. Each motion sent a zing of pleasure to my gut. I closed my eyes and let Presley's vision appear in my mind. The way her long hair shimmered and reflected light like a halo, how her bright green eyes softened to a deep green when her gaze met mine, her lips and how they turned pouty and fucking kissable when she was concentrating on her artwork. I thought about how amazing those lips would feel along every inch of my body. Soft and wet.

I increased my speed and the tightening in my groin signaled the precursor to the pinnacle of my efforts. I imagined her tongue sliding over my balls and up my swollen and stiff cock, and my legs weakened. I leaned over the toilet, bracing myself with my unoccupied hand against the back wall. Her innocent eyes looking up at me while she sucked me off would send me over the edge into an intense release. The mental vision did its job. I muttered a string of cuss words as the weightlifter pumped his load into the toilet. The last of the words to be uttered from my mouth was her name, in reverence and with complete respect.

When my body stopped pulsing, I sensed a presence in the next stall.

The anonymous man cleared his throat. "Don't worry, your secret is safe with me. But you need to get your shit together. If you deserve her, then show her. Otherwise, leave her alone. Presley doesn't deserve a dickhead, even one that has … a *very* nice dick."

Keeping my mouth shut, I cleaned up, washed, and made my way back to the room.

"All better?" Simi asked.

"I think so. Sorry."

"Not the first time that's happened, won't be the last. You think you can do another thirty of the same pose?"

"Yeah." I stripped and took a seat, adjusting to the same position I was in before.

Presley smiled lightly at me. I smirked back with a small raise of my shoulders. The humble move made her smile bigger and more like the Presley of before my idiot ways. Totally worth everything that happened.

"Class, we're ready to start again. Please finish your sketches in the next twenty-five minutes."

I made a concentrated effort to remain perfectly still.

After giving direction to a couple of the girls in the front row, Simi rounded the room. Twenty minutes passed and I heard her usually soft voice change. I brought my eyes up to see what was going on.

"Presley, I love what you're doing. Your lines are textbook, but you've captured an animal quality in the model's eyes." Simi tipped her head. "Intense and sensual, like a lover's eyes. There's a hunger and yearning. Excellent interpretation." Simi moved on to another student.

I cleared my throat, and Presley glanced to me. Her chest rose and fell quickly, her tongue darted out to wet her lips. Every flick of her tongue happened in slow motion.

And I had liftoff again.

This can't be happening. I stood and slid my robe on in one movement, grabbed my bag, and exited the room while motioning with my head for Simi to meet me in the hallway. I was a blur of action, even to myself.

"Jude, what's wrong?"

"It was happening again."

The same giggle was actually comforting. "Really?" She rubbed my arm in a reassuring way. "Most of the students were almost completed. It's not a big deal. Well, I mean what happened isn't a big deal, not that *that* isn't a big deal." She pointed with her eyes, and I shook my head at her. At least she was trying to ease my tension and embarrassment with humor, not that it was working. "Thank you for your time, Jude. I might ask Zane to step in next time, not that you weren't a good subject, but I have a feeling he would be a little more at ease. No matter what happened."

I sighed, releasing tension from my shoulders. "I think that's a good idea. I also know a couple of guys at the gym who might be interested. Give me a call."

"Will do. Have a good night, Jude."

I walked into the bathroom and splashed cold water on my face and my crotch. "Down boy! You already had your moment in the spotlight."

I dressed in jeans, a t-shirt, socks, and canvas shoes and waited in the hall for Presley to exit the art room.

When she did, she walked directly to me, stopping with a few inches between us. With a glance down at my crotch, she asked, "Are you *up* for this?"

"Funny. Yeah, you ready?"

Presley smiled. "I'm ready."

"Want to sit in my truck and we can talk in private?"

Stepping back, she pointed to the door. "Lead the way."

She asked for it. I grasped her extended hand and led her. This was how I would be with her all the time, might as well start at that moment. She inhaled at the touch but surprisingly she wound her fingers in mine. I squeezed gently in support of the move. I grabbed her bag from her other hand and threw it over my shoulder, tucking her sketchpad under my arm.

"Did you finish your sketch?" I held the door open for her.

"Not quite. I'll work on it this weekend."

"Sorry."

"Don't be. I'm sure Simi told you that happens, albeit infrequently, and never twice in one session." Presley eyes danced up through her lashes. "But it has happened before."

"You know why that happened, right?"

"Blood flow and expanding tissue," she answered flatly.

Throwing my head back, I laughed at her blunt but not entirely incorrect response. "Right. I kind of meant what was causing the response to happen, not the physiological definition, more the emotional and psychological reasons."

She didn't answer me. Her eyes bounced around the parking lot.

I helped her into the truck cab, placing her bag and sketchpad on the passenger side floorboard. Rounding to my side, I took in a deep breath before opening the door and climbing in. When I settled in the cab I noticed how far away she was sitting, almost plastered against the passenger side door.

I turned toward her. "Presley, from the moment I stood behind you at the desk before our first training session, I knew there was something special about you. You handled Emerson's bitchiness with grace and more class than most women ever could. I regret inviting Emerson to Brix and listening to those vile words the monster spewed at you. I hope you can forgive me. Blake fired Emerson today. She won't be a problem at Triple R anymore."

"Did I have anything—?"

"No, Emerson caused her termination all by herself. The details aren't necessary, but there is good news that Mitch will hopefully be coming back, if you want to use him as a trainer again."

Presley twisted her hands in her lap. "I don't want to go back to Mitch. I'd like to stay with you, Jude."

"Well, that's a problem."

"Did you get fired, too?" Presley's eyes remained pointed toward the windshield.

"No, but Blake made the decision to move you to Kai."

"I'm sorry. I hope I didn't do something to cause that."

"No, you didn't. I did. Presley, it's good that I'm not training you anymore." I moved a little closer to her.

Her head flipped to me, her eyes brimming with tears. "What?" She shook her head. "Did you invite me into your truck just to tell me you don't want to be my trainer anymore?"

The green pools glistened like grass covered in morning dew, until rolling tears fell over the edge.

I lost all train of thought staring into her beautiful eyes.

She sucked in a jittery breath. "Fine! I get it. We're done, professionally and otherwise. Have a good life, Jude." She grabbed the door handle, yanked her bag from the floor, and swung her legs to exit the truck.

When I recovered my faculties, I reacted quickly. "Shit! Presley! Please wait."

She kept moving. I jumped from my side of the truck to get to her. Her heels were just hitting the concrete when I rounded the truck to the open passenger door.

"Presley, stop, please!" I slid one hand to her waist and one behind her neck. She stiffened as our bodies pressed lightly against each other. When I had her complete attention, I brought my hand from her waist and wiped away her tears. "Presley, it's a good thing. Because now I can kiss you like I've wanted to from the very first day I met you. And this way, I won't get fired."

I tipped her head and met her pouty lips with a soft, gentle kiss. Her eyes opened wide with surprise, then closed in surrender. She dropped her bag to the ground and slid her hands up my chest to the back of my neck where her long fingers tangled into my ponytail. She toyed with the trapped strands and my head spun at how sensual the touch was, and by her soft appreciative moan I could tell she really liked my hair the way it was.

I led the kiss, but everything she did in response was 100 percent better than anything any female had ever done to me. I deepened the kiss. Our tongues rolled in a slippery fusion that seared my memory and taste buds with her sweet essence. Each of us gave a little of ourselves to the other person, and at that moment I'd give her anything she ever wanted. Our bodies heated along with our mouths. My hands searched her back, pulling her closer to me until we were crushed in a passionate vice-like hold.

I broke the kiss, dropping my forehead to hers. "Presley, can we get back in the truck?"

She nodded. Her eyes remained closed and her body shivered lightly.

"Are you okay?"

Not answering, she turned around and jumped back onto the seat.

When I was seated back inside, she slid closer. *Now that's better.*

But her eyes still pointed down and her body tremored visibly. "Don't hurt me again, please."

With those broken and fear-filled words, I wrapped my arms around her. "I'm going to do everything I can to never do that again, and that's a promise."

Her soft eyes fluttered closed and my heart beat fast.

"Jude, I want to trust you, but like always my mind and instincts are telling me to run the other way." Her eyes met mine. "But I think my heart is saying something else. I think it wants to stay and see what could happen."

I guided her body closer. She'd opened her heart to me and I wanted her to know that I was doing the same.

"I like what your heart is saying, Presley."

"I like these muscles." She trailed her fingers along my upper arms, under the t-shirt sleeves to trace my muscles.

"Thanks. I like that you're smart, strong and successful, and you make my head spin with your sexy innocence."

She blushed. "I'll give you the first three."

"Presley, from now on, I will protect you from anything that tries to hurt you. But between you and me, how you handled Emerson last night was fuckin' hot."

Presley giggled, the sound holding the innocence of a child popping bubbles for the first time.

"Thank you, Jude. Don't know what it is, but I've been on quite a roll at standing up to people in the last twenty-four hours."

We both stilled as her fingers continued up my neck, to my face, then traced along my eyebrows and down my sideburns, finally grazing across my lips.

"I like these lips. I've wanted to feel them on mine since the first moment I turned around and said hello."

"You mean ... hi?" I stretched the word like she had.

Presley giggled again and the sound started a chain reaction in my body. I dropped my mouth onto hers and when our tongues met she moaned so loudly I thought maybe I was hurting her, but the way her hands clasped my head and drew it closer, it was clear she only wanted more.

"God, your tongue..." She panted. "It's ... it's..." She slammed her mouth on mine again, forcing her tongue in and making another erotic sound of approval. Her hands searched my chest and dropped lower to the bottom of my shirt, lifting and grazing my abdomen.

I sucked in a quick breath and pulled away from her mouth slowly. "Presley, we're in the middle of a parking lot and there are students milling around. As much as I'd love to continue this, I'm pretty sure there are security cameras filming our first moments together."

Her breaths rolled as fast as mine. "You're probably right. Don't need to end up on the Internet as what not to do."

There was a hard triple tap on the passenger window. Presley shrieked and buried her face into my chest. I chuckled while looking over her shoulder.

"I knew it! Good for you, Prez." The young man pointed at me. "Remember what I said, beefcake. My boyfriend is as big as you and a black belt in tae kwon do. Keep that in mind."

I forced a nervous smile, and the lanky guy grinned.

Presley rocked her forehead against my chest, groaning her embarrassment. "Good night, Edwyn."

"Good night, Gorgeous. Good night, Beefcake." The no-longer-anonymous voice hopped in his Prius and drove away.

I questioned whether to tell her the truth. In the end I trusted her, too.

"He caught me in the bathroom." I rubbed my hand up and down her back.

"So?" Presley nuzzled her nose into my neck.

"The traditional baseball and horrible mental imagery wasn't working and I needed to make my problem go away. So…"

"You owe me twenty dollars?"

I laughed. "Yeah, I think I do."

Chapter Fourteen

Presley

Last night was incredible. Jude and I'd had a good time in his truck, like a *really* good time. He had to be up early the next morning. I'd reluctantly said good night. I understood, kind of. Before we'd left he'd asked me on a date, Friday night. Of course I said yes. He'd kissed me one last time and it was so screaming hot, I'd really thought my shoes were going to melt off my feet. His lips were amazing and his tongue magical. I almost couldn't imagine making my way through forty-eight hours without having those body parts on mine.

I was thankful the dealership was buzzing today, and everyone seemed to be in a good mood. It would help the day go faster. The new incentives came out this morning and they were even better than last month's. *Don't tell the people who bought last month.*

The excitement had the sales staff calling clients they had on their just-waiting-for-the-right-time-to-buy list. I started my phone duties, found a couple of interested clients, set appointments, and finished with calls by lunchtime.

In the break room, I was leaning into the fridge to grab my bowl of minestrone soup and something—or someone—bumped into me.

"Whatcha looking for, Presley?" Drexel inquired over my shoulder.

I made my escape right before his tentacle rounded my waist. "What the hell, Drexel?"

Drexel stepped closer, and I moved to put a table between us.

"Come on, Presley, I was just being playful." His face went pale. "Um … uh … so…"

I stepped back. Hearing Dixless speechless was a little confusing.

He cleared his throat. "Um, maybe you ... maybe you and I could go get a drink tonight?"

I almost believed he was sincere, but then Sam came in the room.

Sam snagged a soda from the fridge. "Hey, Presley. What's going on, Drex?"

"Presley and I were discussing the deteriorating quality of porn sites. She has quite the informed opinion about the low quality of girl-on-girl action."

My mouth dropped open, and Sam laughed.

"Drexel, you are a complete pig!" I calmed myself before I did or said something I would regret. "Not that it's your business, but I happen to be seeing someone. He's a great guy, not the giant jerk that you are!"

"You're seeing someone?" Drexel stepped around the table.

"Yes, and he's the hottest guy I've ever met and unlike you, he's mature." I placed my container of soup in the microwave to reheat.

He leaned against the counter on his hip, crossing his arms and flexing his muscles. "How long?"

"Again, not that it's your business, we've only known each other for a little while but we have a date tomorrow night."

"Where are you going?" Drexel started the most annoying game of Twenty Questions ... ever.

"Why do you care?" I rocked my head and raised my shoulders until they were almost touching my ears.

Sam chuckled. "Cause Drex can't stop—"

"Shut up, Sam," Drexel growled with a pissed-off tone that Sam definitely didn't miss and neither did I. "Just wanted to know where to avoid tomorrow night."

He shook his head and muttered, "Hope this guy knows how perfect you are."

I expected to hear sarcasm in his voice, but it wasn't there. Drexel marched out of the room and Sam followed. To my amazement, I was left to eat my soup in peace.

I searched the Humane Society website and saw the little white dog from Sunday was still available. The picture did her no justice. It was taken before she'd been groomed, and she looked totally disappointed at life and kind of sickly. I stared at the picture until my soup was gone and my name was called over the intercom to meet my next client.

Back at home I enjoyed more soup for dinner with Willow. This liquid diet would have to end sometime. I loved the soup, but I needed red meat ... or any meat.

"You going to Kanyon's tonight?"

"No, we decided to have a night apart. He and Jude are riding over to Council Bluffs for a bike night. Not sure I'm ready to be on the back of a bike yet."

I rolled my eyes. "Live a little."

She pointed to her now-dyed sapphire-blue hair that matched her eyes.

I chuckled. "You know what I mean, Willow. How are things with you and Kanyon?"

I hadn't told her about Jude and me yet. I wasn't exactly sure what to say or how to start the conversation. I told her Jude and I were on speaking terms on Monday, but for everything that happened after Monday she was mostly MIA with Kanyon.

"Good. He's so—"

I rolled my eyes again. "Yeah, I know, amazing in bed. Remember, the walls are thin and he was here last night. Earplugs are now a necessity in my life."

Willow blushed, which I had never seen her do, and giggled, which I had never heard her do.

"Willow, are you in love with Kanyon?"

She stopped and shook her head. "No. No! You can't fall in love with someone in a week, right?"

"I don't know. I think when love happens, it happens."

"I think I could fall for him, but I'm sure he just wants to keep it casual. Maybe. Kanyon is all man, but he's so sweet, too. Remember that coffee burn I had on my forearm?"

I crinkled my nose. "It was nasty! How is it now?"

"Better. Last Friday night while we were … well, you know."

"Yes, yes, I do," I deadpanned, and Willow smiled.

"Anyway, he accidentally grabbed my arm there, and I almost fainted from the pain. He was so concerned that he stopped everything, like stopped dead-cold even though I could tell it wasn't comfortable to cease what we were doing. Then he cleaned, medicated, and redressed the burn. And then,"—she sighed peacefully—"then he made sure there were enough endorphins coursing through my veins to feel *no* pain and I slept like a baby."

I rolled my eyes at her a third time, and she pushed on my shoulder.

"Jude and I made out last night," I said quickly while she took a bite of soup, knowing she'd have to chew and swallow.

"Okay." She stretched out the word after wiping her mouth. "Explain how this happened."

I told her everything, the workout on Monday, Brix on Tuesday, and yesterday at Graphite and Acrylic.

Her silence after I finished was concerning but I hoped she was processing the information.

"Willow?"

"Sorry, just thinking. I'm happy for you, Presley. It's wonderful." Her smile was genuine.

"We have a date tomorrow night. Not sure to where, I was going to text him later."

"A little sexting perhaps?" Willow jested.

I gurgled a groan through a sip of red wine. "Speaking of sex. Question. Do I tell him how little experience I have? Or do I just let him figure it out on his own and be severely disappointed and want to run the other way?"

"One, there's no chance Jude would turn you away in bed. And two, there's no way he'd be disappointed. I've seen how he looks at you, Prez, that boy was interested from day one. I guarantee that's a fact. I think it's whatever makes you most comfortable. Sharing can be kind of romantic and freeing, as long as you're sharing, *not* comparing."

I giggled. "True. But from what I saw yesterday at class, the guys I've been with don't compare to Jude." I raised my eyebrows, and Willow raised one of hers back. "What if I make a mistake? Should I make him wear a condom even though I'm on the pill? Is there a new move I should do?"

"Wow, Prez, you're making me nervous for you. Okay, first, there are no mistakes in sex and all the moves have been created and some of them don't make any sense whatsoever, so just keep it simple. The first time two people get it on is generally pretty awkward no matter what. That doesn't mean it can't be enjoyable, but it's getting to know what each other likes that makes sex fantastic. So be vocal, say what you want, what you like, what you don't like. Work up to actual sex. Start with kissing and fondling, then a blow job, and then maybe sex when you're forty-five?"

I slapped her lightly on the arm.

Willow continued, "And when it comes to the condom, unless you're willing to trust that he's clean, which personally I wouldn't without proof, I'd say, 'No glove, no love'." We both groaned at the pun. She had a million of them stored in that head of hers. "Even though I'm on the pill, I still make Kanyon cover his lover. He doesn't seem to mind. He said he'd go to the clinic and get tested to make sure he's clean but he said he always wears one. I'm not sure I'm there yet with him. Maybe I am? Skin on skin is fucking amazing, it does take the connection to a whole different place." Willow's face revealed her amorous feelings, but she waved whatever she was thinking away. "Anyway, you know Jude is a good guy, Prez. You need to trust him and just talk to him."

"You're right. I will." I stood and grabbed my dishes. "I know it's early and we talked about doing a marathon of B. Cooper, but I be poopered out. I'm gonna take a rain check."

"Be poopered out?" Willow cracked up. "Nice! I should hit the hay, too. Glad I have the weekend off, but I don't have any plans yet. Maybe Jace will go see a Storm Chasers game with me? I think the company she works for has box seats. I could definitely go for some guys in tight baseball pants."

"Good thinking."

"Presley?"

I turned around before reaching the hallway. "Yeah?"

"Don't worry, whatever is meant to be will be. Live in the moment, less thinking, more listening. Remember, you deserve someone as great as you. Okay?"

"And I thought Jace was the Oprah of our group. Nice speech, blue hair. OMG ... blue hair! You just aged yourself!"

"Maybe I need to hit the Early Bird Buffet tomorrow and see how many retirees hit on me?"

"You'd bring old wood to life quicker than Viagra." I laughed all the way down the hall.

After I was in bed, I texted Jude.

Prez: **How was your day? Can you tell me where we're going on the date so I know what to wear? BTW ... I miss your lips.**

I read a new romance book about a moody tattooed guy while I waited for a reply. I started to wonder if Jude had any tattoos, then I remembered I'd seen his body. *All* of his body. And there were no tattoos. I was uncomfortable knowing what I was getting and that he didn't.

My phone buzzed.

Jude: **Great day. Met Mitch, reminded me of my bro, Zane. Triple R has a whole new vibe without Emerson. We're going to dinner and dancing. This time you're not going to turn me down when I ask you to dance. Right? My lips, huh? What about the rest of me?**

Prez: **I miss all of you. When it comes to anything, just ask me and we'll talk. I can imagine your lips on other places than just my mouth.**

Jude: **Want to do a little sexting, Miss Bradenhurst?**

I inhaled a deep breath.

Prez: **Tell me what to do. Please.**

Jude: **Are you in bed?**

Prez: **Yes, are you?**

Jude: **I'm naked on my bed. Strip your pajamas, beautiful**

The vision of him naked slid through my thoughts and made me shiver a little as I slid off my pajama shorts.

Prez: **They're off. I'd like to get a little helper from my nightstand, do you mind?**

Jude: **Not at all but you have to describe the competition for me. I want to know what I'm up against**

Prez: **It's nothing as impressive or sexy as your real thing. Promise. Bullet vibrator, black, three speeds.**

Jude: **You thought I was impressive and sexy?**

Seriously, you need me to validate your penis? Fine.

Prez: **I liked what I saw, although I missed the main events cause I was too busy looking in your beautiful eyes. Are you touching yourself?**

Jude: **Thanks on the eyes. I like what I see when I look at you, can't wait to see more. And yes, I am. Are you?**

Prez: **I am. I've turned on my helper and it's humming.**

Jude: **Rub the bullet over your stomach.**

The light buzzing caused a fluttering deep in my core.

Jude: **That's me placing kisses all over your amazing body.**

Amazing? That's a stretch.

I'd already dropped the phone once on my forehead and twice my chest. With irritation, I texted him.

Prez: **Don't know if I can text and do this at same time, dropped the phone on my head. Maybe we should just wait?**

Jude: **Just read my texts and do what I tell you to, no texting back until you're really close**

Prez: **Okay**

Jude: **Can you imagine my hands on your body? Floating over your breasts, skimming your raised nipples, holding your hips while I crawl between your legs**

He gave me time to let the mental imagery do its job.

Jude: **Move your hand lower, raise your legs. Can you see me lying between them? God, the vision is beautiful, it's making me hard imagining being there with you**

I moaned low and heavy, reading what I was already thinking. My breathing was increasing in speed with every text.

Jude: **My fingers touch you softly, and my lips kiss your thighs working my way toward your heaven**

Jude: **I tease you with my tongue. Slide your fingers where you want my tongue to be**

My heart started pounding and the familiar rush of blood scorched my lower stomach.

Jude: **Turn the bullet up a notch. Tease yourself, lightly, keep it moving**

I turned the small egg to the second setting. At this pace I wasn't going to need the third gear. I was screaming for release right now.

Jude: **Place BOB right on your clit, hold it there, feel how my lips surround you and my teeth tug lightly on you**

I pecked out two words as my body began to shake.

Prez: **I'm close**

Jude: **Baby, come with me. Now, Beautiful!**

I read his words and they took me over the edge into a body and mind rollercoaster ride that rose and dropped steeply, screaming through the corners and causing a weightless feeling in my stomach. I did my best to be quiet, but I couldn't.

After I'd regained consciousness of my surroundings, I grabbed the phone.

Prez: **That was incredible. Thank you.**

It took a couple of minutes to hear back.

Jude: **Was cleaning up. You're welcome. I promise, the real thing will be twice as incredible. I'm not going to let a battery-operated piece of plastic outshine me ;-) Good night, pick you up @ 6:30pm?**

Prez: **6:30 works. Good night, Ponytail**

Jude: **Good night, Beautiful**

In my relaxed state I wondered if Jude was a snuggler.

Hope he is.

Chapter Fifteen

Jude

I sat at the front desk and watched Presley from a distance. We'd played a game of who-could-catch-the-other-person-looking for the last forty-five minutes. I acted like a teenager again and obviously my body had the same reaction. I'd popped two boners since she walked into Triple R.

The sexting last night was damn hot. I'd never done that before, but when she typed, 'Please,' I couldn't help but want her to orgasm, and I needed one, too, not that the release last night was doing anything to help my returning situation.

Kai walked to the desk and picked up her schedule from her mailbox.

"Good morning, Kai." I adjusted my shorts.

"Hey, Jude. Blake talked to me yesterday about Presley. Of course, I got an earful from my roommate Wednesday. Glad I had the afternoon off to enjoy her two-hour bitchfest." Kai glared at me and rolled her eyes. "She hates your guts, but I'm totally positive Emerson deserved what she got."

"She's not my favorite person either. I'm glad she's gone."

"Well, I still have to deal with her but since our lease is up soon, hopefully I can bow out gracefully of living with Satan's bride."

"Good luck. Can I introduce you to Presley?" I was acceptable below the belt so I stood.

"Sure, I'd love to meet her."

As we approached, Presley slowed the treadmill to a walking pace.

"Good morning, Beautiful. How's your workout going?" I leaned against the control tower and smiled.

Presley's sweat-painted and glowing face smiled back. "Good. How'd you sleep?"

"Relaxed." I raised an eyebrow, and Presley blushed. "And how was your night?"

"I slept like a baby. Had some pretty interesting dreams."

"I look forward to hearing about those dreams at dinner." Kai cleared her throat and reminded me why I was actually here. "Presley, I'd like you to meet Kai Thomas, your new trainer. Kai, this is Presley Bradenhurst."

Presley stopped the machine and wiped her hand on a gym towel. She extended her hand over the rail. "Nice to meet you, Kai."

"Hi. Glad I can be of assistance, Presley. I talked to Mitch yesterday about your previous training. Jude and I will talk today about what he's been doing routine-wise and any special workout requests you've made. I'll be ready for Monday, five a.m., right?"

"Bright and too early." Presley's smile radiated sunshine.

"Good. Well, I'll let you two get back to flirting. See you Monday." Kai chuckled while walking away.

"Thanks," we replied in unison.

Presley rounded the machine and stood next to me. "Walk me to the locker room?"

"Sure. Are you okay with steak tonight?"

"God, yes!" she exclaimed on a happy moan.

Instantly I imagined that was the sound she made last night when she came. *Amazing.*

She swung her towel in her hand as we walked. "Willow's been forcing soup down my throat all week. She's a classically trained chef and the soup is fantastic, but I miss meat."

"Good to hear."

Presley turned her back to the wall next to the locker room door, and I stepped close. One hand grasped her waist and the other wound in her damp ponytail, tipping her head upward. I leaned down to her ear. "God, you smell incredible, Presley. Salt and lavender and you."

"You smell really good, too." She moved her head, her nose brushing the side of my neck. "Don't you have to work tonight?"

"Rahl's filling in for me."

Presley cringed. "I need to talk to him."

"I took care of it. I wanted to be clear with him what was going on. He gave me the same riot act that Blake and Prius Boy and Kanyon gave me about treating you right. There are too many guys waiting in the wings for you, Presley. It's a lot of pressure. Oh, and Jace, too." I winked.

She giggled and rolled her eyes. "Edwyn is definitely not waiting in the wings, he loves his boyfriend, Philippe. And Kanyon likes Willow, right?"

I declined to say either way. He was vague about where he was with Willow, and when he told me he'd decided not to invite her along on the bike ride, that led me to believe things weren't so great. Plus, he had a shit-pile of issues with someone from his past, and his life had become complicated. Maybe it was better for Willow if they weren't a couple and she didn't have to deal with his baggage.

"And Blake," she lowered her voice. "I think he'd hate to hear this but I kind of think of him as a brother. Rahl is a super nice guy but on my side there is not one ion of chemistry. And Jace, well, even though she's probably one of the most beautiful people I've ever known, she's just not my type. I prefer a lot more penis on my lovers."

I laughed. "That's good to know."

Presley looked up at me. "So, Ponytail, even if they're waiting for you to mess up and I really hope you don't, I will go back to looking elsewhere."

"Don't expect me to be perfect, Presley, 'cause I'm not." My words were more ominous than I meant them to sound.

"Oh, I don't, and the same goes for you." She reached up and tugged the ponytail at the base of my neck.

"Deal." I dipped my head and brushed her lips under mine, soft and warm. "Okay, you'd bettered get showered for work."

I started to release her and step away, but she pulled me back to her. She came up to her tiptoes and her eyes sparkled. "One more kiss. A good one. Please."

I tugged on her hand and guided her out of the sight lines of the desk and gym mirrors into a cove used for housing yoga mats.

Before she could say anything my lips were on hers, the pressure unforgiving until her luscious lips swelled beneath mine. Her hands teased to my back and plastered our bodies together. She whimpered as my cock responded quickly inside of the compression shorts I wore under my gym shorts. I deepened and slowed the kiss to trap every moment in our memories. I dropped my knees and slid my solid erection against her softness, again and again, until she was writhing under me, meeting my grinding with enthusiasm.

"Presley," I said, and her eyes met mine. "Do you want me to touch you?"

She nodded frantically. "Yes." Her words were breathy. "Please."

I slid my hand into the waistband of her shorts and inside of her underwear. Holding her in a firm embrace and making sure no one was watching, I slipped a finger inside of her swollen slickness. I groaned at how snug and warm she was. Her body coated my hand with her juices. Her forehead hit my chest as she rubbed herself against my hand.

"Shit, you're fucking hot and drenched for me." I groaned into her ear and she moaned against the side of my neck, biting lightly when I rubbed her clit with my thumb. "Presley, I want you to come for me."

My attention was soon rewarded as she moaned softly. A raspy "I'm close, Jude. I'm so close."

"Presley, come now, baby."

She shuddered against my body with a long gasp of release. Her soft velvet rhythmically pulsed around my finger, squeezing me while I massaged her spongy G-spot. I kept her orgasm going with a light pinch of her clit and the waves of pleasure continued to pulse through her body. Her legs wobbled so I tugged her closer to me.

"Presley, you're so responsive, it's amazing." My body took over. "I'm going to come, too," I groaned in her ear while she was coming down. My balls rose in the sack preparing for the discharge. Her hand moved to massage me through my knit shorts, rubbing the head of my erection with her palm. "Shit!" I came with enough force to roll my eyes back in my head. I removed my hand from her shorts and pressed our bodies together as I pulsed under her perfect touch.

When we had both calmed down, I gazed into those sparkling emeralds. "How was that?"

"That was incredible, Jude," she said, her lips swollen and her eyes glassy half-moons from her orgasm.

"I told you I'd blow the vibrating competition away."

She smiled timidly up at me, and I kissed her perky lips.

"Okay, that yoga class gets out in about two minutes, so we need to move on. Can you walk to the locker room?"

"Yeah, you may have made me speechless and weak in the knees, but I'm good to make it to the shower before I collapse."

"Sorry I couldn't wait to do that, but the mix of sweat and soft scent had me hard before I even touched you."

"And I was wet when I walked in the gym's front door thinking of you."

I stopped and stared down at her. "That's the best compliment a guy can get, Prez."

"But now I smell like sex."

"Even better." I placed a quick kiss on her forehead, then guided her around the corner, and she disappeared behind the locker room door.

Cleaning up in the men's locker room, I wondered if I pushed her too fast. She wasn't some bar brat to catch and release. Fucking amazing how we affected each other, but tonight I would make our time all about the non-sex foreplay—the sensuality, the mysterious tension, the flirty part of dating.

I trained my next client when Presley walked out of the locker room, glowing and wide-eyed. After I was done with the session, I got a text from her that told me what I needed to know.

Prez: **Best workout at the gym ... EVER! Thanks. Maybe a repeat performance later?**

I can't fucking wait.

Chapter Sixteen

Presley

"Stop fidgeting!"

I whined at Willow. "Then stop messing with my hair!"

"It's doing that weird thing again. Just a second." Willow cursed under her breath while she ran her fingers through my curls. "That's better. Think you're ready for the god of ponytails?"

"I think so. How's my outfit?"

She stepped back and eyed me up. "Killer. He's gonna come in his pants."

I almost told her that he did that already today, but decided to keep that tidbit of info to myself. That and the fact that he diddled me into a didn't-know-my-own-name-catatonic-state right before grunting out the sexiest sound I'd ever heard. The look in his melting gold-flecked hazel eyes was of complete satisfaction.

As for my outfit, I was in the same jeans as last week, this time with a black fitted jacket over a silver silk camisole with a little sparkle around the neck. I wore black strap Stuart Weitzman braided jute wedges on my feet and simple long silver earrings. My hair was down, styled in soft waves, and apparently one unruly wave.

Swear I was pitting out from nervousness, but with the amount of antiperspirant I applied, every gland from my neck down should be as dry as the Sahara.

"Do you have a date tonight?" I reapplied lip gloss.

Willow completed a last viewing of my outfit. "Kanyon's coming over later." Her shoulders tensed.

"Is there something wrong?"

"I don't know. We were all hot for a few days and I thought we had a great connection outside of the bedroom last weekend, but now it seems he thinks I have a communicable disease. He didn't come over last night after his bike ride like he said he would, and he acted like he had something more important to do tonight but wouldn't freely give up what it was, so I didn't pry. I should trust my gut, and it tells me there's something weird going on. Maybe he's got another girl and I was just a distraction."

"I'm gonna give you advice that a wonderful friend recently gave me. Don't worry. Whatever is meant to be, will be. Live in the moment, less thinking, more listening. Remember, you deserve someone as great as you."

Willow's eyes popped open. "That person sounds brilliant!"

I brought her in for a hug. "She is. Thanks for helping me get ready. I was close to hyperventilating until you came home."

"I got your back, Prez. Always. Have fun tonight and remember, *to avoid a frown, wrap your clown.*"

On that public service announcement, the doorbell rang.

Thank God.

I rolled my eyes at Willow, said nothing to encourage her PSAs from continuing, and grabbed my purse off my dresser while exiting my bedroom. I raised my shoulders really high, then dropped them quickly to shrug off any tension in my body. I'd think the two huge and spirit-altering orgasms in less than twenty-four hours would have me as relaxed as a sloth at the zoo. Not the case.

I opened the door wearing a big smile. "Hi … Kanyon?" My voice deteriorated to disappointment. His gorgeous toothy smile became a half-frown. "Sorry, I thought you were Jude." I raised my spirits. "Hi! Kanyon! Please, come in!"

He chuckled. "Hi, Presley. Ponytail is on his way."

Kanyon strolled to Willow, placed a peck on her cheek, and said something in her ear. She nodded her head.

"Hello, Presley."

I jumped at the sound of a deep voice behind me. I spun to view what was probably a dream, but a damn good one. "Hi, Jude."

In a comfortable black muscle-revealing V-neck t-shirt, dark washed jeans, black casual leather shoes, and a smile from ear-to-ear was the male who made my heart beat out of control … and the pumping muscle started immediately. I stepped forward to him and he placed a soft kiss on my cheek.

"You are beautiful." He produced a bouquet of stargazer lilies from behind his back. "For you."

I gasped. "Thank you. My favorite. How did you know?"

"Good guess?" he offered with a smirk.

"Thanks, Willow," I said over my shoulder. "Okay, let me get these in water and we can go."

Willow trekked to the bathroom, I assumed to get ready to go out with Kanyon. The guys conversed in the living room about some new motorcycle Kanyon was thinking of purchasing.

I overheard Jude quietly ask Kanyon, "How is Grace?" I stopped moving.

Is Kanyon dating someone else?

"She had a concert this week, sings like an angel. Miss her already. Every time is the same, I wish she never had to leave."

"Have you made a decision about what you're going to do?"

"Not yet. It's too hard to think of her not being in my life, but like I said last night, Willow doesn't deserve half a man and Grace needs all of me right now."

From the kitchen, I could hear the affection in Kanyon's voice. I focused on getting the flowers in the vase and on the kitchen table.

"Jude?" I announced my presence and Kanyon shifted uncomfortably in his black biker boots. "Everything okay?"

Jude took the two steps to me. "Great. Ready?"

He grazed my hair over my shoulder and rubbed his hands up and down my arms. For a moment, I wished we were staying here … alone. But the thought of steak filled my brain.

Red meat. Presley needs red meat.

We both gave good-byes to Kanyon on our walk to the door.

"Bye, Willow," I called out.

She yelled from the bathroom, "Bye, Prez. Bye, Ponytail. Have fun, but remember—"

"I remember!" I screamed, not needing to hear another one of her condom usage one-liners. Jude winced at my outburst.

When we were out the door Jude wrapped his arm around my waist. "What was the 'I remember' scream about?"

A resigned sighing noise escaped me. "Willow knows what seems like a million goofy ways to say, 'Use a condom.' I just didn't need to hear another one today."

Opening the passenger door, Jude sounded like an immature teenage boy, "Tell me some. Please. Tell me!"

"Fine. Granted, some of them are pretty amusing. Let's see. Sex will be sweeter, if you wrap your peter. If you go into heat, wrap your meat. Avoid a frown, wrap your clown." I blushed.

He gave me a quick peck on my cheek and I blushed again.

"Don't be embarrassed. It's great she cares about you. I can't wait to hear more of them but from Willow."

He settled in the cab of the truck, but before he started the engine he turned to me. "Presley, I have no expectation that this night will end up with us in bed together. Not that I wouldn't be thrilled if it did, but I'm good at waiting for the right time. Tonight, let's get to know each other better and go from there. Okay?" He started his truck.

"Great idea. Can I ask you one thing before we go?"

"Sure."

"Who is Grace?"

Jude stilled. "You heard us?"

"It's a townhome, not a mansion, Jude." Sarcasm dripped from my words. "Is he seeing someone else? If he is, do you know, does Willow know?"

"I know you want to protect Willow, but I promise Grace is not a threat to whatever is happening between them."

"Okay." I stared out the passenger window.

"You sound irritated."

"A little. I don't like vague answers. Plus, Kanyon sounded like he's in love with Grace."

His warm hand on the back of my neck had me turning my head to him. "Noted on the vague answers, I'll try not to do that when possible. I'm sorry but the answers you want aren't mine to tell. It's up to Kanyon to tell Willow the truth and he will when he's ready. After he does, then I can tell you."

"All right, I think I understand. Let's go. Don't want to miss our reservations. Where are we eating?"

Jude backed out of the driveway. "Omaha Prime downtown. I've never been there. You?"

"Once with my dad." I fidgeted with my purse, wrapping the long strap around my finger and then unwinding it.

"What's his name?"

"Preston. He's a science teacher at Omaha West High School. My mom is Alicia. She's remarried to Rich Rosen. So she's Alicia Greenfield-Bradenhurst-Rosen, which makes her certifiably crazy for expecting people to remember three last names. I don't know what she thinks she is for a profession this week. Cat whisperer? Cirque du Solei aerialist? Third-husband test-driver? Who knows." My bitterness at her never stopped boiling up from the inside.

"When did your parents divorce?"

"When I was twelve. I lived with my dad. My mom followed her first post-divorce boyfriend to New York City. She came back after she caught him cheating, which is ironic since that's why my dad divorced her."

"Wow, rough. I remember you talking about an uncle. Sounds like you are close with him?"

"Yeah, the highly embarrassing story I told you that included my period."

"That's right! You looked like you wanted to find a time machine so you could go back about thirty seconds."

"I wish. Anyway, that's Uncle Thad, my dad's brother. I would spend hours at his garage. I'd be glad to change your oil the next time you need it done." I giggled when I reviewed the sentence I'd just said in my head. "That was weird to hear, wasn't it?"

"Sounded a little suggestive, but I didn't mind it." He reached over and entwined his fingers with mine on my lap. "I think it's great you know how to do those things. If I ever have kids, I'd want them to know those basics of car maintenance, it makes good sense." He squeezed my hand and tingles rode the skin up my arms to my neck.

"So tell me something about you, Jude."

Other than you wouldn't mind having kids, 'cause that information gives me heart palpitations.

"I come from Clive, a suburb of Des Moines. I went to Iowa State University for my bachelor's and master's degrees in kinesiology. My mom is Wendy and my dad is Brian. They've been married for thirty years this coming July. Not that there weren't times I thought they'd be better off divorced, but they've taught me that relationships are difficult and it's harder to stick it out than call it quits, but hard things are usually worth it."

I giggled again.

Jude shook his head. "I think someone has a little gutter mind tonight."

I raised my shoulders in a shrug.

"Anyway, my brother Zane went to UNL, works for Union Pacific Railroad as a night dispatcher. He told me yesterday that he's moving in with his girlfriends."

"Girlfriends?"

"Yep, an exclusive polyamorous relationship. Him and two girls, Yori and Britney."

"I know Yori! We graduated from high school together, took a lot of the same classes."

"Really?"

"Yeah, Simi's sister, Yori Song, right? Stunning girl with full red lips that are every man's dream?"

"Yeah, that's Yori. Small world."

"Omaha is the smallest big city you'll ever live in. I find it comforting when I see someone in the crowd who I know, makes my existence seem real, connected to something bigger than me. Anyway, good for Zane, hope to meet him and Britney sometime and catch up with Yori."

"Maybe you can come over on Sunday for a cookout? Supposed to be really nice in the evening."

"Um…" A familiar anxiety rode through me like a dark wave of moonlight in Van Gogh's *Starry Night*.

He squeezed my hand. "I'm sorry, Presley, I'm getting ahead of myself. Tonight is all that matters."

It was reassuring that he understood my need to take whatever was happening between us semi-slow.

I know. I'd let him—*and encouraged him to*—fondle me into a euphoria that had my knees collapsing earlier, but that was different. It was … I didn't know what it was that made me do that! Totally unlike me. But it was an incredibly mind-blowing experience I'd never had and I was fine with that.

In an attempt to be honest with myself, I wrestled with the fact that I wanted to let down every protective wall I'd ever put up when I was around Jude. Completely West/East Berlin those bitches to the ground and send a piece of brick to every asshole jock and bitchy girl I'd let into my head with their judgment and vile words. Then guide Jude in regardless of passport or citizenship. Unfortunately, the wall had become a shelter for my head and heart. My chest kicked as I stared at his handsome profile, wondering if what was built inside of me couldn't be permanently removed.

We made it to our reservation. The steak was exactly what I needed after a week of liquid diet.

I took a sip of my wine. "I saw that dog is still on the Humane Society website today. I've looked at her picture almost every day since Sunday."

"I think that means something, Presley. What keeps you from adopting her?"

"I don't know. I think I'm afraid I won't be good—" I closed my eyes as my heart started to pound.

Be open.

I swallowed the lump in my throat. "I'm afraid I won't be good enough for her. That I'll fail her somehow."

His hand cupped my face. "Hey. You're good enough. I'm sure you'd make a great pet owner."

I opened my eyes. "I'll think about it."

Constantly.

"How was work?" Jude inquired while cutting off a hunk of his twenty-ounce T-bone.

"Drexel was an ass yesterday and again today." I downed half my wine at the memory.

"How was he an ass?" He gripped his knife a little tighter.

I concentrated on cutting my filet into small pieces. "Well, he said something weird to me on Wednesday, something about my body and him looking at it like artwork. I chased him into the men's restroom to bitch him out and walked in on my boss at the urinal. Not a good day." I brought my eyes to Jude as he took a deep, controlled breath I couldn't miss. "Yesterday he came up behind me and tried to…" I stopped talking when a flush of what I imagined was anger flared through Jude's face.

"Tried to what, Presley?"

I waved away what I was going to say. "You know, it's not a big deal. I've handled Dixless, that's what Willow nicknamed him, for the last two years. I can handle it."

Jude set his silverware down and reached across the table to give my wrist a reassuring squeeze. "I'm listening to be supportive. I know you're a strong person and can fight your own battles. Now what happened?"

I shook my head in exasperation. "Well ... he came up behind me and tried to put his tentacles on me."

"His testicles?" Jude asked loudly, and the people at the next table stopped talking.

I giggled. "No. Tentacles. As in his slimy, creepy arms."

Jude tipped his head indicating the clarification did not make the story any better.

I thought it did.

I talked in a lower voice and finished the story quickly. "And then he asked me to go get a drink with him and when I told him I was seeing a guy he got all flustered and said something about how perfect I am. Today he trapped me at the copy machine and told me some story about how he'd like to get a drink to talk about why he's such a jerk to me. He tried to paw at me that time, too."

Jude's strong jaw hardened. "Presley, I guarantee that guy is interested in you, in a majorly fucked-up way."

"Dixless is only interested in being an immature, self-centered jerk. Always has been. Now tell me about *your* week."

Jude took a minute to collect himself, and although I would never consider myself a damsel in distress, it was kind of nice to see him get all worked up over Dixless's juvenile but harmless antics.

He cleared his throat. "I have nine clients now, after losing my favorite to, hopefully, a much better relationship."

A warm flush of happiness tickled my cheeks.

He drank his beer and cleared his throat. "After Emerson was let go, the week went smoothly. Management is interviewing for her position. I hope Blake is a better judge of character this time."

"What do you know about Kai?"

"She's ex-military, just out of school, and she likes to do new, fresh workouts with her clients. Oh, and she's gay."

I perked up. "She's a lesbian?"

"Thinking about Jace?"

"Yeah. Her girlfriend dumped her last week. Do you know if Kai is dating anyone?"

"She's available. I remember her talking about needing a date for a black-tie event. I jokingly declined before she could ask and she made a comment about how my combination of chromosomes weren't of interest to her. I suspected before, but that confirmed my suspicion."

When he'd finished every morsel of his steak, he insisted on paying the bill. I argued only until he leaned across the table and kissed me silent.

Jude placed his napkin on the table. "You want to walk around for a while, maybe stop off at The Berry & Rye for a craft cocktail?"

"Never been there, sounds interesting."

We leisurely walked around the Old Market, holding hands and gazing in windows at the contemporary and vintage finds that mingled effortlessly behind huge picture windows. The brick streets provided an antique-looking background to every block of history-filled buildings.

He paused when we were outside of The Berry & Rye, moved his hands to my waist, and pulled me closer. "You are beautiful, Presley. I consider myself the luckiest man on Earth tonight."

I brought my hands to his firm chest. "Cheesy, Ponytail, but I like cheese, so that's Gouda for you."

He laughed as he dropped his forehead to mine. "Gouda to know. And I like cheese, too."

He kissed me with a tenderness and genuineness I'd never felt from a man before, like his emotions were right there for my lips to read, wordless movements that had so much meaning. Not going farther than lips on lips, the connection was the epitome of innocent and dreamy. My head floated full of desire, my body responded with a soft sigh of happiness, and my fingers tightened in his shirt. This kiss made every "perfect" movie kiss seem ridiculously phony. This was real.

"Ready for a drink?" he asked after a couple of affected breaths and a quick hug.

"Sure."

He led me inside the bar to where Kanyon and Willow were sitting on stools at a beautiful oak high-top table in the corner.

"Hi, Willow, Kanyon. Been here long?"

"Long enough to see the whipped male show outside." Kanyon raised an eyebrow.

Jude grunted. "Being open to PDA doesn't make me whipped." He pulled out a chair and motioned for me to sit.

I glanced between Willow and Jude. "What's going on?"

"Well, I remember you and Willow like to dance, so I invited them along."

"Where are we going dancing?"

"The Max," Willow and Jude said simultaneously.

I released a joyous girlie scream. "I've never been there and I've always wanted to go!"

"Yeah, a little birdie told me that, too."

I stared at Willow. "Did you already know about our date before I told you?"

The guilt was obvious in her lowered eyes.

I shook my head. "Why didn't you just ask me?"

"Cause it wasn't mine to say something, it was yours."

I glanced to Kanyon. Our eyes met and his body fidgeted in his chair. His normal attractive-arrogant attitude withered into awkwardness.

Willow continued, "Plus, it would have ruined the surprise."

The waitress arrived at the table breaking the semi-awkward moment. "What can I get you?"

"I don't know." I reviewed the menu for the third time.

"Do you mind if I order for you?" Jude asked.

"Please." I gave his thigh a squeeze.

Jude covered my hand with his, trapping it with warmth. "Okay, the beautiful Presley will have a La Floridita, and I'll have the Southern Savior."

"You two doing good?" the waitress asked Willow and Kanyon, and both nodded their agreement. "I'll get this right in."

Jude moved his chair closer. "Watch the bartenders. This is a religion for them. The actual creation of a cocktail is only about ten percent of their job, the rest is creating the essences and clear, pure ice and fresh juices that go into the cocktail."

"Wow, impressive. How long have you bartended?"

"About four years. I started to pay the bills while I was in the master's program at ISU."

"Working as a bartender and other things," Kanyon said with a smirk.

"What other things?" My eyes wandered back to the mixologists at the bar carving strips of orange and lemon peel perfectly into curly-q shapes.

"You'll see later." Kanyon smirked again and Jude rumbled his irritation.

"So, Willow." Jude leaned forward, resting his arms on the round high-top table. "Presley gave me a few samples, but I'd love to hear more of your prophylactic public service announcements."

Kanyon gave a hearty laugh. "What?"

"Yeah, apparently Willow is a walking phrase generator of ways to say *wrap your willie before you get silly.*"

Willow pretended to be lifting off a top hat in recognition of his efforts. "Nice. Maybe some other time, when we're not in public. But I'm adding that one to my repertoire, Ponytail. How was your dinner?"

After Willow changed the subject the conversation remained light and carefree while we enjoyed our delicious cocktails. Jude's drink was good but mine was delicious, with just a hint of vanilla and cherry. I slid my chair closer to his and rested my head on his shoulder, his arm wrapped around my shoulder.

We walked to the dance club around ten o'clock. The doorman questioned my driver's license because truly I looked nothing like in the picture. Jude made it crystal clear I was one and the same person, and the bouncer should drop the inquisition. The hunky black guy raised his eyebrows suggestively and told me how great I looked now.

Jude pulled me along quickly. "See? The vibrating black item in your nightstand isn't my only competition. I hate to think how big his thing is."

My eyes rolled in a huge circle. "Whatever."

"So, hip-hop or pop?" he asked, pointing to different rooms at opposite ends of the entryway.

"Hip-hop? To start?"

"Hip-hop it is." He led me in, and although it was early, the dance floor was almost full. We found a table and Kanyon parked his cute ass on a stool.

"Not a dancer?" I slipped off my jacket, draping it on the back of a chair.

"When the mood hits me. That, or ten shots of tequila."

"I guess you just get to watch." Willow did a little grind on him and he pulled her backside to his front and gave her a slow kiss over her shoulder.

"Nice PDA," Jude declared when they detached lips.

"There's a time and place for everything, Ponytail."

I followed Jude to the dance floor as Pitbull and Kesha's "Timber" started playing. The first thing I noticed was *all* of the females—and *most* of the males— were gawking blatantly at my dance partner. The second thing I noticed was my dance partner knew how to dance, and it wasn't that he was a good dancer, he was an *excellent* dancer. I gaped at the view for a minute. Soon Jude spun me on the dance floor, and I was laughing and not caring what anyone was looking at.

After the song ended, two cute girls grabbed Jude's hands and dragged him from me. He stared at me questioning intervention or disapproval. I smirked and shoulder-shrugged that I wasn't going to stop them. I continued to dance alone, watching the unfolding scene. The duo of admirers helped Jude onto a stage in a place of honor in front of the DJ. Jude appeared totally comfortable as the center of attention. The music changed, and Willow joined me on the dance floor. Jude started a muscle-popping body roll that caused Willow's mouth to open in awe. Kanyon must not have liked the ogling of his friend by his—whatever Willow was to him—because he slipped in behind her and said something in her ear to which she let out an energetic laugh.

Pretty sure I know what Jude did to earn extra money besides bartend.

His jean-covered hips gyrated in what could only be described as a Channing Tatum movie-inspired way. He teased the edge of his t-shirt up giving a small glimpse of his Adonis lines and half of his hard abdominals. The girls in front of him screamed like the club was on fire. His movements weren't distasteful, just a surprise.

And surprisingly hot.

Even across the dance floor, Jude never took his eyes off mine. He ignored the attention of every pawing and transparently interested female and quite a few males in the club. After spotlight dancing to a couple of songs and providing a pretty spectacular show, Jude received a crowd full of disappointed jeers when he jumped down from the platform.

We continued our emotionally charged stare-down as he meandered his way through the packed dance floor to me.

His eyebrows rose before he spoke. "Can you guess what I did to earn extra money?"

"I don't care."

His brows snapped to a furrow. "What?"

Having the four-inch wedges on my feet was offering up a smaller height advantage on his side, I wrapped my hand around his neck and drew his ear down to my mouth. His large hands grasped my waist, and his fingers teased under my shirt and across my dewy skin.

"I don't care what you did before, but I do care what you do from this point forward." I collected myself as my heart pounded to the pulsing rhythm of the music. "Jude, I don't like you *only* because you can dance better than Magic Mike himself and not *only* because you have a godlike sculpted face and a dazzling smile, and not *only* because your body is ridiculously amazing and every girl is jealous of me right now, and not *only* because you can be the most genuine man I've ever met." He leaned back to collect my gaze with his green- and gold-splattered brown eyes. I pulled him to me again. "Jude, even if any of those amazing things changed, I'd still like and want you because of who you are on the inside. I like *all* of you."

When he took a step back, I wondered if I put too much of myself on the table and he was going to run like the club was actually on fire.

He began to move, his hard body grinding sensually and his hands holding my hips, leading me to circle against him. My very own standing lap dance with Jude. He spun me so my back was to his front and we danced intimately with the beat of the music in our own world. My hands wound up around his neck, his hands skimmed my body, and his velvety and hot lips seared against my neck. The heat of our bodies crushed to each other, the pounding beat of the music, the explosive flash of the lights, our carnal body movements, my head clouded with erotic images of the two of us unclothed in the same position, more than a physical attraction leading our bodies to connect. The moment was emotionally closer to any man than I'd ever been.

We continued dancing for several songs, until we both agreed a break to hydrate was in order. I joined Kanyon and Willow back at the table while Jude went off to buy a beer and a vodka and diet.

"What do you think of Jude's dancing skills?" Willow asked.

"Um, am-a-zing!" I fanned myself.

"Are you going home with him?" Her eyes watched me closely.

I blinked rapidly. "I don't know, we haven't discussed anything."

"I'm going to Kanyon's tonight."

"Sounds good. I'll text you what I decide."

"Please, remember it's up to you, Prez. If you do … *wrap that bait before you mate … cover his diddle then let him fiddle your middle.*"

I groaned while Kanyon burst into gut-busting laughter.

Willow got serious. "You know I'm just joking. Prez, please, don't feel pressured to do anything. Just cause he bought you an expensive slab of dead cow and put on an erotic dance show worthy of a chain of one-dollar bills around his insanely seductive hips, you don't owe him anything."

"I understand. But most of me wants it to happen."

"Make sure *all* of you wants it to happen. No regrets."

"No regrets."

I mean it.

Chapter Seventeen

Jude

"Have a good night, Kanyon, Willow."

They gave a last wave as they entered Kanyon's truck.

We left the club a little early and there was still a half hour before closing time.

"Wanna go get one last craft cocktail at House of Loom?" My arm wrapped around Presley's waist, pulling her closer to me. The other hand held her jacket as we walked to my truck at the city parking lot a couple of blocks away.

"Actually, I'm kind of wiped out."

"No problem."

I helped her into the truck through the driver's side and for the first time she took the middle spot. The innocent move made me smile. I started the truck, adjusting the air to cool us down after dancing for almost three and a half hours.

I turned toward her and her hands wound around my neck and into my hair. I took the hint and did the same to her. Our gaze held while our mouths moved closer. The kiss was dancing tongues, grinding and teasing each other while our hands search each other's bodies. My hand slipped under her shirt, my fingertips glided over her sweat-dampened, velvety skin. I slid up to her breast and grazed past her firm nipple through her bra. She released a whimper of approval. I pulled the lacy cup down to release the tender flesh, cupping her in my hand.

"Presley…"

She moaned as I pinched her peaked nipple in my fingertips.

"Presley…"

This moment wasn't about me. It was about her needs, her desires, and most importantly, her trust.

Her passion-charged eyes opened. "Jude…"

"Would you like to come to my house for the night?"

Her eyes searched mine. "I'm not quite ready to spend the night with you."

I leaned my forehead against hers. "I understand. It was a great night. I'll take you home."

"Thank you."

We rode in silence. Presley's exhausted body leaned against my shoulder with her head resting lightly. My hand cupped her knee. By the time we hit west Omaha, innocent noises escaped from her into the silence, not snoring, but melodic little whimpers of a dream state. The drive to her house seemed shorter with her sweet, entertaining sounds.

Nearing her place, the pleasant hums changed. They were less like whimpers and more like desire-charged moans. Moans like she was really enjoying whatever she was dreaming about. After parking the truck in the driveway, I watched her for minutes as her breathing changed and her eyes darted rapidly behind her eyelids. Her mouth opened in a small pant and her body writhed as she moaned my name.

"Presley, beautiful, wake up. You're home." I tried to call her softly from the dream. I said the words louder and still got no reaction.

Turning my body so her head was against my chest, I tipped her head up at me and kissed her lips softly. She released the sexiest sound I'd ever heard. It was a whimper-moan, a melodic coo. In seconds, I was hard as steel as the sound charged my body with craving for her.

While our lips stayed connected, her hands searched my chest and quickly moved below my belt, raking along the swelling bulge in my jeans. Although I would've loved to continue what was happening, every lucid thought, there were only one or two, believed it was less than gentlemanly to encourage Presley to touch me intimately in her sleep. Mind-numbing desire to be with the sexy raven-haired siren filled every corner of my brain, but I heaved myself from my hormone-induced haze.

"Presley! Wake up!"

Her eyes opened slowly while her hand still cupped my erection through my jeans.

"We're at your house." I pushed pieces of her hair out of her eyes, while she blinked away the dream.

She glanced down and her eyes widened while she pulled her hand back to her body.

"I'm sorry." Her rosy pink blush glowed in the moonlight.

I kissed her forehead. "Don't be. I was enjoying whatever dream you were having. Do you remember what it was about?"

"Same thing as last night. You ... and me ... on your motorcycle." Her sleepy voice was gravelly from waking.

"Taking a ride?"

Her fingers tangled in my hair. "In a manner of speaking."

"Oh." I inhaled a long breath to calm my heightened body as the insanely erotic image flashed in my mind. "That sounds like a really great dream."

Presley's sleepy eyes were only slits of green peaking from her lashes like mini-moons of seduction.

"Okay, I'd better get you inside. Come on." I opened my door and stretched my legs to release the tension in my groin. I tugged her body to the edge of the seat. Her long legs wound around my waist as her fingers played with my ponytail. She slid closer to me and her hips met mine. I growled at the connection, and her eyes opened wide as every ounce of blood returned to the weightlifter.

"Damn, you are so fucking sexy, Presley."

"Right." She dropped her gaze.

I raised her chin. "Yes, you are. I don't know what makes you think so poorly of yourself, but Presley Bradenhurst, I swear to you, you are the sexiest woman I've ever met. And it's not only because you're smart and funny and an incredibly talented salesperson and artist. And it's not only because you have the body of a goddess, shapely and toned. And it's not only because your huge emerald eyes sear a path straight into me, causing every cell in my body to stand at attention, some more than others."

She smiled shyly.

"Presley, everything about you—brain, humor, profession, creativity, body, eyes, heart…" My thumb brushed over her puffy bottom lip. "Everything is sexy. I wouldn't want to change one single thing."

Her chest rose and fell and her open-mouthed erotic pant had my head spinning like a spring tornado. I slammed my mouth to hers. She released a series of moans into my mouth, building my storming libido. Our bodies thrashed against each other. Her legs pulled me closer until my hard cock rubbed against her jean-covered softness. Her moans swirled around us as frantic pleas for more.

She broke the explosive kiss and hot breaths flowed between us. "I've never wanted someone like I want you, Jude. It's frightening me. I try to always be in control, guarded and protective of my head and my heart

… and my body, but you…" Her eyes glossed over. "You make me want to drop every defense I've ever had and give myself to you."

I caught a tear as it rolled down her lust-blushed cheek. "Fuck! See? So damn sexy."

We stared into each other's eyes for minutes, neither of us wanting to interrupt the hot and hungry gazing.

Her forehead fell to my chest. "I really wish I could just say yes and give myself to you, but I can't. I want to, so badly, but I just can't."

I caressed her back. "Prez, I will wait for you. It doesn't mean there is something wrong with you. That you don't jump into bed without knowing where you're at emotionally and physically is actually refreshing. Not that I'm judging the opposite way. I'm saying I respect your decision either way."

Her fingers played with the V of my t-shirt. "God, you're incredible. I think every girl and the majority of men in that club would have gone home with you tonight. They'd think I was crazy for not dragging you into my bed." She looked up and rolled her eyes. "Maybe I am."

"I don't care what they think and neither should you. Let's get you inside and locked in." I guided her from the seat and onto her legs.

At the door we shared one last hot kiss to, hopefully, bring back her motorcycle dream. That dream would haunt me tonight, too.

****

The next morning, after a long run, I cooked breakfast when my phone buzzed on the counter.

Prez: **Good morning. How are you?**
Jude: **Good, finished 10 mile run, making breakfast. How are you?**

Prez: **10 miles? Good for you! I will go biking today ... later. You want to come over this evening?**

How I wish I could, beautiful.

Jude: **I have to work tonight. Sorry**

Prez: **Don't be sorry, I should've remembered**

Jude: **Maybe tomorrow?**

Prez: **After you get off of work at 2Fine tonight is considered tomorrow, right?**

I re-read the text.

Jude: **Yes**

Prez: **Would you like to spend the night at my house tonight? I mean, it's on your way home and you'll be tired. I'm only concerned about your health and safety ;-)**

Okay, I don't want to assume, but...

Jude: **Should I ride my motorcycle?**

I was thankful that Zane was with the girls. My gym shorts didn't hide that one part of me was definitely up for a motorcycle ride.

I had confidence that I read correctly into what she was really talking about but I glanced at the screen every ten seconds for a return text. The response took what seemed like forever but it finally arrived.

Prez: **Your choice, but I don't think we'll need it tonight. My bed is very comfy. I promise.**

Yes!

I typed quickly.

Jude: **Work's over at 1:30am, 2:10am if we're really packed. No band tonight. Shouldn't be that busy**

Prez: **Have a good day and I'll see you tomorrow** ☺

I did some quick calculations in my head.

Jude: **57,600 seconds and counting down**

Jude: **57,559 seconds**

Jude: **57,558 seconds**

Prez: **I get it. :-) You're really looking forward to tonight/tomorrow. I am, too, Ponytail.**

Jude: **Have a good day, Beautiful**

Prez: **You too.**

While I cleaned the kitchen from breakfast, Zane lumbered in through the side door.

I talked to him over my shoulder. "Hey bro, I have a couple of hours. You want some help moving?"

"I'm not moving any more of my shit. If anything I'm moving my shit back over here."

I glanced at him and saw him rubbing his bloodshot eyes. "Wanna talk about it?"

Zane plopped down into the chair in the living room. "Fuck! The two of them!" He threw up a hand aimlessly pointing to the other side of the duplex. "They … they … they…" Zane sputtered like a skipping CD. He dropped his head and grunted something inaudible.

I tried to finish his sentence. "Hate you. Can't get along. Make you crazy. Need medication. Have STDs. Spit it out, Zane."

"They won't let me get any sleep! It's a fucking competition to see who can get off and get me off more times. I think I'm close to dying from overexertion or busting open a nut."

I finished drying the omelet pan while laughing hysterically. "I don't think you can die from too much sex, Zane. But I get what you're saying. Your relationship can't be about sex only." Zane nodded into his hands. "Bro, you need to talk to them." I clasped his shoulder and gave a caring squeeze before moving to the couch.

"I try, but we end up having sex 'cause my honesty turns them on." He lowered his voice, real terror in his eyes. "I think they're nymphos."

"Maybe, but you seemed to enjoy that fact two days ago." I shook my head in exasperation. "Okay, do the talk somewhere neutral, a park with kids near, but not too near, or in a busy restaurant. That way the situation can't get heated. Be firm. Jesus, everything sounds sexual after you say nymphos!" I laughed, but got serious at how he held his head in his hand. He was truly not in a good place. "Zane, relationships aren't easy. Dad told me there were a few times he thought about leaving Mom, but then he'd stop and remember the reasons he wanted to stay and there were always more of those. Are there more reasons to stay? Besides the constant sex?"

Zane threw his body back into the chair, rolling his head in the headrest. "Yes. I'm just exhausted. Can I sleep in your bed for a couple of hours? Then I'll go back and talk to them ... again."

"Only if you text them and tell them where you are. If you care about them, they deserve to know you're okay."

"Then lock the door! I guarantee they'll come over." His eyes alternated between both real and fake panic.

"I'll tell them they have to go back home. Go get some rest."

He stood and wavered on his legs. "Thanks, Jude."

"No problem, bro. Plus, it's still your place."

"Good point. Good night." Zane shuffled zombie-style to my bedroom, then the thud of his body on the mattress, followed by light snoring just a couple of minutes later.

"Good night." I closed the door, chuckling to myself.

Didn't expect to be a safe haven for the sexually exhausted today.

Like Zane predicted, ten minutes later, the demanding duo showed on the front step. I intercepted them before they pounded on the door.

I jerked opened the door, and they both jumped. I kept my voice calm and quiet. "He's fine. He needs some rest. Sounds like he can't seem to get enough when he's over there." I nodded across the driveway. "You two need to start acting like people who love my brother and care about his health."

Britney's hands clamped onto her womanly hips. "Whatever, I don't think we need relationship advice from Mr. Celibate."

Yori gripped Britney's arm. "Come on, Brit. Let's go. If Zane needs some alone time, we should respect that."

She shook off Yori's hand. "I don't have ta do any such thang." Her southern drawl came out in full when she was pissed.

I stepped onto the front porch and closed the door. "Well, then maybe he won't be coming back. Is that what you want, Britney?"

"Is he really that worn down?" She drawled "really" like she still didn't believe the truth.

"Yes," I said with no room for questions. "I think you two need to find other ways to spend some of your free time—an entertaining hobby like gardening, knitting, reading, whatever, just give something else a try. Please. I understand what sex can add to a relationship, but there are diminishing benefits when it's *only* sex, and sex is *never* a competition." I thought of how I'd want to be treated, if I were in Zane's shoes. "It's a connection to be savored in the moment, not for a just moment. Have a good day, ladies."

I turned and stepped back inside. Before I could close the door, Britney stuck her boot in the doorway.

She rolled her eyes. "Fine. But he doesn't come back by dinner and I'm kicking down the door."

"I wouldn't expect less from those shit-kickers, Britney."

"I'm sorry I called you Mr. Celibate."

"No, you're not."

"You're right, I'm not. But I was worried about Zane. Sorry I took it out on you." Pools of tears formed in the badass country girl's eyes.

I stepped back onto the porch and pulled her into a hug. "Hey, he'll be fine. He loves you both, just return the sentiment with a little more listening to how he's actually doing."

She nodded into my shoulder.

Yori smiled at me behind Britney's back and mouthed, "Thank you."

I mouthed, "You're welcome" back.

I watched as they left and made their side of the duplex.

What a situation. Of course my brother could fall in love with two women.

I chuckled and returned inside. Resting on the couch, I scanned a magazine, but in a few minutes, I was deep in an afternoon nap. My phone alarm buzzed on the coffee table, waking me from my dreams about tonight. They were good dreams, none involving my motorcycle, but that was a dream I would love to make a reality.

I woke Zane and he rolled to his feet, his eyes much clearer and his stance stronger.

Walking him to the door, I told him what happened. "Your ladies showed up. I gave them a little speech. I don't think you'll have any problems talking to them and them listening now."

"I told you, and thanks. And hey, my balls say thank you too."

****

Two Fine Irishmen was busy. My body stayed active but my brain was elsewhere. I took some time to send Presley a couple of texts to let her know I was thinking about her, but I didn't continue the possibly annoying countdown.

Jude: **How are you doing this evening?**

Presley: **Good. And you?**

Jude: **Only thinking about you.**

Presley: **Awww. Thanks, Ponytail**

If today had taught me anything, it was that sex wasn't what really mattered. It was good communication. And having a hobby or some outside interests.

A couple hours later I received...

Presley: **I'm all ready for you. Counting down the seconds here ... 5321 ... 5320 ... 5319 ... :-)**

I was a little busy and it took some time for me to get back to her.

Jude: **Good to hear, can't wait. Thanks for the countdown update. Should be there soon.**

Without a band, the crowd thinned after midnight. Sage hit the stage and sang a couple of songs. She had an incredible voice and it always seemed to me like she was singing to someone in the crowd. I watched her closely but I didn't see her concentrate on anyone in particular, but then again the Ogre wasn't here. I suspected Rahl was her muse.

Sam gave me the nod that my time was done. No use paying three bartenders and I didn't blame him. I was totally fine with being the one he was letting go early.

I finished up washing pints and sent Presley one final text to let her know I was on my way. I ran to my truck.

Five minutes was all that stood between me and a beautiful girl.

Chapter Eighteen

Presley

Asking Jude to spend the night with me, even by text, was the most difficult thing I'd ever communicated to a guy. With the other three guys, sex just kind of happened, but asking Jude to be with me was empowering. I took charge of my needs and wants. After last night's screaming-hot truck cab action and how I was feeling about him, I wanted to make the move. Even if it wasn't forever, we could still be right tonight. And I couldn't imagine Jude being anything but a skilled and understanding lover.

I spent some of the day getting prepared. Normal things any woman would do knowing she was going to be hooking up later. I shaved all necessary body parts—legs, pits, and the hoohoo. Ate light—no beans, no cabbage, and no onions—nothing that might offend or cause gas later. Picked out an outfit that was comfortable, but easily removed. Yoga pants and a fitted t-shirt with soft socks worked. Applied minimal makeup. Nothing said *not sexy* like waking up with raccoon eyes. And finally, I consumed a bit of alcohol—two sweet tart martinis between ten p.m. and midnight. I wanted to be relaxed, not smashed.

At midnight, I realized the two martinis might have been a mistake on the little amount I ate to keep my stomach flat. The second one went to my head. I giggled at the infomercial on TV and couldn't stop giggling when Kanyon and Willow returned home from their date. Willow seemed concerned, and I explained everything, in way more detail than necessary with Kanyon present. Kanyon chuckled and Willow elbowed him. He coaxed her to see the humor in my situation before they headed off to bed.

By one a.m., I drifted in and out of sleep. I curled up on the sofa and quickly entered an alcohol-laced sleep. My dreams crept up on me.

I was in high school, walking down the hallway being pointed at while horrible names were thrown my way. Someone made cow mooing sounds as I'd walked by. I'd shuffled around the corner of the lockers and my body shook with embarrassment. Waiting in the girls' bathroom until most of the perpetrators of my pain had left for the afternoon, I walked home or Willow drove me home after she was done with all the extracurricular activities I couldn't or wouldn't do for fear of being teased or making a fool of myself.

I'd told myself I wouldn't eat. I'd just go to bed, sleep off the memories. But once inside the house, and without a second thought, I'd hit the fridge and was halfway through a half-gallon of ice cream before I'd stepped off the linoleum floor. The ever-present regret crashed into me, and I'd run to the bathroom to purge the contents of my stomach, wrenching in tears, remembering all of the cruel words the kids had thrown so carelessly in my face. I'd cried myself to sleep on the floor in front of the toilet, my stomach clenched and my throat burned from the damaging acid.

The dream morphed. I was at Triple R. Emerson was in the locker room. She'd pointed her white-tipped acrylic nail at me while talking to one of her workout friends. They'd both snickered and made gagging sounds as I'd rounded the corner to the shower. After showering, I'd returned to my locker, gathered my items, and carried them into a changing room.

"Do they just let anyone join this gym?" her friend had asked, and Emerson had answered, "The owner took pity on her cause she gave him a good deal on his truck. She's probably thinking he'd give her more than free lessons. Mitch has to put his hands on her. I bet his amazing cock cringes when he does. You think she ever gets laid?"

Even though I'd tried to fight it, my stomach wrenched and I'd thrown up in the trash can in the changing room. Years of purging taught me how to be silent while I expelled. I'd sat on the dressing room bench and wept until the tears dried onto my cheeks, only leaving Triple R after I was sure the other girls had left the locker room.

I faintly heard something foreign in my dream. My eyes flashed open, and I grabbed my phone from the coffee table.

Jude: **On my way, Beautiful.**

The doorbell rang. My legs were moving but my body floated inside a dream. My hands dripped with sweat while my heart pounded until the vein in my neck thumped against my skin. Opening the door with a trembling hand, I held the other hand up to stop him from entering.

"Shit! Presley, what's wrong?"

"I ... I can't. I don't know what I was thinking."

He started to move in the house, but I shook my head violently. He stopped. His eyes searched my face for the answers that I wasn't going to give him. Answers I couldn't even put into words.

His voice was smooth and calm. "Presley, we can just talk. Please, let me come in." He reached for me and I shuffled back. "Please, Beautiful." His requests sent my heart into a frantic rhythm.

"No, you ... you don't belong with me. You belong with someone like Emerson, someone who looks like you do, someone who will always be the same."

His eyes narrowed. "What are you talking about? I don't want Emerson. I want you, Presley. I don't care if we don't have sex. Just talk to me, Beautiful."

I'm not beautiful!

"No. No!" I yelled, and Jude flinched. "I don't want to see you. I can't…" The tears rolled as my breathing constricted to choppy gasps. "Please, just leave."

Arms wrapped around me from behind. "Prez, come on, sweetie. Let's get you to bed."

Thank God, Willow.

My legs started to collapse as she rounded my waist with her comforting hold.

"Jude, I've got her."

"Please, let me help. Willow, please."

"I'm sorry, but you can't. Good night, Jude."

We passed Kanyon on the way to my bedroom, and Willow said something I didn't actually hear through my wailing. She sat with me while I cried, reliving my dreams. She told me everything would be okay. I didn't believe her.

I was messed up. Again. I didn't mess up. I *was* messed up. Years of social failure and body image issues, and just being me, had led to this moment. The moment I turned away a great guy and told him to his face that I wasn't good enough for him. But maybe he would have found out for himself?

And which situation, I wonder, would be worse? Cause this feels like I'm dying.

Chapter Nineteen

Jude

I stood dazed in the doorway while Presley and Willow disappeared down the hallway. Kanyon rounded from the end of the hallway, stopping Willow with a few words, before he strode to me.

"Need a drink?" He clasped my shoulder and I dipped my head, unable to form words. I followed him outside. "Let's go to my place. I have plenty of beer, tequila, and whiskey."

"I'll take all three," I mumbled as I climbed in my truck.

The drive was a series of flashbacks trying to figure out what had happened. Only a few hours before the massive crash, we were on smooth pavement joking and flirting and out of nowhere came a brick wall of screaming.

"Hey!" Kanyon tapped on my driver's side window, and I jolted from my daze. "Come inside."

I didn't even realize I'd come to a stop in his driveway.

He brought all three alcoholic beverages to the kitchen table. I pointed to the Wild Turkey. He poured a shot. I downed it. The liquor acted as a lighter fluid-like fireball all the way down to my gut. He poured another, and the amber liquid was gone as quickly. He started to pour a third, but instead he stood, found an actual glass tumbler, and filled it.

"If you're gonna make me play bartender all night, we're gonna cut to the chase."

"Ice?" It was the first word uttered since I left Presley's.

He harrumphed. "Prima donna?"

"Your whiskey sucks, needs to be cold to dull the pain … in my throat and my head. Ever heard of the term 'top-shelf'?"

Kanyon chuckled and collected three ice cubes from his freezer, plopping each one in my glass ceremoniously as the liquid rose to the top. I flipped him off as it teetered at the rim.

"Wow, never seen Ponytail have his boxers all in a wad. Wanna explain that whole spectacle to me?" Kanyon opened a beer and swigged a large gulp.

"I am fucking clueless."

Silence.

"Jude…"

"I really can't even think right now."

"Okay."

Instead of talking, we drank. Him, in support. Me, to dull the volcano of emotions. Confusion. Why? Valid concern. Is she okay? A little hurt. What did I do or what didn't I do? Reasonably heavyhearted. What could I have done differently? And somewhat pissed. Why isn't what I've done enough to show her who I really am?

Kanyon's phone rang "Black Sheep" by Gin Wigmore and I had to smile a little at his choice for Willow.

"Hey, Willow." His eyes looked everywhere but at me. "She gonna be okay?" His body language gave nothing away. "Okay. See you tomorrow? I think he's okay. We're having a couple of drinks at my house. I'll put him up here for the night. Yeah, me too. Good night, Gorgeous."

"Well?" I asked with enough attitude that I wanted to slap myself.

"Presley fell asleep."

"And?" The word still held a dick-like vibe.

"And Willow's worried."

I slammed back the rest of the liquor in the glass. "Makes two..." I looked at him. He nodded. "I guess three of us."

Kanyon passed the liquor bottle to me. "That girl has something she's not over. The way she was screaming, that was something else. Willow couldn't get dressed and move fast enough from the bedroom. I could tell her concern wasn't just for Presley. I think she was worried for you, too."

"Again, that makes three of us. I wish I knew what happened." I poured more liquid fire in my glass. "We had a great night last night. She asked me to come over after work. I would have been fine even if we didn't have sex but she was damn clear I wasn't getting anywhere near her. She looked like a beaten and cornered dog and for some reason I felt like I was holding the weapon that inflicted her pain."

"Willow admitted last night that she was waiting for Presley to crack," Kanyon said quietly.

"Because?"

"Jude, come on! Even girls who have had high self-esteem from day one of their lives probably have problems believing they're good enough for what you have been blessed with. Good looks, gentlemen-like class, you dance like a girl's wet dream and you're interesting to talk to. Bastard."

"So what? I'm not supposed to shower for days, start calling every woman bitch, slut, and ho, never enjoy myself on the dance floor again, and pretend to be a dick just to fit the mold of every other asshole from Presley's past?"

Kanyon laughed. "No. I'm saying it's going to take patience. However, patience isn't your thing. Noticed that the first time you came into the store and walked right to the Panigale S. Have you two done anything besides kissing?"

My jaw tightened. "Yes."

"Now, I can see that gentlemanly 'I don't kiss and tell' attitude coming out in that short answer. Here's the deal. You can either elaborate or we can call it a night 'cause I could give a fuck less if you ever get some from Presley or anyone else. But since I think you genuinely like her, I'm trying to help. What's it gonna be, Ponytail?"

"We sexted to completion," I admitted. Kanyon smirked and I grimaced. "I got her off at Triple R." I held up my hand, Kanyon grimaced. "And last night we made out pretty hot and heavy in my truck."

"All clothes on, right?"

"Yeah."

"You really like her?"

"I do."

"Then you need to try everything to have patience, 'cause she's afraid to show you her body."

"That's crazy. She has a great body." I refilled my glass and sucked down a big gulp.

"But what if she didn't? Willow told me about Presley's efforts to get healthy. What if she still thinks of herself the way she used to be?"

"I wouldn't care. I like her for more than her…"

Then I remembered all of her words last night, her adamant speech about how she'd still like and want me if I changed. And then how I didn't say the same to her. If anything I said the opposite. I told her she had a rockin' body, not that I'd still want and like her if she didn't.

"She's worried she'll return to the way she was before and I'll leave her," I said. Presley's fears rolled through me, and the feeling wasn't enjoyable.

"Probably. She's not exactly comfortable in her own skin yet." Kanyon blew out a big breath. "I can read people pretty damn well. I'd bet a case of craft beer she was treated like shit by lots of people in her life, maybe used by her parents, maybe teased or tortured at school, maybe shit on by past boyfriends. If you have the patience to stick it out and you can get through to her, she'll be yours forever, Ponytail."

Forever? With Presley?

I pulled out my phone.

Jude: **I'm not giving up on you, Beautiful. I'm here for you when you are ready to talk.**

I showed the text to Kanyon and he gave the acceptable nod. I hit send, then picked up my glass and chugged the rest of its contents.

"I need some sleep. Where's this bed you were talking about to Willow?" I slurred every word in the sentence as the whiskey irrevocably numbed my brain.

He motioned with his head. "You're looking at it."

I glanced over his shoulder at the couch. "Great."

"Hey, it's a lot more comfortable than you're imagining. Or I could call you a cab and you can pay through the nose to get home. Which will it be?"

"I think I'll need another shot so I pass out."

"I think you're done if you want to be in any sort of shape to see Presley tomorrow."

I relented, stumbled to the sofa, and smacked down face-first onto what was actually very comfortable.

"Good night, Ponytail." Kanyon said, throwing a blanket over me.

"Stop calling me Ponytail! That's only for Presley."

Kanyon chuckled. "Okay. Fair enough. Good night, Saylor."

"Night, Hills."

Chapter Twenty

Presley

I ignored my phone in the morning. I wasn't ready to read any texts or hear any voice mails.

What happened last night was ... hell, I still didn't even know. Maybe it was a combination of lots of things. The alcohol, the dreams, the anxiety, the fact that Jude was so incredibly amazing and the undeniable detail that I still couldn't believe I was in his ballpark, let alone his league of attractiveness. That I insisted he go to Emerson tore a piece from my heart.

Hope he didn't take me up on my demand.

I headed out for a bike ride, exercising cleared my head. Thought about going to Triple R, but there was a bigger chance of running into him there so I nixed it for now. Plus, I had a training session tomorrow morning.

Maybe Jude and I could talk after?

My ride ended up being a long one. It was in the lower 70s and there was just the slightest breeze around the lake. I circled twice, feeling an incredible rush of endorphins that reduced my anxiety and helped me to see a few things clearly.

First, I needed to stop running *from* and start talking *to* Jude. If he still wanted to talk to me. That might be a huge *if*.

Second, I needed to sincerely apologize. Not because I wasn't ready for sex, but for how I treated him. Screaming was unnecessary, very immature, and very rude. I had a right to feel, but I had no right to take my harsh emotions out on him. I needed to tell him what I was feeling. I had been doing a better job lately. And then last night happened.

Lastly, I was falling for Jude Saylor, and there was no more hiding that from myself. If he didn't feel the same, that was on him, but it was time I put a name on my emotions and feelings to own them. If I was scared I was going to say so. If I was upset I was going to tell him. If I was horny, I was going to tell him but not expect him to do anything about it.

Well, maybe I would.

Willow was right. It was time I took a chance.

By the time I arrived home I had just enough time to shower and rush to my Sunday standing appointment with the barkers and meowers. My time with them was always a bright spot at the end of my weekend. When I made it to the shelter, I met up with my contact, Sheri.

"Presley, Yolanda had a family emergency and she can't walk the dogs today." She grabbed a clipboard from a nail. "Is that something you'd be interested in?"

"Of course!"

I loved being outside with the dogs, and they always seemed to agree that it was a much better place to be. Anything not to scoop poop and mop kennels, but I never complained about those chores either. Whatever it took.

Before I entered the kennels I stood at the heavy metal door. A pit of dread hallowed my already-empty stomach into a cave.

Is she still here? Or is she ... gone?

I pushed the door and skated my feet along the concrete floor as I walked the first row of dogs. No white little dog. My heartbeat quickened as I rounded to the second row. The barking of the dogs set my heart into a frantic rhythm. I approached the last block of four kennels, then looked around the edge and sunk to my knees.

There she was.

She still cowered in the back, but she was here.

I pulled her card and shoved it in my back pocket. The move meant she was on hold for someone. No one else would be adopting her today but I still had work to do.

"I'll be back, sweetie. Give me a few hours and I promise we'll talk."

I started with a few of the bigger dogs. Most of them were very well behaved. Minus a male Great Dane who wanted to drag me like a sled behind him. I did my best to stay upright. I could tell he was a gentle giant, just really, *really* excited to be outside.

I'd finally made it back to the little ball of fluff. She was a mix of two or three or four small dogs. Maybe poodle, Chihuahua, and … oh, heck, she was a mutt and I didn't care. The breed wasn't important, it was the love and that tug deep inside of me that told me she was the one. White with a grey chest and soft curly hair, she probably could do with a grooming soon, but to me she was already beautiful.

I spent time coaxing her to the front, gaining her trust to get her on a leash, and finally, getting us to the back door. Once the timid little lady walked outside, she gained a spirit and played like a puppy even though she was definitely a mature dog. The ball of white glanced behind her to make sure I was still there during the walk. She never demanded attention, but offered hers in small doses that seemed to help her feel at ease. The fact she could tell I needed some unconditional love was uplifting. We sat on the ground and shared the happenings in our lives. Actually, I did all the talking. She was a remarkably good listener.

"So, there's this guy." The dog cocked her head. "He's cute, like *really* cute," I whispered. "Actually, he's a cat person, but we won't hold that against him, will we?" She found a leaf on the ground and attacked it.

"They say you need some special attention. Well, there was a time when I did too. I know how it feels to be alone but I think I've found someone who might end that feeling. I'd like to give you all the attention you need, if you're interested." She sat beside me and stared into the park. "Well, I suppose I should get you back." I stood and the ball of fluff scuttled away at my quick movements. I'd have to remember to take it slow.

By the end of our time together, the little package of love and happiness was definitely coming home with me. When I filled out the paperwork for adoption, the counselor was just as direct as she would have been with anyone adopting the tiny dog.

"Now, Presley, she has some issues. She's overweight and she's shy."

"Now wait a minute. Maybe she's got a couple pounds of extra something on her frame and *maybe* she needs a little extra exercise and socializing, but I can tell she can change. Even if she didn't … I'd still love her."

The counselor grinned. "Well said." She looked at the ball of fluff sleeping on my lap. "I think you're going to be very well cared for, little girl."

After the normal adoption procedures, I made my way home with an adorable eleven pound, soon-to-be nine-pound dog in the seat next to me.

I guess the loaner car will be mine after having my dog in it.

Chapter Twenty-One

Jude

"Good morning, Pony ... I mean, Jude." Kanyon shoved a large trough of black coffee at me.

"Don't drink the stuff." I stretched and rubbed my eyes.

"Right. I'll get the whole-grain-loving, granola-eating, kale-crunching creature inside of you a glass of orange juice?"

"Water, just water," I groaned. "Please."

Sitting up, I ground my teeth at the jackhammer pounding in my head. I squeezed both sides of my skull hoping to either crush the pain ... or my skull.

Whatever it takes to make this pain go away.

"Ah, so half a bottle of Wild Turkey in an hour and a half probably wasn't a great idea, especially with only five hours of sleep?" Kanyon cracked up while placing a big glass of water on the coffee table, which even only inches away seemed too far to reach.

"What time is it?" I asked with only one eye open.

"A little after nine. I'm going to get Grace for breakfast, so..."

"Got it. I'm on my way out." I pulled on my boots, downed the glass of water, and stood all in a minute. I was positive that someone lit a stick of dynamite inside of my head and the blast cleared all the cognitive function but left the pain recognition. I trudged toward the door. "Thanks, bro. I'll let you know if something happens. You seeing Willow today?"

"Yeah, I'm supposed to go over there. She's making dinner tonight. I think it's time to tell her about Grace. She needs to know."

"Have a good time with Grace." I pointed to the picture on the entertainment center. "She sure is beautiful, blonde hair and green eyes, quite a combination … on a girl. They're only okay on you."

"Not everyone can be a god like you, Jude. Have patience today, okay? Give Presley some time to process what happened."

"I'll try. Thanks for letting me crash here. Not a bad sofa."

We bro-hugged and in ten minutes I crawled into my own bed. It was after one in the afternoon before I woke up again. My phone buzzed on the nightstand making my brain buzz in my head.

Willow: **I'd like to meet today and talk about last night.**

Jude: **Is Presley okay with that?**

Willow: **Wouldn't know, didn't ask her. She's volunteering today.**

This is probably an unwise idea. Good things come from unwise ideas, right? Don't have a good example right now but…

Jude: **What time? Where?**

Willow: **4pm, here. Come prepared to stay, she gets home at 5pm**

Jude: **Not sure that's a good idea**

Willow: **She left phone here. She didn't read your text. She'll want to see you. I promise.**

Jude: **If you say so. See you then.**

Willow: **Don't worry, Ponytail**

Jude: **Only Prez can call me Ponytail**

Willow: **Noted. See you later, Horsehair**

I shook my head.

Jude: **Not better.**

Willow: **I guess it's Ponytail then :-)**

I fixed myself food, and not granola or any of the other items Kanyon offered up as potential fodder. I cooked a grilled cheese sandwich and heated a can of tomato soup. Hopefully my stomach would calm down enough to keep everything down. I was successful.

Damn whiskey.

Lying on the couch I watched half of two movies, not interested in either. After showering and dressing, I motivated to head over to Presley and Willow's place. I parked on the street enjoying the cool air blowing in the truck cab and wondering what I was really doing here when Willow stepped onto the front porch.

After hiking to stand in front of my truck, she yelled, "What the hell are you waiting for?"

Hell to freeze over and my head to stop screaming at me.

"Can you stop yelling, please?" I dropped my forehead to the steering wheel. "I have a hangover from the cheap-ass whiskey Kanyon served me last night."

She came around and opened the door. "I'm sorry. Come on." She pulled on my arm. "I'll get you a sports drink and some pain relievers."

My ass hit the sofa with a tired *thud*. I took the pills and drank half of the electrolyte-replacing liquid in one chug. I could tell why Presley loved Willow. She was a natural at caring for people.

"So, overdid it a little last night?"

"Little," I replied, refocusing my eyes and rubbing my face with my hands. "What did you want to talk about?"

Willow sat in the chair across from me. She pursed her lips and inhaled a breath like she was going underwater for a deep, deep dive. "Presley really likes you. Please give her another chance. Last night wasn't the real her. She drank a couple of martinis to relax and they went to her head because she didn't eat a whole lot yesterday so her stomach would be flat." I scowled at that revelation and Willow rolled her eyes. "Girl thing. Anyway, she fell asleep on the couch before you came over and had a bad dream about high school and another one about Emerson. And that's why she freaked out. It had nothing to do with you, really." She inhaled after releasing all the information she wanted me to know.

I thought over what Willow told me for a minute. There was nothing that changed how I felt about Presley.

"Okay." I rubbed my hands on my jeans.

"Okay?"

"Yeah, if I want to know Presley better and she won't tell me what I need to know and you will, then I guess I'll go with it for now. She'll have to open up to me sometime. You can't be an information liaison forever."

"True."

"Is that everything?"

"No."

"What else?"

"There are things from Presley's past that make her untrusting of people."

"No shit," I replied dryly. The retort was the hangover talking. My humor took a serious hit today.

Willow giggled and I smiled.

Get to your point, Willow.

"Yeah, the events and what happened in her past aren't funny, but sometimes when she gets out of control, her actions can be a little amusing in a really twisted way. I can tell you're a good guy, Jude, but it might take Presley more time to see what I see. She doesn't have rose-colored glasses when it comes to men and sometimes women. Too many mean and thoughtless people and too many years of cruelty have clouded her glasses to gray. I'm hoping you can help her to see clearly and in color again."

"That's a tall order, Harper."

"I know, but I haven't ever met anyone else who's even come close to being right for Presley."

"You seem pretty sure of yourself."

"I am. Just like I knew Kanyon was the one for me the moment you pointed him out at Two Fine. I really think I had a mindgasm just viewing him across the room. I don't think I need to tell you what it's like when we're in the same room ... together ... alone."

I held up a hand. "No, you don't. You're making him dinner?"

"He decided to take me out. Said he needed my full attention 'cause he has something to tell me. Plus, I figured it would be okay to be gone so you and Presley can talk. I'll plan on spending the night at his house, unless he decides otherwise."

"Who says Prez will want to talk?"

"I know her. Right now she's trying to figure out how to apologize and make amends."

"Maybe I'll make her beg for my forgiveness?"

"No, you won't. Plus, she might be begging for other things. She was really looking forward to last night."

My eyes opened wide.

Shit, condoms...

"What?" Willow inquired, tipping her head curiously.

"Nothing."

"No, really, what, Saylor?"

"I forgot to get condoms ... again."

Willow's youthful laugh matched her colorful hair. "So you didn't even have any protection last night?"

"No, it's been awhile. I kind of forgot my end of the deal. I really didn't think anything would happen tonight. I guess it won't."

"She might have some, if not, top drawer of my nightstand, but bring your own from now on."

I smirked. "Thanks."

Just ask her.

"Um, Willow, is Presley a—"

"Virgin? No. Now, that's not to say she's had a lot of sex and she's pretty anxious that she's not going to live up to some ridiculous perfection she's engineered in her head, so go slowly and give her the support she needs. You'll be fine." Willow glanced to her cell phone. "Kanyon's outside on his bike." She slipped into a hot pink leather jacket. "I hate that I'm wearing leather. I swear I smell dead cow but Kanyon won't let me ride without the gear. What we do for lo—" Willow sucked in a quick breath and stood frozen.

My eyes shot to Willow. I could finish the sentence for myself.

"It's okay, Willow. I won't tell anyone. Have fun tonight."

She relaxed but still appeared a little dazed. "Okay, thanks." She tugged on black combat boots. "Here's the remote to the TV. There are DVDs in the bottom drawer, help yourself to food and drink." She snickered, raising her eyebrows. "And condoms." Her smartass attitude returned and she smiled, giving a last wave.

"Thanks, Willow." I switched on the TV and sat back into the sofa.

After five thirty p.m., I wondered if maybe Presley decided to go somewhere else. I picked up my phone. There was a text from Kiera.

Kiera: **Hey, haven't heard from you in a few days. Going to be in Omaha tomorrow. Maybe dinner?**

Kiera's text was correct, I hadn't even thought of contacting her for the last few days. She had to know that meant something, and I definitely knew that meant something.

Jude: **Don't know. Kind of in the middle of something. I'll let you know.**

Then I texted Presley.

Jude: **Hey, would like to talk to you. Can I come over?**

Actually, I'm already here.

I heard her phone buzz on the kitchen table. That's right, she doesn't have it.

My phone buzzed.

Kiera: **No problem. I'll text you tomorrow. Have a good night.**

After another ten minutes, I stood to leave, but Presley entered through the front door.

"Willow?" she called while her back was turned to close the door. When she spun around, she was not alone. She finally took her eyes off of the white ball of fluff in her arms. "Jude!"

I flinched from the decibels in the small space.

She stepped toward me. "Are you okay?"

"Hangover." I held my throbbing head, with one eye open and one eye clenched shut to stop the throbbing inside of my orbs, which was thankfully starting to lessen from the pain relievers.

She softened her voice. "Poor guy. What are you doing here?"

I restarted the conversation. "Hello, Presley."

Her smile widened. "Hello, Jude."

"I came over to make sure you're okay. Willow let me in. You really had me worried last night."

Presley stepped closer and the ball of fluff in her arms tried to worm its way into her body.

Presley saw my concern. "She's a little scared of people only until she gets to know them. Where's Willow?"

I kept my voice low. "Dinner with Kanyon. He's going to tell her about Grace."

"So can you tell me about Grace now?"

"Sure. But first, introduce me to your new friend." I stepped closer to Presley, closing the distance between us to mere inches.

"This is my new dog. She's very loving but a little timid until she gets to know you. I haven't named her yet."

I reached out to pet her. "Can I?"

"Of course." Presley slipped the soft trembling cotton ball with long legs into my arms and the dog hid her long snout in the crook of my elbow. "Give her a minute. Some animals don't trust instantly." Presley pointed to the sofa, and I sat. She rested on the coffee table to face me. Leaning forward, she rested her hands on my knees. "Jude, I'm really sorry for the way I handled things last night. I let my insecurities get the best of me ... well, that and the two sweet tart martinis I had to relax."

"I'd say you were anything but relaxed, Prez."

Her face blushed the lightest shade I'd seen yet.

She cleared her throat. "I'm really embarrassed by the way I acted, I shouldn't have yelled at you and gone all crazy-woman. There's no excuse for treating you like that. I'm sorry."

The dog brought her head out and licked my forearm. I petted her and soon she wiggled around on my lap, feeling more at ease.

"Presley, if you don't want to do something or are unhappy with a situation, you always have the right to say so. Like with Drexel, you have the right to ream him when he makes you feel uncomfortable. And I wish you would. I accept your apologies, but you need to start telling me about your past so I can understand you better. Because I'd like to be a part of your future. "

Presley's breath caught and she smiled sweetly. "Can we just enjoy tonight? I promise, I'm not stalling."

I grinned.

She rolled her eyes. "Okay, maybe I'm stalling a little, but after last night, I think we need a do-over?"

"I'll agree to that only because I need food and like soon. But after the food?" My eyebrows went up to emphasize that she wasn't going to get forever to tell me.

Her fingers dawdled up my thighs and back to my knees. "I'll tell you what you want to hear. No, that didn't come out right. I'll tell you what I want and need to tell you about my past."

I relaxed. "All right." The dog had relaxed, too, and its gray eyes stared up at me. "What are you thinking of naming this little one?"

She squirmed on my lap.

"And I think she needs to go outside." I placed the wagging ball of fur on the floor.

Presley walked to the kitchen. "Not sure of a name. Ideas?" She whistled for the dog while opening the sliding door and encouraging her to leave the security of the house.

Standing behind Presley, the scent of her perfume wafted lightly from the spring breeze. I moved closer, wrapping my arms around her waist. Her back tightened for a second but relaxed as quickly and her head fell back against my shoulder, rocking against me. We stayed like that, watching the still nameless ball of fuzz bounding across the fenced backyard.

I turned her in my arms to face me. "Presley, you are the best thing that has happened to me since I moved to Omaha. Please let me into your life, and I can be the best thing that's ever happened to you, too."

"Cocky much?" Her green eyes softened and her eyes skipped to my lips.

I gave her my best smirk to make the view worth the look. "Only when I need a beautiful girl to really listen to me."

I cupped her jaw in my hands and softly kissed her forehead, moving down to her nose and sealing on her waiting lips. Her body softened against mine. She released the embarrassment and hurt of what had happened last night in one long peaceful and contented moan into my mouth.

"That's better," I whispered.

Woof. Woof.

We both looked down to our feet as the round globe of white with grey eyes scampered happily around our ankles.

"I think she approves," Presley said, smiling.

"I approve. I missed your smile."

"I missed you." The amazing words resonated through my body.

"Okay. So, food?" I asked.

"Chinese or pizza?"

I released my arms. "Pizza, pepperoni, I need the grease and carbs."

"What did you drink?" She picked up her phone from the table.

"Low-quality whiskey."

Her sparkling tear-filled eyes came up from the phone. "Thank you for not giving up on me."

"I know you're worth it, Presley. Now please, order food. I'm starving." I picked up the dog, and she squirmed frantic happiness in my arms. "So what should Prez name you? You ever watch *The Muppets*?"

Presley cocked her head. "Yeah. Long, long, long time ago."

"I was watching an episode with Grace a couple weeks ago and Miss Piggy's dog's name is Foo-Foo. What do you think of that?" I rubbed the dog's head and she playfully bit at my hand. "You look like a Foo-Foo."

"How old is she?" She brought the phone to her ear.

I glanced down at the dog after I placed her on the floor. "I don't know, maybe two, three?"

"Grace is two or three?"

I chuckled. "No, Grace is six."

"Grace is six?" With extreme confusion, Presley held up a finger to me as the line connected. "Yes, I'd like to order a medium pepperoni pizza and a small veggie pizza. Thin or regular crust?"

"Thin."

"Thin, please, for both." Presley relayed our choices, giving a quick good-bye. She spun to me. "What are you talking about? Grace is six years old?"

"Yes, Grace is Kanyon's daughter."

The fuzzy ball with a droopy pink tongue bit playfully at my canvas shoe.

"Wow, Kanyon's a dad." Presley leaned against the counter. "What's she like?"

"She's beautiful. Big green eyes, long blonde hair, and as sweet as you are." I caged Presley in with my arms, and hers wrapped around my neck.

"I wasn't so sweet last night."

"Hey, I accepted your apology. Let's move forward. I have a feeling you look back and regret the past a lot more than you should, and you probably never should, Presley."

"Guilty. Well, Grace makes a whole lot of sense now. School concert, right?"

"Yeah. Kanyon is a great dad. He's thinking of fighting for joint custody. Didn't even know Grace existed until a year ago when he received a notice for paternity testing."

"That's crazy! One-night stand?"

"Yeah, girl didn't even know his name, just that he had a unique tattoo and green eyes like their daughter, and apparently, she barely remembered those things. Her dad ran into Kanyon and laid into him in the Ducati store. Kanyon didn't remember the girl. Unfortunately, he said that out loud, and the guy dropped him to the floor with a blow to the chin. Now the granddad of Grace realizes that Kanyon's a great dad and his daughter, Moriah, is the questionable parent."

"Wow, again. Glad he wants to be a part of her life. Willow would make an awesome mom. She's great with kids."

"She's also great with adults, took care of my hangover headache like a pro."

"How?" Presley's body tensed.

I threw my head back and laughed. "With pain relievers and fruit punch sports drink … not sex, Presley."

"Speaking of…" Her eyes dropped and closed.

I lifted her chin, and glassy-green mottled marbles shined at me. "We don't have to talk about that right now."

"But I need to."

She laid her cheek on my chest. Her fingers dug into my back jeans pockets, and time rolled by, but I was okay with waiting.

"Jude, not sure you're going to want to hear this, but I need to get it off my chest. I've been with three guys. The first was a good guy and we had fun, but we fizzled quickly after we had sex. I've always questioned if I was bad in bed even though he said he was just ready to move on. The second guy, he was an ass, bossy and controlling under and outside of the covers. I dumped him and he retaliated with a deluge of crap about how awful I was in bed. I questioned if he was truthful or only trying to hurt me, but still the words stuck in my mind. The last guy was almost a year ago and he was a one-night stand. It was okay. He gave it his best." She squirmed. "But the universe didn't explode for me. I guess I'm not the kind of person to have no-strings-attached sex. I need an emotional connection." Her eyes came up and held to mine. "Like I have with you."

"I need that, too, Presley. That's why I haven't had sex in over six months. I've only had six partners in eight years and one of those was a monogamous four-year relationship. The other five were girls I dated numerous times or knew for months as friends before we got physical. Not that I'm judging, but I don't have one-night-stands. A physical attraction isn't enough for me, there has to be time and effort *and* an emotional element that I don't get with many girls. But, God, I have that emotional element bad, in a good way, for you. I want you to be only mine."

"I want that, too, Jude."

I leaned down to kiss her and the doorbell rang.

"Pizza." She moved forward, pushing on my chest while placing a soft kiss against my throat. I groaned at our moment being cut short. "Later, Ponytail. Come on, I need to go pay."

She grabbed her purse from the table, but I made it to the door before her and paid the delivery driver.

255

****

"Thanks for dinner, Jude." Presley leaned back on the sofa after finishing one slice.

"You're gonna eat more than that, Presley."

"No, I'm not."

I finished the last bite of my third piece. "I would think you're gorgeous no matter your size, Presley."

"Right. That's what they all say, until you're actually that size and it's not so gorgeous."

I blew out a big breath of frustration. The dog tipped her head at me, and I shook my head back at her.

Stay calm. Patience.

"Okay, it's up to you, but I'll tell Kai to take it easy on you tomorrow 'cause that piece of pizza wasn't enough to workout on, especially if you didn't eat well yesterday. Your glycogen stores would be gone in minutes of even semi-intense cardio and you'd fatigue easily making you at risk for injury."

Presley narrowed her eyes. "Okay, smartass. I think having a personal trainer for a boyfriend is going to be both good and bad, right?"

I shrugged and ate another slice.

It is true, Prez. I can be so good and so, so bad. You'll see.

Chapter Twenty-Two

Presley

Coming home to find Jude there was what I needed. He was what I wanted and needed. Opening up to him was still hard. Maybe it always would be? I hid things from people for so long that it was almost a gut instinct to be jaded, guarded, untrusting. It was time to change or I'd end up being alone for the rest of my life.

And right now, I could get used to being with him for the rest of my life.

We finished our pizza. After his encouragement, I ate three slices of the veggie and cheese-covered triangles. He was right. I needed the food. My emotions had controlled my stomach lately.

I signaled him to stay sitting as I cleaned up.

"Want to watch a movie?" I asked as I sent Foo-Foo outside.

"I'd rather make out with you," Jude replied honestly. I stuck my head out into the cool spring air to clear my hormone-clouded thoughts.

Foo-Foo bounded back inside. I set up her water and food dishes and a small bed I bought her. She sniffed around, inspecting the cushion from all angles, then jumped into it, spinning in a circle and curling into a small white compact ball in the middle.

I gave her a couple of pets and walked to Jude. "Okay. It's your turn for a little attention."

His big hands encircled my hips, pulling me between his open legs. He raised my t-shirt until a sliver of stomach was showing and he kissed the sensitive skin with the barest of pressure, igniting every nerve south of my waist.

"God." The word lengthened as he grazed his teeth across the same area.

Jude's lips smiled against me, then floated from one hip to the other, right above my low-rise jean waistband. He stopped. His wet, hot tongue flared out to tease right below the silver button closure. I shivered uncontrollably. Jude chuckled at my reaction as he sat back and tugged me to straddle his lap.

I pulled the ponytail holder from his hair, combing the silky strands loose with my fingers. "That was so hot." My hands wrapped around his neck, the muscles rippling beneath my fingertips.

He tilted his head forward. His nose met mine and circled tip to tip. "That was the mini-preview to the special feature movie this evening. This one stars only you and me and time to get to know each other. No pressure."

Riding his lusciously full lips along my jawline, Jude took his time to pay special attention to parts of me that had never been touched, much less kissed by a man. Hot breaths in my ear sent my body into tingling spasms everywhere.

I lifted at the hem of his t-shirt. He took the hint, pulling the grey fabric over his head, his abs clenched, and my eyes popped at the mouthwatering view.

I ran my fingers over his Adonis-inspired face. "My boyfriend, you are gorgeous, outside … and inside."

My hands skimmed down his chest slowly. Those hazel eyes fluttered closed as he leaned back into the couch, letting me get my fill of his body. At the moment, I was sure I'd never actually get my fill. This want was a bottomless glass of desire. I leaned forward and shared one of the deepest, most meaningful kisses I ever had with a man. Jude let me kiss him, making my statement that he was mine and I was his. My tongue found his and glided against the wetness from every angle. My teeth nipped lightly at his slick lips. I skidded down his jaw, down his neck, down to his toned, firm chest, repaying the mouth-attention he'd given earlier.

Slithering my body off his lap, I knelt on the floor between his long legs. My tongue made its way down his six-pack abs, dipping in and out of every inch of taut skin. His treasure trail deserved extra attention. I circled my fingers down and back up the thin trail of hair leading into his jeans. He sucked in a quick breath. His eyes opened and the orbs glazed with sparkling gold shavings before melting into pools of craving. Jude's hand wound into the hair at the base of my neck, giving a small squeeze of support for whatever I decided to do. My breath rushed from me as his gaze held mine.

Without overthinking anything, I worked frantically. I unbuttoned his jeans, slid down the zipper, and pulled the material open. I tugged at the waistband, he lifted his hips, and the jeans dropped to his knees. My whole body was on fire. Every part of me wanted so badly to have him. Make him all mine. I tugged the band of his blue boxers and he lifted again.

Before he realized what was happening, my lips were suckling at the tip of his rock-hard cock, my hand wrapped firmly at the base.

His body shook. "Presley, that's amazing." His hips bucked. "Like *really* fucking amazing."

The erotic growl that accompanied those words was enough to start my ascent toward my own pleasure, but I wanted this to be about him. I needed him to know what he did to me, what I felt for him, how worked-up I got knowing he was mine.

I dropped my mouth down the length of him. His long erection struck the back of my throat and forced a small gag, but I didn't stop. I twisted his shaft lightly in my hand and his hips jumped off the sofa. I continued the action, increasing the speed.

"Presley." He moaned my name like it was the only word in his vocabulary that mattered at all to him. His testicles rose up and his breathing became rough.

"I'm ready for you, Jude. Please, let me have all of you." My mouth returned to worship his cock, sliding the soft skin smoothly in and out of my salty, pre-cum slickened lips.

His hands gave me a thoughtful warning squeeze behind my neck. He gritted out, "Your mouth is mind-blowing, Beautiful."

Our eyes connected as the head of his manhood enlarged and his shaft pulsed in my hand. His long fingers dug into my neck as his body tensed and released repeatedly. I slowed my movements to swallow every sticky drop of him as he loudly grunted his release.

I shivered with elation. I loved consuming him in that very intimate way.

His eyes were still closed when I straightened. I leaned forward and planted a kiss on his collarbone. Taking me by surprise, he wrapped his arms around me, raised me up, and rolled us together until he was on top of me on the sofa.

"I'd say that was about the hottest fucking scene ever in a movie." His lips turned up at the edges. "Now I think we need to create a scene that's all about Presley."

My heart beat anxiously. "Not necessary, Jude. I'm happy to just lay here with you."

His fingers traced my lips. "But here's the problem with that, Prez. I could tell how worked-up it got you to give me head. And, Beautiful, that was the best blowjob I've ever had. I promise it was fucking fantastic."

I blushed.

"Do you know how happy it will make me to go down on you?"

I shook my head.

"It's all I can think about right now."

"But..."

He pushed himself up, his arms straightening and tensing to hard-sculpted rolls of muscle.

"Okay, here's the deal, I won't if you can tell me *exactly* why you don't want me to, but I get one chance to change your mind."

I started to protest.

"Without touching you," he added.

I closed my eyes and released exactly what was holding me back. "I have disgusting stretch marks from when I was really..." I couldn't finish the sentence. I shook my head. "They'll never go away and I hate them. I don't want you to be turned off."

Jude rose from the couch.

That's it. He's leaving.

I opened my eyes to see his naked body on full display. The view was spectacular and disorienting.

"See these?" He pointed to his hips.

I rose onto my elbows and squinted. "Are those...?"

"Stretch marks. Yes. Look here." He turned so his backside was in my face.

I giggled. "I'm sorry Jude, I don't see anything but your amazing ass."

"No, above!" He chuckled as he glanced over his shoulder. "But thank you. See that?"

I bit my lip. "More stretch marks," I mumbled.

He spun around, pulled his boxers and jeans up. "Don't want you distracted, you need to concentrate." His smug smirk said everything.

"I don't know, Jude."

He sat next to me on the sofa. "Presley, I *do* know. I know I want you so badly that I can already taste

261

your sweet softness on my tongue. I know I want to feel your legs wrapped around my head. And I know I'd love to hear you scream my name when I make you come."

I sucked in an alert breath.

He brushed a piece of hair out of my eyes. "And I know you're going to want me to do it again and again, over and over."

"There's that cocky thing again." My body betrayed my brain and the words came out heated and breathy.

Jude's hands cupped my face. "Hey, we can call it a night if that's what you want, but I'd love to give you what I think you deep-down really want."

"Okay, fine. But don't be disappointed if it doesn't go the way you're expecting."

"Presley, if I can get you off with a kiss and my hand, I'll blow your mind with my mouth."

Cocky was a good color on Jude. Turned me on more than I would ever let him know. I suspected he already knew what his words did to me, though. What *he* did to me.

He lowered me back to the sofa. "Relax. Enjoy. Don't think. Just feel."

My eyes went lax as his hard warm body laid on mine, hard muscle pressed into me everywhere. His strong arms and abs held him in a comfortable plank position as his silky lips started their journey down to mine. He grazed and skimmed and tickled and teased me. I rumbled unhappy noises that he wasn't deepening the kiss and he chuckled.

While Jude's lips spent time on the soft underside of my neck, his hand made its way down my body tenderly, stopping at the hem of my t-shirt and lifting. His hand cupped my breast and my back arched as his warm fingers dug into the skin around my bra. He lifted the cup over my breast and released the small but perky globe.

"These are incredible."

His head lowered and he raised my t-shirt all the way. His lips surrounded my nipple and his teeth nipped lightly. My body jerked with every pinch of combined pain and pleasure. He placed kisses all over that breast, then went to work on the other one. My body responded with equal ache to his additional attention.

"Jude. Oh, my ... Ponytail."

"That's right, keep saying my name."

"Which one? Jude or Ponytail?" I panted the words.

He raised his head and beamed. "You keep moaning and moving like that and you can call me whatever you fucking want."

When he moved farther down my body, I started to recall when I had masturbated to the thoughts of him doing just that.

I gripped his head, our eyes met. "Stop at my belly button and tease me, please."

"I love it when you tell me what you want, Beautiful."

I watched every movement of his mouth. My body shuddered as his tongue lapped deeply across the indentation. He teased in and out quickly, and little quivers of pleasure started building south of where he was.

"Jude..." My body tensed, a little anxiety, a little anticipation.

"I've got you, Presley. I'm here for you."

He unbuttoned my jeans and in one smooth motion both the denim material and my underwear were on the floor. I observed his face as he took everything in.

There was not one sign of disgust and not one moment of repulsion.

"That is…" His hungry eyes connected to mine. "You, Presley, are beautiful. Every inch of you."

His words wrapped around my soul. "Thank you, Ponytail."

"I will tell you every day until you believe it, too."

"When you say it, I do believe it."

Jude's eyes sparkled up at me. "Now hold on, because I'm about to make your universe explode."

He wasted no time. He raised my legs and his head disappeared, his soft long hair tickling the insides of my thighs. My pink tissues were swollen and firm as his warm wet tongue glided along the inside ridge slowly like he was collecting and savoring every drop of my juices. His hands opened my folds and his tongue dove deep inside of me. I hummed with an intense flutter of pleasure and my blood pumped through my body with the force of an F5 tornado.

I'd never had a guy so skilled at giving me pleasure, so patient and talented. I closed my eyes to just sense everything he was doing to me, in me, for me. His tongue flicked up to my clit and my hips jolted as little strikes of electricity zapped and zinged through me.

"Presley, you're sweet, everywhere. This is a flavor I'll never get enough of."

His teeth grazed my clit right before his tongue soothed the thrumming nub. He was brilliant, heightening the experience with a little pain so the pleasure was that much greater. He did the yin and yang move again and the pressure of a climax began to mount.

"Oh, my God…" I grabbed his head in my hands.

As he pressed firmly with his wet tongue on my clit, he drove a long finger inside me, stroking gently.

"Jesus, you're fucking tight and dripping wet."

His lips returned to my swollen bud and in one motion he both bit down and sucked on the nerve-filled point. The combination released the heavens and shooting stars came at me from every direction.

I sucked in a deep breath and screamed his name. My hips rolled as the orgasm engulfed my mind, body, and soul. A buzz of emotional electricity pulsed through my muscles and psyche.

"That's it, Beautiful, ride it out, all the way." His tongue darted back inside as his nose pressed on my clit causing another chain reaction to flood through my body.

My thighs clenched around his head. "I'm still coming, Jude..." I extended his name to almost a melodic chain of letters.

Keeping his attention fluid, he allowed my body to ride the waves of pleasure until I was panting, and my body went limp. He slowed his movements, bringing me down gradually from a place where I wasn't even sure I knew my own name.

I think I just had a stroke.

His body moved to lie on mine.

"Universe?" he asked smugly, brushing his fingers over my face.

I opened my eyes. "Shattered into a million fucking pieces, Ponytail."

We laughed and held each other.

It was even better than he promised.

Chapter Twenty-Three

Jude

"Good morning, Presley." I poked my head out of the break room as she walked by.

"Good morning, Jude. How are you today?" With a sexy and satisfied grin, she backed up a couple of steps to face me.

"I'm great. How are you?"

"Same."

I leaned against the doorframe. "Would you like to come over for dinner tonight?"

Her smile faded. "I work late. Maybe tomorrow night?"

"That works."

"Can't wait."

She turned to leave, but I circled her waist with my arms and dropped a soft kiss onto her lips. Her body responded with a purr of happiness.

I lowered my mouth to her ear. "Is that enough to last you until tomorrow night?"

Presley blushed. Her eyes relaxed into mossy swamps as her fingers brushed over my jaw and around my neck. "Honestly, I'll never get enough of you, Jude."

My heart heard the words. The innocent but full-of-meaning statement meant we were getting somewhere. She was opening up to me and letting me in, but I wanted her to be ready before I gave her more. Giving her all of me too soon would make her run faster than a whitetail deer in October.

"If you ever do, you let me know. Deal?" I winked.

My question brought out a small smile. "You'll be the first to know."

"I'll cook tomorrow night. Anything you don't like?"

She leaned forward and took a long draw of my bodywash scent, making the sexiest raspy moan. "Mmmm...pistachios, creamed corn, and ... I'm allergic to kiwi."

That's specific.

"Okay, no pistachios or creamed corn and definitely no kiwi. Not sure I've ever bought a kiwi."

"My tongue swells."

"Are you serious?"

"Yeah."

I embraced her. That was a little unnerving. Plus, I liked her tongue the way it was.

Just the way it is.

"Okay, I'll text you with directions to where I live."

"I'd bettered get to my training session or Kai will think I flaked on her."

"Have a good day."

"You too, Jude. Talk to you later." Her warm lips pecked my cheek and I smiled.

"Bye, Beautiful."

"Bye."

I talked to Kai briefly this morning about Presley's workout, suggesting an emphasis on developing a little more junk in the trunk. Kai punched my arm. Really hard! She claimed that choice was only up to Presley and until Presley said she wanted a bigger butt, Kai was going to maintain *not* growing any part of Presley. Then she punched me again. I wouldn't want to meet Kai in a dark alley or really piss her off. Not sure what branch of the military she was in, but Kai definitely knew how to strike with accuracy and force.

I admired the view from afar as Kai led Presley through a tough workout. An interesting part of the routine didn't get by me. Kai added in more lunges and three sets of prone leg lifts on a stability ball and she had Presley do the stair machine for cardio. All three were highly effective ways of developing—or at least tightening—the glutes.

Thank you, Kai.

However, Presley was as perfect, inside and out, as I had ever wanted and dreamed for. No matter what, she always would be. Perfect was a lofty aspiration but when you were patient, which I'm usually not, and you kept your eyes open, which I usually don't, it could happen. She had qualities I'd come to appreciate in a woman, some of the same qualities I'd found in other women I loved … honesty, humorous, adventurous, and successful, all in a beautiful package that made my head and heart know I'd love to be hers, if she would trust me and let me in completely.

My phone buzzed in my pocket.

Kiera: **Hope all okay. I'm in Omaha for couple of nights on business. Can you do dinner or are you still busy with your "something"?**

Kiera was a good friend. I could talk about Presley to her.

Jude: **I'll make you dinner, my house 6pm?**

I prepared for my next appointment.

Kiera: **Great, text address. See you then.**

Jude: **Will do.**

Kiera: **Lots to catch up on. Have a good day**

Jude: **Me too. Later.**

My four scheduled clients did a great job to help the day move along. This was what I was meant to do, helping people be healthy and create the body they've always wanted or keep the body they've always loved. I felt like a Frankenstein wannabe—in control, but without all the electricity and dead bodies. I liked my clients alive, and I attempted to keep them that way.

I met with a new client. Jack had been given doctors' instructions to lose weight or, as he told me, "I'll be dead in five years." When someone said that to me, the pressure was huge. I wouldn't let him down. Now my job was to keep him coming here so together we could help him get healthy. We set up a reasonable plan for commitment. Baby steps.

After work, I bought groceries to make dinner. I showered and prepped the meal while drinking a beer and listening to a Fitz and the Tantrums CD. I texted Presley while I waited.

Jude: **Missing you. Have a good evening.**

I stopped and considered telling her that Kiera was coming over. It was just two friends getting together. She didn't need to worry. She would. I decided against it. She texted back almost immediately.

Presley: **Hi. Missing you, too. Enjoy your night. Get some rest, you're gonna need it. See you tomorrow after work.**

Great that she's coming out of her shell.

Jude: **Looking forward to it.**

Presley: **:-)**

****

The doorbell rang right before six.

"Hey, Kiera."

"Jude, God, it's been forever."

I ushered her in and she walked into my chest, her cheek planting against my collarbone, her arms wrapped me in a long squeeze. The moment felt good but the usual physical attraction wasn't there.

She took in the surroundings as I took her in. Kiera's crystal blue eyes and deep violet-red hair had always been a potent combination. Add in her peachy clear skin and she turned heads faster than a Playboy centerfold. And her body ... curves, curves, curves. She was *all* woman, everywhere. Successful as a contractor in the information technologies field, a powerful woman in a mostly man's world, and she liked it that way.

"Great to see you. What brings you to Omaha?"

"Well, let's have a seat and I'll tell you, Mr. Impatient."

Maybe I've always had that personality trait?

"Let me check on dinner."

"Smells great." Kiera rounded the corner to the kitchen.

I pointed to the breakfast bar seats. "Thanks. White wine or beer?"

"You're a bartender and all you have is white wine and beer?"

I sighed loudly. This was the way we were. She busted my balls, and I enjoyed every minute.

"Beer, please," she said with a cute smirk.

I got her a bottle and checked on the chicken and rice dish.

Mom insisted Zane and I learn to cook. Got a dump truck-load of shit from my friends about how "Mommy needed to turn her big boys into little girls," but I'm pretty sure those assholes are the ones eating what tastes like shit now, cause I could cook just about anything. I'd be the first to admit Mom was right. A guy who can cook is, as she would say with that tone that told me it was very important, "A very, *very* attractive quality to a woman, Jude Elliott."

"I'm moving to Omaha, Jude," Kiera said to my back.

I closed the oven door and removed the oven mitts. "That's great. Can't wait to introduce you to—"

I turned around and Kiera was right in front of me. She had backed me into the countertop.

"I'd like us to start over."

Her hands wrapped around my neck and yanked my head toward a kiss. It took a moment for every part of me to comprehend what was happening and I pulled away from her. When I raised my head, my eyes didn't meet Kiera's blue ones. They stared over her head into shimmering green ones outside of the kitchen window. I stayed locked to those gorgeous eyes and Kiera spun to see what I was looking at.

And the emerald gems were gone.

"Presley, wait!"

Kiera jumped. I moved her out of my way and sprinted to the door. My heart pounded to the quick beat of my feet.

"Presley! Stop! Please!"

As I hit the driveway I only saw taillights of a white sedan screaming down the street. I pulled out my phone and dialed Presley. No answer. I turned around and in front of the garage was a bag full of Chinese food, dropped. A surprise. For me ... for us. Containers broken open, like Presley surely felt.

"Shit!"

I ran my hand through my hair. With her trust issues, this wasn't a smart idea. She was my girlfriend and even if I thought she wouldn't like the truth, she deserved to know that I was having another woman to my home.

Man, you messed up. No, you fucked up royally.

"Jude, are you okay?" Kiera's voice called from the porch.

"Yeah. Give me a minute," I returned almost calmly.

She headed back inside.

I picked up the bag and scooped up its contents, opened the garage door with the keypad, and dumped the bag into the trash. I tried Presley's phone one more time.

Please, answer.

I resorted to a text.

Jude: **Please give me a chance to explain. What you saw was a moment—not the full story. She's an old friend**

I stopped typing because that was not the truth and she deserved the truth. I backed that bullshit off the screen.

Jude: **Please answer your phone and give me a chance to explain. If I don't hear from you in ten minutes I'm calling you again.**

Back inside, I explained to Kiera what was going on. She apologized. I reminded her that she couldn't have known. I didn't tell her and I should've.

"Jude, you want to go find her?"

"Kind of, but I also want Presley to realize that I'm a good guy and I wouldn't hurt her on purpose. I want her to trust me."

"You trust her?"

"One hundred percent."

"You love her?"

I smiled at what I used to think was my future. I didn't hesitate. "One thousand percent."

"Wow." Kiera took a long drink of her beer. She cleared her throat. "Honestly, a little hard to hear, but I'm happy for you, Jude. I'm glad you found someone. She was beautiful, from what I saw streak past the window."

"She is. What do you think? Do I go after her? Give her the night to sleep on it? Text her? I texted her I would call her."

"Then call her!"

Woman, you were always so bossy, but usually right, too.

"All right." I held up my hands in surrender at her redheaded temper.

I dialed. No answer, again. My shoulders dropped.

Kiera pounded her fists on the table. "Fucking text her!"

"Okay. Okay!"

Forgot how overbearing she could be.

Jude: **Here's the truth. That was my girlfriend from ISU, Kiera Maxwell. She's in town for the night. I invited her to dinner at my place. No, I didn't tell her about you and no, I didn't tell you about her. Didn't think there was anything to tell. She told me she was going to be moving to Omaha and she tried to kiss me. That's what you saw. I did not kiss her. Then I ran after you, because Presley, I only want you. Beautiful, I want YOU! Not her.**

Before sending the text, I showed it to Kiera.

She frowned. "Well, the start is okay, except say *ex*-girlfriend—not girlfriend." She rolled her eyes and I made the reasonable change. "And delete 'I didn't think there was anything to tell.' Are you asking to be slapped? Of course you should have told her you were having dinner with another woman!"

I mumbled a curse word under my breath.

"You're not gonna unless you make this right," my irritating friend responded under her breath before taking a drink of her beer.

I chuckled. "Okay. Then…" I motioned for her to continue her mocking and pseudo-helping me.

"The rest is good, until 'Beautiful, I want you!' I can't believe I'm actually doing this! I'm getting you together with another girl? I've got to be nuts 'cause I know what a catch she's getting. Judas!"

"You know that's not my name … Kiki."

She smiled. "Just wanted to hear you call me that one more time." She narrowed her sparkling blue eyes at me. "You'd bettered find me a nice guy here in Omaha for this. Pronto!"

"I think I have more important things to work on right now, but I'll see what I can do. *After* I get my girlfriend back."

Kiera chuckled and leaned back in her chair.

I tapped my fingers on the counter. "So what about 'Beautiful, I want you?"

"Take it out. It's begging. No woman wants a man to beg. We want you to find your fucking balls and testicle up! Be a man. Tell us what you want, what you need, admit when you're wrong, and tell us how you're going to make up for it—but don't beg for it."

I looked over the words again. I knew Presley and the words felt right but I deleted them. "All right."

Jude: **Here's the truth. That was my ex-girlfriend from ISU, Kiera Maxwell. She's in town for the night. I invited her to dinner at my place. No, I didn't tell her about you and no, I didn't tell you about her. I'm sorry, that was wrong. She told me she was going to be moving to Omaha and she tried to kiss me. That's what you saw. I did NOT kiss her. Then I ran after you, because Presley, I only want you. Not her.**

I showed the text to Kiera. She nodded and I hit send.

Kiera blew out a long breath. "Well, I wanted to get screwed tonight. I guess I kind of did."

"I think we both did, Kiera. Let's have some dinner."

Chapter Twenty-Four

Presley

Mondays were not my favorite. Plus, knowing I had to work late tonight was going to make the day drag. To top off my dread for the day, Drexel was being weird. Like really creepy weird. When I walked in the door, he asked me how I was doing and seemed sincere … and my skin tried to eject like a parachute off my body. I demanded it remain where it was.

I avoided him for the rest of the day, but around four p.m., he poked his blue eyes in my office door.

"Hey, Presley, was talking to Sam and we both like your headshot for April's Salesman … shit! I mean Salesperson of the Month. Great picture."

I rolled my eyes, but I had to admit, Mark did a great job. The picture wasn't like Drexel's. His was all business—suit, tie, serious. Mine was much more me. Soft and approachable, not stuffy. I was thinking of getting a copy for Jude to have. After all, I had a picture of him … all of him. I wouldn't admit to him that I kept a copy of the drawing, but I did.

Drexel sighed. "Anyway, I have some follow-ups coming in tonight, you want me to cover your late night?"

"Really?"

"Yeah, go on. Sam's staying and so is Marcus. We've got it covered."

"You're just trying to keep me from being the May Salesperson of the Month." He shook his head. "Aren't you?"

I noticed how friendly his smile could actually be. I sent back a genuine one.

"No, I'm done being a jackass to you." He shoved his hands in his pockets. "Um, you have a beautiful smile, Presley."

"Thanks, Dix..." I coughed. "Drexel." That was a scary almost slip-up. "If you're sure, I'd love to surprise my boyfriend with dinner tonight."

His face paled. "He's your boyfriend?"

"Yeah." I glanced to make sure my computer was shutting down. When I looked back, his eyebrows almost touched to one another. "Are you okay, Drexel?"

"Well, I ... I was wondering..." His face flushed deeper with each word of the broken sentence and he leaned back into the hallway. "Yeah, I heard you, Sam. I'll be right there." He leaned back in. "Can we talk tomorrow?"

"Sure." I stood and grabbed my purse from my top drawer. "Thanks again for covering my shift, Drexel. I owe you one."

"I'll be looking forward to payback, Miss Perfect."

I tipped my head at him. He looked me up and down, sighed and left.

That was weird.

I texted Willow on the way to my car.

Prez: **Can you find out Jude's address from Kanyon? Want to surprise him with dinner...and something else? ;-)**

Stopped at a light, I checked my phone.

Willow: **It's 11008 White Street the north side of the duplex. Have fun. Text if you'll be staying ALL night. I'll take care of the panting fluff ball.**

Prez: **Thanks! Will do and her name is Foo-Foo.**

Willow: **I will never call her that ridiculous name.**

I laughed.

After stopping off to let Foo-Foo do her thing, I picked up Chinese food. God only knew what Jude ate on a daily basis. A never-ending supply of protein bars and shakes? Gross.

I pulled in behind a blue sedan with a rental sticker on the back bumper at the address Willow texted.

Maybe the girls next door have someone over?

I balanced the food while I reached for the doorbell when movement inside the house caught my eye. I turned to my right and my body froze as I glanced inside. A beautiful tall redhead had her hands on Jude's face. When his eyes connected with mine, the moment was like a plug to a socket. Electricity flowed through us and I was electrocuted from the inside out.

I spun while hearing Jude yell my name. My body moved independently of my thoughts. I tripped on the last step and the food crashed to the ground. I left the brown bag and contents littering the driveway. The frantic beating of my heart and the bile rising in my throat had me on one mission. Get the hell out of there.

I squealed the tires from the driveway, driving way too fast and shaking uncontrollably. Stopping the car blocks away and over a hill, I let go of every emotion, and after opening my door, the contents of my stomach. I had to force myself to stop vomiting, knowing it wasn't healthy. I had to keep better control of my physical response to my emotions.

My phone rang in my purse and without seeing who it was, because I knew who it was, I turned the phone off. I collected myself for the drive home. How could I be so stupid?

Inside the house, Foo-Foo ignored her food and took care of me instead. Her body nuzzled into mine, trying so hard to make me feel better. And I did, marginally. I crashed in a crying heap onto the bed while she stared up at me from her bed on the floor.

He seemed so genuine. So real. And so right. At least you found out before—

I woke up exhausted. My sleep was sporadic. Remnants of mascara and eyeliner ran down my face in charcoal lines of pain. It wasn't a great look.

"Fucking men!" I gazed into the mirror at what was scary enough to chase any testosterone-based life-form away. Foo-Foo tipped her head and lay down prone while yapping her own disgust.

A shower and coffee did their part in getting me to a more presentable state of being. The dealership was almost comforting. Safe and friendly. I tried to put pep in my step to fake happiness until the emotion was real. I failed miserably.

Late in the afternoon I was having a mini-meltdown alone in my office, my chair turned away from the door.

"Hey…" Drexel rounded the corner into my office.

I wondered if I was actually in hell as I spun my chair to face him.

His All-American boy features softened when he saw me. "What's wrong, Miss Perfect?"

"Nothing," I mumbled. "What do you want?" I wiped my face with a tissue.

"Stand up!" he declared, almost as a demand.

"Drexel, I don't need any of your bullshit today. I'm not in the mood. Please leave." The words came out through broken sobs.

He closed my door, walked around my desk, pulled me from my chair, and wrapped his arms around me in a warm hug. Without warning, I detonated into a mass of blubbering XX chromosome in his arms. It was heartbroken female Chernobyl in my office and people walking by the glass-fronted door scampered by like the emotional radiation would seep out and contaminate them. I didn't know how long I continued to make a scene but when I slowed the leaking fluids, Drexel glanced down and smiled at me. Like ... genuinely smiled.

What the hell?

"Okay, got that out of your system?" He wiped the tears from my cheeks.

"Yeah, thanks." I tried to step away and his arms continued to hold me firmly.

"I take it New Guy was an ass?"

"How'd you figure that out?" The sarcasm was veiled by a small whimper of sadness when the memory of Jude and the redhead filled my thoughts.

"Not that I'm proud of it, but I've made one too many girls look like you look, Presley ... lost, hurt, destroyed." He softly rubbed my back as he spoke.

"Yep, basically how I feel, just add foolish and betrayed."

"So tell me the story."

"You don't want to listen to my verbal blubbering, Drexel. Thanks for the offer. You can leave and pretend you didn't see anything." I pushed him away and sat back down.

"Nope, not going anywhere until you spill. I'm here for you, Presley." He plopped in a chair.

I gave him the abridged version, more to get him to leave than for support.

"Sorry. That sucks." He cleared his throat. "Presley, I don't want to be the unsupportive jerk you probably already think I am, but do you think that maybe it was all a mistake? Maybe just bad timing and circumstances? Have you talked to Jude today?"

"No, and I'm not going to." I wiped my nose. "I'm going to move on and be okay."

"Well, in that case ... um ... want to get a drink tonight?"

My head snapped up at his question.

Does Drexel actually like me?

His baby blue eyes roamed my face before dropping to my desk and examining my nameplate like he'd never seen it before.

"You weren't lying last Friday in the copy room, were you?" I leaned forward and rested my elbows on my desk.

"About what?" He messed with the paperweight on the edge of my desk, spinning it like a top.

I placed my hand on top of his to stop the juvenile fidgeting. "About actually being interested in me."

His eyes slid up to mine. "I wasn't."

I went to open my mouth but he held up his other hand to stop me.

"And I know what a prick I've been to you. If the dealership was an elementary school playground, I've figuratively pulled your pigtails for two years. Hell, I kind of ripped your hair out at the roots. I'm sorry for that."

"So, even before I lost the weight?"

"You've always been perfect to me, Presley, that's why I call you Miss Perfect. I mean it." His eyes softened and he swallowed hard. "The way you sell cars is fucking hot, your sassy and strong personality is fucking hot, and now your amazing body is fucking hot, but that one didn't matter to me. It only adds to your hotness factor."

"Holy shit, Drexel." I drew my hand from his slowly. "I don't know what to say."

"Say you'll have a drink with me. You owe me one for last night."

"I don't know, Drex. I'm messed up. I'm confused, and I really just need a friend."

He was silent for a moment, then he asked, "Do you hate me?" He leaned back in his chair and grabbed the arms as if to brace for bad news.

"No, of course not."

"Would you ever want to be my friend?"

I paused to consider my answer carefully. "I think we could build a friendship, if *this* Drexel is for real. Honestly, I don't think I'd ever feel more."

He rose from the chair and turned toward the door. "Friends it is. I'll see you at six. Does Firebirds sound okay?"

"Sounds good. See you later."

"Later, Miss Perfect."

****

I closed a sale and was feeling better by the end of the afternoon. I grabbed my phone from my purse and after turning it on I avoided the messages from Jude. All five text messages and two voicemails. *And* two e-mails? How did he even get my e-mail address? Triple R! Talk about stalker.

I called Willow.

"Hey, Prez," she answered with a reserved tone. "How are you?"

"You heard me last night, didn't you?"

"Yeah, when I got home from Kanyon's. Wanna talk about it?"

"I went to his home and saw him with a redhead through the window."

"What the fuck? Are you serious?"

"Yes, I am."

"Did he say anything?"

"He yelled for me to wait but I didn't. He's texted a few times. I'm not going to read them. He left voice mails. I'm not going to listen to them. He even found my e-mail in my Triple R file and sent me two e-mails—not interested in what they have to say. But actually, that's not why I'm calling."

Willow cleared her throat. "Maybe you should listen to the messages, Presley."

"I can't. I thought he was different. I thought he…" I started to choke up but I gritted my teeth. "Anyway, I'm going to Firebirds to have a drink with Drexel after work."

"Presley, come on … Dixless? He's never been nice to you."

"He admitted he likes me, always has." Realizing I was tired of not saying the three-letter word that held some imaginary grasp on me, I added, "Even when I was fat. That's why he always calls me Miss Perfect 'cause he actually means it, even though I'm far from it. I'm not going to jump from one guy to another. I don't like Drexel that way. I'll be fine."

"Prez, please…"

Just the tone she started the sentence with told me it wasn't something I wanted to hear right now, even if it was the best advice in the world. She couldn't always be by my side to coddle me and make things better. I needed to stand strong by myself.

"I only called to let you know what was going on so you wouldn't worry. Have a good night. Good-bye, Willow."

Chapter Twenty-Five

Jude

I focused on work after I texted Presley again. The third one today. Had a feeling I wasn't done. Far from done. I left two voice messages, both simple, asking for a minute of her time to talk. They still sounded like begging. I went a step further to reduce my manhood and e-mailed her twice, misusing my authority to gain access to her e-mail address. Getting fired was the least of my worries today. I guaranteed my balls were ready to jump off my body in a revolt of my behavior, and I was pretty sure Kiera would suggest a testiclectomy if she heard I had done exactly what she'd told me not to. I was a certified begging nut-bag.

Before I left Triple R, I texted Presley one more time.

It was confirmed. No testicles.

But in reality, I was doing this because I *had* testicles. I'd let this woman into my heart and as much as I wanted and needed her, she wanted and needed me, too. I wasn't going to give up easily and if she thought we were done, she was wrong.

Shit, I sound like an obsessed man. Really, I wasn't. I was just in love. Painfully, and maybe hopelessly in love with Presley Bradenhurst.

I drove home on autopilot. My phone rang in my gym bag. Normally I didn't answer while driving, but I was hoping it was Presley. It was Willow, and my curiosity still got the better of me.

"Hi, Willow."

"Hey, Jude. You still at Triple R?"

"No, almost home. What's up?"

"Hey, I think you need to hear something."

"Okay."

There was a long silence. I pulled the phone away to see if the call dropped but the signal was still connected.

"Willow, you still there?"

"Yeah, just wondering if I should interfere or let Presley make her own mistakes."

"Now you're worrying me."

Mistakes? Am I one of those?

"You should be. She's going out for drinks with—"

"Don't say it!"

"Yeah, Dixless. He's fed her some bullshit line about how he's always liked her even before she lost the weight and that she's his Miss Perfect. Now either he's truthful and he's the most emotionally stunted jerk ever, or he's playing her to get in her pants. Either way, I don't like it."

I don't like it either.

"And where are they having this drink?"

Willow made a strained noise. I couldn't do anything to change what happened last night, but I could do something about what might happen tonight. I fucked up, but not again.

"Willow! I love Presley. I need her, I want her, and I will be hers forever, if she'll take me back. And if she doesn't, I will compare every girl to her for the rest of my life. If not for me and not for Presley, then do it for those girls who will get their hearts broken when they can't live up to what *I* think is perfect."

Willow's voice was gravelly with emotion. "That was beautiful." She cleared her throat. "Up until the weird and creepy logic at the end but the fact that you admitted you love Presley, well, that means something to me. So, Ponytail, explain the redhead to me before I decide to tell you or not."

After I finished with my story, Willow sighed into the phone. "I figured. She just can't let the past go. Firebirds at Village Point. Go get her, Jude, and please keep your tongue out of anyone's mouth that isn't Presley's."

I chuckled. "There was no tongue, but I got it. Thanks, Willow. How are things with Kanyon?"

"I get to meet Grace tonight, so you tell me."

"That's great. She's an amazing little girl. She adores her daddy, though it might take a little time for her to warm up to you." I pulled into the driveway of the duplex.

"I know, just hoping she will someday."

"She will. Wish me luck."

"Ponytail, you don't need luck. You have love."

I disconnected the call on that comment because I wanted to keep the words fresh in my memory.

After a quick shower and fresh clothes, I headed back out the door at half past six. I tapped out a frantic rhythm to Eminem's "Berzerk" on the steering wheel. My brain buzzed with a million questions.

Should I wait outside and talk to her at her car? Should I make a huge scene and tell her I love her? Should I creep from afar, unless he touches her? Wait until their date is over to approach her? Should I just beat the crap out of him?

I wasn't a violent or short-tempered guy, but Dixless might change my ways.

I parked my truck next to Presley's sedan. From where I was, I could see them on the patio. Bringing out my phone, I texted Presley one last time. If this went badly, I wanted her to know how I really felt.

I took a few deep breaths and stepped out.

****

Presley

We walked into the restaurant and agreed the patio was a good choice. The weather held in the upper 70s and a light spring breeze flowed through as we took seats at a high-top table. The sunset provided a beautiful background, and the easy listening music filtering through the air calmed me. An acoustic version of "Someone Like You" came on and the words sunk into me, making me question what I was doing here with Drexel.

My mind kept wandering to yesterday morning when Jude stopped me at Triple R. There'd been a new intensity between us. Something had been left unsaid.

What if Drexel was right? Maybe I should let Jude explain? Maybe I'd made a big deal out of nothing and if he explained I would laugh at the truth.

Yeah, that would never happen.

I cared for Jude too much to be that flippant with our relationship. Maybe that was the point? If I didn't care, I wouldn't react? I missed him so much that every heartbeat chugged along in my chest, every breath wasn't full of life, and every smile held less happiness.

Brought back from my attention wanderlust by Drexel's tenor voice, I was afraid that conversation between us wouldn't happen easily, but I was proved wrong. We talked about baseball, work, and family. I didn't know he played ball for the Kansas City Royals for two years before having to leave his pitching career due to an injury. I didn't know he started out as a detailer at a dealer when he was in high school and although he liked car sales, he didn't love it. He would rather go back to school and get a master's degree in counseling to help kids with behavioral issues. He had a brother and a sister. His sister stayed home with three kids and his brother was a doctor. His brother and partner were adopting this year. Drexel's blue eyes twinkled and his smile beamed when he talked about his two musically talented nephews and his baseball-loving niece. Apparently she had him wrapped around her finger, and from what I could tell, he didn't care. In fact, it was clear that he loved it.

Everything he said was honest and real. He could be charming when he wanted to be. We moved to a different place with each other. Friendship. As long as he didn't return to his reign in Jerk City, I was good with keeping our relationship right at this level, but there would be no moving up in the ranks of affection.

He had a lot to offer someone but he didn't have the things I'd found in Jude. The things I couldn't imagine living without.

Like his cocky but restrained cockiness.
I smirked at the thought.
His impatient-patience.
I bit my lip.
His ability to say just the right thing to me.
I sighed loudly.

Just talking to Drexel cemented that I had found the person I wanted to spend the rest of my life with and trying to fit someone else into that mold would be both heartless and pointless.

There was no substitution for Jude Saylor and his ponytail. I needed to bow out of this and find him.

Drexel started a new conversation about travel. My phone buzzed in my purse and I dug to find it.

"Sorry, Drexel."

He waved my apology off and called the waitress over to order me another martini and some appetizers to share. He handed the waitress something, said something ending with a loud sigh, and the waitress gave him a friendly smile. I typed in my access code and Jude's texts hit my screen. I tried to get rid of his newest message but

I didn't move fast enough as the text flashed on the screen.

I inhaled sharply.

"What?" Drexel's eyes narrowed.

I reread the text and my eyes watered.

I started from the first text Jude sent me last night and read through today's texts. What I should've done before I agreed to have drinks with another man.

Jude: **Here's the truth. That was my ex-girlfriend from ISU, Kiera Maxwell. She's in town for the night. I invited her to dinner at my place. No, I didn't tell her about you and no, I didn't tell you about her. I'm sorry, that was wrong. She told me she was going to be moving to Omaha and she tried to kiss me. That's what you saw. I did NOT kiss her. Then I ran after you, because Presley, I only want you. Not her.**

My chest constricted.

It is a misunderstanding.

Jude: **I'm sorry. I know they are only words but I really do mean them. I don't want to be vague by text. Please let me explain.**

My heart pounded.

He means them and he remembers I don't like vague answers.

Jude: **If you are still awake, can you please just let me know that you are okay? I'm worried about you.**

My lips quivered.

He worries because he cares ... about me.

Jude: **Good morning (well, not good). Again, I'm sorry for what happened last night. I want to say thank you for trying to surprise me with Chinese food. That was very thoughtful. I'm sorry you're the** one who really got a surprise. I'd like a chance to talk to you, just hear me out for five minutes, please.

My hands shook.

He wants to talk.

Jude: **Hope your day is going okay. We're supposed to have dinner tonight. If your schedule is still open, I'd still like to make you dinner and talk. Please, Presley.**

My stomach dropped.

It should be Jude sitting across from me.

Jude: **I feel like a stalker. I don't know what more to say. I already miss you, Presley. Kiera told me women don't like men to beg, but I'm going to ignore her. Please, Presley, all I ask is a few minutes to talk. Please.**

My heart rose.

He was ignoring her advice because he knew what I needed to hear.

And the text he just sent me.

Jude: **I should have told you yesterday morning when I wanted to but I thought saying the words would make you run from me. That happened anyway. I have nothing to lose. Presley Bradenhurst, I love you and I always will.**

My eyes closed.

He loves me, too.

Drexel reached across the table to squeeze my other hand. "What's wrong?"

"Presley."

My heart exploded in my chest upon hearing the familiar deep-tone boom.

Drexel released my hand and turned in his seat.

When I brought my eyes up, like always, I wasn't prepared for the vision of the beautiful man that had painted his name across my heart in a colorful script.

"Hey." Drexel eyed Jude up and Jude stepped to the table.

"Jude Saylor." He held out his hand.

"Drexel Mason." They shook hands while I wiped my tears. "So you're Presley's boyfriend?"

Jude didn't hesitate. "I am. And you're the guy who acts like an ass to her because you would like to be her boyfriend, but you're not."

Drexel's jaw ticked, but he chuckled lightly. "Yes, Jude, I know what you have, and honestly, I'm pissed as hell at myself that I missed my chance." Drexel stood. "But after sitting here and having her a million miles away, I'm assuming thinking about you, I know I'm too late. Right, Miss Perfect?"

I nodded the tiniest of nods to let him know he was right.

Jude stepped closer to him. "You don't get to call her that *ever* again, Dixless."

After having a long stare-down with Jude, Drexel twisted to me. "Is that what you call me?" His bright blue eyes dimmed.

"I'm sorry, Drexel. My roomie made up the nickname after you sprayed my white dress-shirt with water in the break room."

Jude grunted his disapproval at that bit of information.

It was a long time ago.

Drexel closed his eyes and shook his head at himself. "All right, maybe I deserved the nickname." He reopened his eyes and smirked. "That was an entertaining day though, very eye-opening."

I rolled my eyes.

"It's time to leave, Mason." Jude's body language was like a peacock ready to defend its mate.

Fitting.

"Okay, okay!" Drexel held up his hands in surrender. "I get the point. No need to go all protective mammal on me, Saylor. See you at work tomorrow, Miss … Presley. Good night and good luck, Jude." Drexel turned and walked out the side fence to his car.

Jude watched until he drove from the parking lot.

The waitress came over with the appetizers and my second martini. She skimmed Jude up and down. I cleared my throat at her. She dropped the food and drink and hightailed it away.

Jude rounded the table, stopping beside my chair. "Did you get my messages?"

"I read the texts right before you showed. I'm assuming Willow—"

"Yes, she did. Can we talk, please, Prez?"

"There's nothing to talk about."

His face washed of all emotion, his hazel eyes clouded to a smoky brown, and the glitter of gold disappeared. "So we're done? I can't believe you won't just—"

I tugged his shirt and guided him in between my legs. We'd gained the attention of most of the guests on the patio, but I didn't care. I ran a hand down his handsome face, the whiskers tickling my palm. "I should have told you yesterday morning when I wanted to but I thought saying the words would make you run. Now I have everything to gain. Jude Saylor, I love you and…" I gazed deep into his beautiful eyes as they gained back their sparkle. "I always will."

The gasping of onlookers gave me goose bumps.

Jude cracked his smirky smile. "No more running, Presley."

The words were a demand, not a question, and at this moment it was clear—I never would run, ever again.

"Couldn't even if I wanted to." I winked. "Asthma."

He chuckled but stopped and sighed. "I love you, Presley Bradenhurst."

"I love you, Ponytail."

Using the grip I had on his shirt, I tugged his body to mine and he closed the distance. His lips met mine. The cheers around us made us giggle against each other's mouths.

"Wanna come to my house?" I asked in his ear.

"No."

I started to back away.

"No, Presley, I want you to come to my house. I have a motorcycle we need to ride."

I puffed a desire-filled breath into his ear and nuzzled into his neck, grabbing the soft skin with my teeth, leaving a light red mark.

My mark.

"Get ready to call in sick tomorrow cause I'm gonna shatter your world over and over and over again," he whispered into my ear, nipping at my lobe which sent shivers of anticipation through me. "Let's go."

"Need to pay." I called the waitress over.

She stepped to the table. "Your other guy got it. Told me he had a feeling he'd be leaving early and alone."

Jude threw his head back laughing. "At least Dixless knows when he's struck out."

After playing major league baseball, he really does.

Chapter Twenty-Six

Jude

I followed Presley to her house. She collected Foo-Foo's dog items and her own to stay over while I played with the dog in the backyard. I could feel the anticipation in the air and a little anxiety on Presley's side.

"Jude, I'm ready," she yelled from the kitchen.

I picked up the tiny ball of white and dropped my mouth to Foo's ear. "Foo-Foo, you need to be nice to my cat, Ninja. Don't expect you to be friends right away. Give him time and he'll come around. Or I guess you'll be mortal enemies and that's okay, too."

She barked and I laughed.

When I got to the door, Presley's smile told me I had done something she liked. "What were you telling Foo-Foo?"

"I was letting her know that Ninja's not a huge dog fan, but not to take it personally." I stopped inside the door. "Are you okay, Prez?"

She tipped her head and nodded but her silence spoke more than a multi-volume novel.

"Anything you want to know about last night?" I asked.

Presley bit her lip. "How long did she stay?"

"Until nine."

"Did she kiss you?"

"No."

"Do you still have feelings for her?"

"Nothing more than friendship."

"Are you going to see her again?"

"Only if you're there with me."

"Do these questions make me seem psycho?"

"Yes, but I love your kind of psycho."

She laughed and pulled on my arm. "Let's go. There's a motorcycle I'm dying to ride."

I snarled low and animal-like at her and she let out a shriek of fake fear. If my imagination was anything like what would happen on that bike, it was hot and I was going to need to clean it up. The bike, not my imagination.

Before we made it to the door, I shuffled to a stop. Presley turned. "What's wrong?"

I stretched the words. "You have any condoms?"

"What? I have to bring my own protection?" she said with fake shock while she moved her hand up to my neck. I adjusted Foo-Foo to sit under one arm so I could pull my girlfriend close.

I kissed down the side of Presley's soft neck. "We can stop and I'll get some. Not a problem."

"I have some in my bag. Have you always been safe?"

"Yes, and I've been tested ... clean, no partners after my test."

"Then I'll let you decide. I've been on the pill for years. I can't say an accident wouldn't ever happen, but as far as I know, I'm covered. And since I've only had sex about a dozen times, and we used condoms, I'm 99.9 percent sure I'm clean, too."

A dozen times?

I dipped my head and grazed her lips. "Honestly, not to scare you, but someday in the future, to have our baby inside of you will be the greatest gift, besides yourself, that you will ever give me, Presley."

Then I realized we'd never talked about kids and if she wanted them, but what I saw in her eyes wasn't fear of the idea. It was love. And it rocked my world as well as the weightlifter's. I raised my eyebrows and her eyes widened.

"Apparently, somebody really likes that idea." She moved closer to me, pressing my erection against my lower stomach. "Really, *really* likes that idea, and you know I can't say I disagree with him. Are you sure you don't want to stay here?"

"Yes. I'm sure." The blood started to stream from my head to below the belt. "I think." I took a deep breath. "Let's go before I change my mind."

After the quick drive, Presley and I had Foo-Foo settled in my side of the duplex. Ninja came out of hiding and acted like the little dog was completely annoying but that he couldn't care less. She licked his face and he jumped onto the back of the chair, looking down on the playful fuzzball as if to say, "Felines rule, canines drool." Presley drew her hand down Ninja's back, and he was in heaven.

"Are you hungry?"

"Not for food," she returned with a husky timbre.

"Presley…" I pulled her against me. "I want to make love to you, but I haven't eaten since eleven this morning. I have to eat or I may just pass out from the blood rushing to my weightlifter."

Shit, did I just say that?

"Weightlifter?" Her head shook on the word.

I looked down and shrugged my shoulders.

She broke out laughing. "You did not name your penis the weightlifter!"

My ego took a small hit, but I recovered quickly. "I did." I walked backward to the kitchen. "Want a glass of wine?"

"Yes, please. Well, I'm pretty impressed with the weightlifter. I hope he's ready to *get pumped*." She said the last words like a 'roided up bodybuilder.

Oh, I'll show you pumped.

I spun and picked her up, and she released a happy little squeal of surprise. I set her on the counter and started our night out right. My mouth covered hers, my tongue licked along her delicate lips, and teeth pulled at the plump flesh. Her hands rounded my neck, pulling me as close as I could be. I tugged her forward on the counter and our bodies connected intimately through our clothes. Her thin yoga pants didn't provide any substantial coverage to prevent the bulge in my jeans from being evident. I rolled my hips, rubbing the hardness against her. The friction caused her to moan deeply. Her head crashed into the crook of my neck, vibrating her want against my skin.

"How's that for pumped?" My lips were right at her ear, pulsating the words in time to my hips.

Her fingers dug through my hair, nails scraped across my scalp and sent skin-rippling tremors down my spine.

"Do you really need to eat?" Her breathy voice weakened my knees. She turned her head and her eyes glowed with passion.

"I could eat you instead."

I slid my lips down her neck, pulling the skin through my teeth.

Presley's hands gripped my head and brought my eyes to hers. Her eyes heated to green fireballs. "Please."

I made quick work of getting her yoga pants and underwear off, then I dropped to my knees and lost myself in her heaven. I loved hearing her gasps as her fingers dug into my scalp when she was close to cresting. I brought her to the edge and back down several times. Her body trembled and calmed. It was a fine line between torture and building the height of her climax but since she was so responsive, I could tell when she was close but not going to shatter. She was at the point of no return when she gave me the raspiest moan, almost pained but in a good way. I helped her over the threshold into bliss and her body trembled beautifully. My hands grasped her hips and held her safely in place. Her mouth released my name in time with the waves of her orgasm, like a mantra of appreciation. I brought her down slowly and stood to view her beautiful green eyes ... so soft and so satiated.

I leaned in to give her a kiss.

"Jude?" Zane called out. "Hi, there. Who are you?" I heard him say to Foo-Foo and the tiny dog scampered into the kitchen.

Shit! I didn't even hear the door.

"Zane! Don't come in here!" I yelled before he walked into the kitchen. I moved to shield Presley's body in case he misunderstood the urgency of my words.

"Are you masturbating in the kitchen, dude?"

Presley burst out in a full-body laugh, throwing her head back and slamming it against the upper cabinets. I grabbed her head and kissed the pain away, and she continued to laugh.

I helped Presley to get her clothes back on.

"No, I'm not!" I called back. "If you can't hear, there is a beautiful female who is laughing wildly at your jackass comment. I'm not alone."

"Dude! Sorry. I can come back later. Just needed to grab something from my room."

Presley indicated she was fine with meeting him but she rolled a finger around at my face, signifying I needed to clean up.

"Wait a second, Zane." I helped Presley off of the counter and cleaned up at the sink. "Better?" I mouthed.

"Yes." She wiped my chin with a paper towel.

Presley kissed me deeply, her tongue searching for the flavor of her juices on my tongue.

"I taste good," she said, her voracious voice intoxicating.

"Fuck me," I moaned.

"Dude ... I heard that." Zane chuckled.

I led Presley into the entryway. "Presley Bradenhurst, I'd like you to meet my brother, Zane Saylor. Zane, this is Presley, my girlfriend."

"God, you're gorgeous. I mean, nice to meet you, Presley." Zane shook Presley's hand and held on for a moment, acquiring her full attention with his hazel eyes.

"Nice to meet you, too, Zane. I see both of the Saylor boys have the same excess problem with confidence."

Zane chuckled. "I like her, Jude. Sorry to interrupt, um, dinner?" Zane said, raising one eyebrow.

"Oh, don't worry. Jude only finished his first course. The main course and dessert are just heating up," Presley replied calmly and my eyes popped from my head.

Zane rolled with laughter while I yanked Presley close to me.

I laughed into her ear. "You are going to get it!"

"I hope so." Her fresh confidence made me want to chase Zane away to his own side of the duplex.

"Bro ... your shit. Get it now and leave." I kept my eyes on Presley.

Zane stopped laughing, caught my drift, and made his way to his room, returning with a bag full of items. The whole time he was gone I laid a long kiss on Presley.

Zane cleared his throat. "Nice meeting you, Presley, and maybe we can..." He squinted like he was trying to figure out the answer to the meaning of life. He shook his head. "Well, double plus-one date with you sometime?"

"Great idea. I know Yori from high school. Please tell her I said hello. Look forward to meeting Britney." Presley's hands were doing fantastic things to my ass inside the back pockets of my jeans as she spoke.

"Cool. Have fun, bro. Later, Presley." Zane closed the door behind him.

Presley pulled her hands from my jeans. "Okay, we'd better actually eat. My stomach is growling. Want help making something?"

I pecked her forehead with a kiss. "No, I've got it. How about pasta with sausage, tomatoes, and spinach?"

"Uh, what? You can actually cook?"

"Yeah." I pulled out ingredients and pans.

"So you don't have a fridge full of power shakes and cabinets full of power bars?"

I shook my head. "No. Is that what you thought I ate?"

"Well, that and probably delivery or carry-out?"

"My mom taught Zane and I how to cook real meals. I cook. Zane eats whatever someone sets in front of him. So does pasta sound okay?"

"Sure." She stretched the word like she didn't really believe the meal was going to happen or be edible.

She ended up eating two helpings and the sounds of approval she made while she was eating tortured me.

We cleaned up, the tension building, knowing that the evening was quickly progressing.

I walked Foo-Foo to wear her out, but picked her up and ran her back to the duplex when she indicated she'd had enough. When we made our way back inside, Presley wasn't in the kitchen or living room. I stepped into my bedroom and she was lying on her side, her beautiful black hair draping down her exposed shoulder.

"God, you look sexy as hell on my bed."

She looked up, her eyes hooded. "Your bed smells like you. An incredible combination of something sandalwood and cherry and a clean soapy scent. I've loved that smell from day one." Her sincerity flipped my heart in a way that had me wondering if she was for real.

I instructed Foo-Foo to lie in her dog bed, and she curled into a ball. I crawled onto the bed, facing Presley. My heart thudded like I was running a marathon. "Presley, I don't want to pressure you. We can wait if you need more time."

"I love you, Jude, and I want to make love with you. I want to fill every recess of my brain with memories we create together."

She stole the words from my heart.

"Me, too."

She rolled over me and straddled my waist. Our gaze connected before she lowered slowly to my chest and we united in a deep, wet kiss. Her hot tongue fluttered over mine, setting everything below my chest on fire. I loved how her hands roamed insistently but calmly over my body. Scorching fingertips trailed under the hem of my shirt. I grabbed the collar and pulled the fabric over my head. Her pupils expanded and her breathing quickened as she floated her soft fingers over my jumping flesh, gliding through every muscle with a fascinated gaze that I would remember forever.

"Presley," I moaned as she moved her hands lower on my body, outlining my hard cock through my jeans.

She unzipped the jeans and slid her hand inside, skimming along the weightlifter's length, causing a shiver through my body with every soft pass over its sensitive head. Hugging her to me, I rolled her and took a moment to gaze at the beautiful woman beneath me. My body responded with what felt like a blast of fire through every cell.

Pulling her t-shirt over her head and making quick work of the front-clasp bra, there was little question how beautiful she really was. My hand slid down her ribs. She had a large watercolor butterfly tattoo, a representation of the metamorphosis from caterpillar to butterfly.

"That's beautiful." I skimmed the butterfly's journey.

"I got it while I was losing the weight. It's my journey. Every twenty-five pounds I went back and got a new addition of the transformation to butterfly. That's a hundred pounds of tattoo, Jude."

"Presley, I can see in your eyes that you're worried about the weight coming back, but sweetheart, with the amount of exercise I have planned for you, well, you'll be working off lots of calories, both vertically and horizontally."

"I hope so."

Normally those words were almost a question but not this time. She meant them.

I cupped her supple breast. Lowering my head, I circled her nipple with my tongue, teasing the baby-pink skin and blowing air across it to watch it pucker to a stiff peak.

"Jude…" Her back arched at the combination.

I warmed her other breast with my mouth, enjoying her response as well as mine. My body kicked into high gear, hardening to an almost painfully aroused state. I kicked off my jeans and underwear while she watched, licking her lips, creating a dewy look that I couldn't resist. I pulled her to a sitting position and kissed her like tomorrow would never happen.

"I need you in my life forever, Beautiful."

"I need you, too, but like now!" She panted the words.

"Okay, hint taken."

After removing her yoga pants, I glided a finger inside of the slickened and engorged tissues that already tensed in small vibrations around my finger. Her body was ready. I just needed to know where her head was.

"Are you sure it's okay if I don't wear protection?"

Her hands searched my face. "That's up to you, but, please, Jude..." She extended my name as I rolled my thumb over her clit.

My heart crashed against the wall of my chest.

"Presley, I know you have my heart because every time you say *please* it makes that me want to make you happy, whatever it takes."

She jerked on my ponytail with insistence. "Then, Ponytail, *please*, make me happy."

I laid over her, soft body to hard body, lifted her legs around my waist, and in one smooth motion I thrust deep inside her welcoming body, flesh in flesh. The gasp we both released was full of excitement and a little apprehension.

"Are you okay, Beautiful?" I waited to move. Although she was slick and seemed ready, she was also tight and my concern seemed warranted.

She took several quick breaths with her eyes closed. Her long onyx lashes parted and the green orbs flashed. "I've never been better. I'm full of you. My heart, my body, my soul are all so full of you, Jude."

The words entered my body through my ears, but they stayed in my heart.

Our bodies synched and found a tender rhythm. Our eyes never left each other's, a circle of love. I reached between us to stroke lightly across her hard clit, and she inhaled quickly at the touch.

"Yes," she sighed. I rubbed again, her internal walls quivering along the length of me. "Jude! Oh, my Pony…" Her body began to spasm before she released the rest of the word. The sight of her lost to reality brought me closer to my own.

Presley's back arched and her whole body trembled. Her slickness embraced me, like every part of her wanted to hold onto me. I bucked against her faster, enjoying the continuing waves of fluttering pressure against me.

Heaven … pure heaven.

"Presley, I love you."

I reached my own release. My face burrowed into her soft hair as the relaxation traveled through my body, and her hands trailed over my backside soothingly. When we both regained our strength, I rolled us onto our sides, disengaging our bodies. She let out a sigh that was satisfied but told me she already missed our connection.

"How are you, Beautiful?"

A gradual and amorous smile slipped across her face. "My universe isn't shattered, Jude. It's better. It's complete."

I drew her in close and we fell asleep in each other's arms.

I may run for exercise, but I would never run from her love. More importantly, she would never run from me again.

She can't … asthma.

Epilogue

Jude

"Bro, chill out." Zane came up behind me and muttered semi-supportively but mostly with irritation in my ear.

I paced in the kitchen, pretending to get steaks ready for the grill.

I glanced over my shoulder. "I'm trying to."

"I've never seen you this nervous." Zane's hand gave my shoulder a squeeze. "Jude, she's going to say yes, and with all the work you put into this, if she doesn't I'm pretty sure any woman out there would marry you when they hear your speech of how much you love Presley." He carried the steaks out to the grill. "You got this. You're a Saylor. We're a natural at love."

Four months ago, the girl of my dreams was going to run from my life, from me. But, thankfully, I was able to help her see what a relatively nice guy I was, and most importantly, we were meant to be together. She moved in a month after and there wasn't a single day that I didn't have a smile on my face.

Waking up next to her was having sunshine in my life from the moment I opened my eyes.

We were throwing a Labor Day backyard fest with twenty-plus of our friends and I was ready to ask Presley to be my wife. It was quick, but it was love. No need to wait. I wasn't nervous like Zane assumed. I imagined the excited anticipation was making me act a little crazy around her.

Maybe I should just do it and enjoy the rest of the evening with my fiancé in my arms?

"Hello? Jude?" a voice called from the entry.

"Come in! I'm in the kitchen, Kiki," I yelled back.

My redheaded friend rounded the corner and kissed my cheek. "Hey, thanks for inviting me. Here's the dessert. Where's that beautiful woman of yours?"

"Thanks." I examined what looked questionable as a dessert, or even food. Kiera was never known for her cooking or baking skills. "Um, Prez is outside with Willow and Sage."

"Sage is here? Oh, I can't wait to see her!"

Thankfully, Kiera, Presley, Willow, and my ex-coworker, Sage, all hit it off and they hung out together. It was kind of odd having my ex-girlfriend and my current girlfriend as good friends, but I rolled with it.

"Jude, hey, Zane wants the veg—"

I scanned over my shoulder to see what stopped Drexel from talking when he normally didn't shut the fuck up. Ever.

Never thought Drexel and I'd end up friends. I continued to use the term "friends" loosely and always guardedly. But since he sincerely apologized to Presley *and* she forgave him *and* she asked me to make an effort *and* since she said *please* in the sexiest, I'm-gonna-rock-your-world-if-you-do-this-for-me kind of way, I didn't say no.

Drexel isn't bad. He's just ... Drexel.

"Hi, Drexel Mason." He beelined to Kiera with an outstretched hand.

Over my dead body, Mason.

"Hi, Kiera Maxwell."

"Nice to meet you, Kiera. Let me help you get something to drink. This way to the outside bar."

He tagged the plate of vegetable kabobs for the grill and guided her to the side door to the back patio. Quite like a gentleman. Then he spun to me and shared a juvenile hip-pumping movement before following her out.

I shook my head and he chuckled.

Drexel, grow up.

"Honey…" Her soft voice filled my ears. I put down the knife I used to chop tomatoes, washed my hands, and turned around. An arm wrapped around my waist and the other hand raked through my hair. "Jude, what's wrong? You've been acting weird and uncomfortable all day, actually all week. Are you getting sick?" She touched my forehead and frowned.

She was right. This week I'd been different. I wanted to make tonight special so I dismissed her advances at every turn and every night there was a sharp turn to avoid. In a couple of instances my efforts had almost killed me. Those eyes and that body, they spoke a different language, and my lower half acted as interpreter for my body.

"No. I feel great."

She frowned even deeper.

I slid her closer and skimmed my hands up and down her toned back.

"Then what is it?" She swallowed hard and brought a hand up to my mouth to stop me from talking. "If … if you've decided I'm not what you want and you need me to leave … I won't lie, it will hurt, but I want you to be happy."

I chuckled, and she leaned away. Her emerald orbs shimmered as her lips quivered.

She thought I was unhappy? How far from the truth that was.

I couldn't bear the thought of her torturing herself all night over what might be going through my mind.

Gazing into the eyes that confiscated my heart to be hers, I dropped my head to meet her lips-to-lips, joining our bodies in a kiss that was infinitely soft and tender. My love conveyed right at the connection of our bodies.

I rested my forehead onto hers. "Presley, my heart has never been as full with love and happiness as it is with you in my life. Every moment of every day has a smile because of you. The way you love me, the way you comfort me, the way you know when something is up with me. I really can't imagine any day without you. I want forever with you, Beautiful."

"Jude, but…" She inhaled quickly as I lowered to one knee.

I pulled out a silver box with a burgundy bow from my cargo shorts and held it toward her. Presley smiled down at me, her glassy eyes shimmering green pools in the afternoon sun.

This moment is perfect … just us.

I opened the box to show her what cost almost as much as a Ducati Panigale S, but she was worth more than that bike ever would be to me.

"Presley Bradenhurst, will you do me the honor of being my wife?"

"Oh, my God … yes, Jude Saylor, nothing would make me happier than to spend forever with you."

I placed the diamond ring on her finger. She leaned down and sealed our engagement with a tear-soaked kiss. I stood and guided her into an embrace.

"Thank God. I couldn't live without you," she mumbled against my shoulder.

"I couldn't live without you, either."

"I love you, Ponytail."

"I love you, too, Beautiful."

The back door opened. "Presley, our pale green-eyed friend is turning green. She needs an antacid. Pregnancy is a biotch." Willow bounded into the kitchen on a mission but stopped when she saw us holding each other. Her eyes narrowed at me and she screamed. "Oh, my God, you did it without us?"

Presley giggled at her friend. "You knew?"

"Do you like the ring?" Willow ran toward us, her jet-black hair reminding me of her continuing depressed emotional state. The color was gone from her and her hair, but there was hope that the color would come back.

Maybe tonight she can move on.

My fiancé held her hand up, examining the diamond. "It's stunning. I bet you had something to do with that?"

"Congratulations, I'm so happy for both of you." Willow's blue eyes churned dark like the midnight sky, filling with shimmering waterworks.

Presley and I exchanged a look and both stepped forward into a group hug while Willow sobbed between us for a couple of minutes.

Things had ended between Kanyon and Willow right after Presley moved in with me, and three months later, Willow still hadn't recovered. Her perpetual state of sadness made me want to throttle Kanyon into next year. I took Willow's side. Only because he was being the idiot this time and wouldn't own up to his idiocy. His reasoning for breaking things off wasn't even remotely worth mentioning to another human. He and I texted occasionally about doing something that rarely happened, and I stopped by the store a couple of times to chat for a few minutes, but we weren't the same.

"Come on, let's go tell the girls!" Willow snapped from her self-pity and wiped her cheeks. She yanked on Presley's hand, and I gave her the go-ahead nod.

"I need to do something first." Presley peeped up into my eyes. A secret sparkle told me I was going to like what she needed to do.

"Okay, see you in?" Willow smirked and raised her onyx eyebrows.

Presley pulled on my hand. "Give us at least thirty before you send out a search party."

With a mischievous grin on her face, my amazing fiancée led me into the garage and to my motorcycle. It was a dream she was going to make come true.

This is going to be the best ride of her life.

The End

www.julesdixon.com

EVERNIGHT PUBLISHING ®

www.evernightpublishing.com

61798069R00188

Made in the USA
Lexington, KY
20 March 2017